The
New York

**Other books from Alyson
by Felice Picano**

The Book of Lies
Looking Glass Lives

The New York Years

Stories by Felice Picano

 alyson books
los angeles | new york

MANUFACTURED IN THE UNITED STATES OF AMERICA.

THIS TRADE PAPERBACK ORIGINAL IS PUBLISHED BY ALYSON PUBLICATIONS, P.O. BOX 4371, LOS ANGELES, CALIFORNIA 90078-4371.
DISTRIBUTION IN THE UNITED KINGDOM BY TURNAROUND PUBLISHER SERVICES LTD., UNIT 3 OLYMPIA TRADING ESTATE, COBURG ROAD, WOOD GREEN, LONDON N22 6TZ ENGLAND.

FIRST EDITION: MAY 2000
(FIRST PUBLISHED SEPARATELY AS *SLASHED TO RIBBONS IN DEFENSE OF LOVE: AND OTHER STORIES* BY THE GAY PRESSES OF NEW YORK IN 1983 AND AS *AN ASIAN MINOR: THE TRUE STORY OF GANYMEDE* BY THE SEA HORSE PRESS IN 1981.)

00 01 02 03 04 a 10 9 8 7 6 5 4 3 2 1

ISBN 1-55583-522-8

LIBRARY OF CONGRESS CATALOGING-IN-PUBLICATION DATA
   PICANO, FELICE, 1944–
      THE NEW YORK YEARS : STORIES / BY FELICE PICANO.—1ST ED.
      COMBINED ED. OF: SLASHED TO RIBBONS IN DEFENSE OF LOVE, AND OTHER STORIES; AND, AN ASIAN MINOR.
      CONTENTS: SPINNING — THE INTERRUPTED RECITAL — SHY — TEDDY: THE HOOK — MR. WORLD BUNS: A STORY WITHOUT A MORAL — AND BABY MAKES THREE — XMAS IN THE APPLE — SLASHED TO RIBBONS IN DEFENSE OF LOVE — EXPERTISE — HUNTER — A STROKE — AN ASIAN MINOR: THE TRUE STORY OF GANYMEDE.
      ISBN 1-55583-522-8
      1. GAY MEN—NEW YORK (STATE)—NEW YORK—FICTION. 2. NEW YORK (N.Y.)—SOCIAL LIFE AND CUSTOMS—FICTION. I. PICANO, FELICE, 1944– SLASHED TO RIBBONS IN DEFENSE OF LOVE, AND OTHER STORIES. II. PICANO, FELICE, 1944– AN ASIAN MINOR. III. TITLE.
      PS3566.I25 N49 2000
      813'.54—DC21   99-089539

CREDITS
•SOME STORIES FROM *IN SLASHED TO RIBBONS IN DEFENSE OF LOVE: AND OTHER STORIES* ORIGINALLY APPEARED IN OTHER PUBLICATIONS: "SPINNING" IN *STALLION;* "THE INTERRUPTED RECITAL" AND "SHY" IN *GAYSWEEK ARTS AND LETTERS;* "MR. WORLD BUNS," "TEDDY," "EXPERTISE," AND "XMAS IN THE APPLE" IN *BLUEBOY;* "HUNTER" IN *DRUMMER, ON THE LINE* (CROSSING PRESS), AND *PHILADELPHIA GAY NEWS;* "SLASHED TO RIBBONS IN DEFENSE OF LOVE" IN *CHRISTOPHER STREET* AND *APHRODISIAC* (COWARD McCANN). VARIOUS © 1975, 1976, 1977, 1978, 1979, 1980, 1981, 1982 BY FELICE PICANO.
•AN ASIAN MINOR: THE TRUE STORY OF GANYMEDE © 1981 BY THE SEA HORSE PRESS
•COVER PHOTOGRAPHY BY DAVID WATT.
•COVER DESIGN BY PHILIP PIROLO.

Contents

Preface

The stories in this book were written in the decade between 1972 and 1981 and first published either in periodical or book form between 1978 and 1983. Rereading them today I'm less embarrassed than I expected to be when Alyson Books suggested reprinting them. I can be immodest enough to say this for several reasons. First, these pre-AIDS stories feel less dated than I dreaded they would. Of them, only "Spinning" really seems to belong to the disco-drugs era in which it was written. The other tales could have been composed last year or even last month. I don't know whether it's because they are about what might be termed "timeless" subjects—particular characters and specific situations—or because when you come down to it, gay life and gay men haven't changed that much in the intervening years.

Then too, several stories have gone on to lead independent lives—which may be responsible for their feeling contemporary. All but two were previously published before they appeared between covers, and that account constitutes a miniature history of earlier gay publishing. "The Interrupted Recital" and "Shy" appeared in New York's first real gay newspaper, *GaysWeek,* in its quarterly Arts and Letters section, in March 1978 and March 1979 respectively. "Slashed to Ribbons" (written in 1972) was published in *Christopher Street* magazine in February 1980. "Spinning"— originally titled "Fantasy and Fugue"—came out in *Stallion,* a skin mag, in September, 1980. "Hunter" was printed in the leatherman magazine *Drummer* in October 1980. Four stories, "Teddy—The Hook, "Xmas in the Apple," "Expertise," and "Mr. World Buns," first appeared in *Blueboy* magazine (October 1980, November

1980, May 1981, and June 1981) during that publication's unre-
peated year-long flirtation with quality fiction. I wrote the second
of the four at the behest of the editor. "A Stroke" first appeared in
the quarterly *New Sins* in the spring of 1982.

To put this period a bit in perspective, these fictions fit between
the first edition of my poetry book, *The Deformity Lover,* and my
novels *The Lure* and *Late in the Season.* A wider 1981 outlook
would include my contemporaries: while these were coming out,
Andrew Holleran published *Dancer From the Dance* and *Nights
in Aruba,* Edmund White published *States of Desire: Travels in
Gay America* and *Nocturnes for the King of Naples,* and Larry
Kramer excreted *Faggots.*

Since their collective publication, four of the stories—"Slashed
to Ribbons in Defense of Love," "A Stroke," "Expertise," and
especially "Hunter"—have been reprinted in anthologies. In a one-
year period of 1997-98, "Hunter" appeared in three compendi-
ums—in England, Germany, and the United States.

Of the two stories included here that first appeared in book
form, both are novellas and both belong to a sequence of narra-
tives I at the time thought of as "impossible" or "improbable"
loves. *An Asian Minor* came out in a slim volume with illustrations
by David Martin in 1981 and promptly went through two more
printings. "And Baby Makes Three" appeared only in the Gay
Presses of New York volume. (The other titles in this "impossible
love" group were published separately: *Late in the Season* in
1981 and as a Stonewall Inn Classic in 1997, and *Looking Glass
Lives* by Alyson Books in 1998).

The entire collection, *Slashed to Ribbons in Defense of Love
and Other Stories,* had the good luck to emerge during a brief
short story renaissance and was widely reviewed. It was spotlighted, in glamorous company, with books by Raymond Carver, Alice
Munro, Ann Beattie and Donald Barthleme in *Writers* magazine
and was reprinted three more times in five years.

Three of the stories have led lives outside their prose fiction
form. I performed "Spinning" as a monologue on New York City's
"alternative" FM radio station WBAI on September 23, 1980, and
later at Three Lives Bookstore in Greenwich Village. I heard it read
by DJ Jorge Villarosa and watched it "acted out" on the dance
floor of the Manhattan discotheque Paradise Garage on October
26, 1980. It was repeated there and at the Ice Palace. Another
tale, "Xmas in the Apple," was dramatized by City Lit Theater of

Chicago and presented July 11–30, 1983. (I cannibalized it for my novel *The Book of Lies,* Alyson Books, 1999).

But it was *An Asian Minor* that really ended up starstruck. It was adapted by myself and stage director Jerry Campbell as a "Play with Music and Dancing" at the request of the Meridian Gay Theater. Retitled *Immortal!* it opened at Manhattan's Shandol Theater and ran 13 weeks in the spring of 1986. The casting was memorable. We had put a call for auditions in *Variety* that read "Wanted—The Most Beautiful Young Man in the World. 18-22." When we arrived at the tiny theater, the line was around the block. Jerry looked at me and said, "Too bad you're not single, I plan to get dates today for the next five years." TV soap stars, guys in their late 30's, even a young woman disguised with a fake mustache (we hired her for another role) were on that line. We cast the entire nine-person production in two days from the group. Available until recently from Dialogus Press, *Immortal!* may still be found in some gay and theater book shops.

Subsequent to the 1983 volume, I have written and published several new gay-themed short stories—mostly for anthologies but once for an online magazine. I call them "True Stories" because they are from incidents in my life and are narratively unaltered from how they occurred. The present collection contains two earlier True Stories—"A Stroke" and "Shy"—both of which happened pretty much as I wrote them. Readers have asked me for years, so I'll now acknowledge that the movie star in "Shy" was the beautiful, tortured Montgomery Clift, whose ghost is said to haunt the 14th floor of Hollywood's Roosevelt Hotel.

Two other stories here are strongly autobiographical; "Teddy—The Hook" and "The Interrupted Recital" are both based on young men I knew. In the second, the anecdote originally concerned a concert pianist, not a cellist, and was told to me by his hustleresque nemesis, with whom I then had a brief, tumultuous affair. And of course I dated someone who "worked lights" in the DJ booth of a large dance club. That experience gives "Spinning" whatever authenticity it may possess.

A note about the amazing cover photo. It was taken a quarter century ago, in late October 1974 at 9 A.M. on the roof of New York City's famous (and infamous—it then housed the gay Continental Baths) Ansonia Hotel, looking down 21 stories to the street at Verdi Square—Broadway and 72nd Street. It was photographed by someone I've since lost contact with, David Watt, using a 1933 Hasselblad camera with a 60 second lens that languidly revolved 180 degrees as I stood and waited...and waited. The back quarter of the photo was cropped to become an "author shot" on the inside back cover of my first published novel, *Smart as the Devil,* put out by Arbor House on February 22, 1975, my 31st birthday.

—Felice Picano, Los Angeles, January 2000

Spinning

(Author's comments: "Spinning" has an interesting history. Several years ago I was beginning to do enough poetry readings to become dissatisfied with them. Reading poetry requires a great deal of concentration and is so discontinuous that even with experimentation and practice, I found it difficult to "build" an evening toward and away from satisfactory climaxes. I decided to write prose pieces to fill in the first half of the program, sensing that by telling a story, I would get attention faster, and my listeners would feel rewarded faster.

One of these pieces, "Absolute Ebony," was read aloud and picked up for the premier issue of Twilight Zone magazine (along with a story by Joyce Carol Oates, of all people!), and later was published in a hardcover anthology, Masters of Modern Horror. The second piece was another attempt at the Ganymede legend, and conceived some five years before as—wrongly—a mock epic poem. That piece, of course, became An Asian Minor. "Spinning" was the third piece, and while I wrote it to read at Three Lives & Company, it was first aired over WBAI for Gay Pride Week in 1979. That station—and Radio Pacifica in San Francisco still play it every once in awhile.

It was conceived—where else?—dancing one night at Fire Island's Ice Palace, but was written only after I'd spent almost an entire night and morning inside the booth of a discotheque of equal stature in Manhattan.

When I read the piece aloud, I give specific intonation and inflection to the voice of "The King of Smooth." He is casual, tough, clipped at first, then a little spaced out, neither Brooklyn nor Bronx, but definitely New York. He's also in command of the club. Think of a transcontinental 747 pilot bringing the ship in, week after week.)

This number walks into the club, onto the dancefloor which is not heavily occupied as it is only just after midnight and the party won't get going here until after two. Bonnie Pointer is belting out her re-mix of an old Supremes' hit, "Can't Help Myself." I'm spinning. There are five or six couples to my left—bridge and tunnel traffic mostly, who've managed to wrangle someone's membership card. A group of ten or eleven guys to my right—a quartet of them already twisted—dust and MDA I'd guess, with a brush-on of Coke in the bathroom a few minutes ago. They don't care who's here or why. Another dozen or so men hanging loose around the perimeter of the dancefloor, trying not to look conspicuous, although by not dancing and it being so empty, they can't help themselves. Easy to see why I pick out this number.

Easy to see also he's not one of the usual crowd. The way he's dressed says that, the way he walks—very classy. The way he puts two hands up behind him, lifts himself easily to sit on top of the Double XM Boom—a speaker I only turn on for the dark and dirty music at, say, five a.m. when most of these creeps will be beddy-bye, or worse, screwing each other. Please don't ask me to picture it for you.

Maybe not him though—the number. He's different. Not clean-cut. No, I wouldn't say that. No facial hair, though. Sort of blonde—silver blonde or strawberry blonde, depending on the lights. A v-neck sweater—pale grey? No shirt underneath. Looks like a slender, flat body. No jeans. He's wearing creased trousers, of all things. Real shoes too. No sneakers or boots. Maybe he's a model. Or European. Dutch. Tony used to say for real romance go to Amsterdam. He met Andre at the D.O.K. I don't know. I like it fine here.

At any rate, the number lifts himself up and back in one motion, and although it's some thirty feet away, he starts to stare across the swirls of Butchie's lights on the dancefloor, at guess who? As though he knew me.

"Hey Butchie," I say. "Who's that number?"

Butchie looks up from the lightboard he's been working, squints across, and says:

"Ain't one of mine."

His head bobs down to the board: he's back to work. No Einstein, Butchie's managed somehow between reform school and drug dealing to learn computer programming, and he's had Herb and Ghost Music Ltd. build him a computerized light board that's better than any other club's. He has two panels of program modules filled with lights and switches he presets, another panel of the same for free wheel lighting, and a variable finger module on the edge of the board that looks like the keyboard of a rainbow colored piano. Butchie mostly plays with the programs and free panel, but when he's really hot, he runs up and down that keyboard like Arthur Rubenstein. Right now, he's setting up some basic programs for the first few sets.

"Looks like a refugee from Studio," I say to Butchie, then explain, "The number."

"Ain't one of mine," Butchie says. "Must be one of yours."

"The blonde?"

"What blonde?"

"The number," I say. "He's blonde. You know I don't go with blondes."

"Wait a minute, will you," Butchie says, "I'm busy doing the pancake with stars."

I see him blacken the room, then throw on a light peppy strobe. He blacks that, replaces it with a pin-hole pattern, twirls the pattern, blacks it, and on go the strobes again.

"That's blinking," I say.

Butchie's offended. "That's my own invention. Pancake with stars!"

"Riccardo calls it blinking. Watch me," I say. I do an imitation of Riccardo at the lights. I tap my own shoulder, then, as Riccardo, I turn around to my imaginary self, bat my eyes, and say, "Wai' a min', huh, I'm blinkin'."

"He's German," Butchie says.

I look at him as though he's crazy.

"Riccardo? He's Cuban. Or Uruguyan. Something like that."

"No. The number."

I look at the number. He might be at a football game or tennis match. He's not watching the guys against the walls. He isn't watching the couples and groups dancing—pig-dancing, if you ask me, wait 'till the pros arrive. No. He's watching me.

The song's about to end.

"Aretha, next," I say.

"Candi Staton," Butchie snaps back.

"Anything?"

"Anything by Candi Staton."

I decide to compromise, and put on Sam and Dave, which I brought to play especially this evening.

Butchie moans when he hears the result of my segue. But then he begins tapping his fingers against the board, before he catches himself. Fucking kids don't know good music when they hear it. Rhythm and Blues, Daddy! Not this plastic shit with soaring violins electrified over nothing. Musak. But then, half of them are on Ethyl. What do they care what they hear.

The number has not shown me he gets off on Sam and Dave. Screw him!

German, huh?

More people come in. If I lean a little out of the booth I can see the checkroom. It's getting busy. People upstairs coming down. Not getting down. That'll come later. If ever. Sometimes it doesn't. Remember last week? A real dud.

"He's not one of mine," I say to Butchie, who shrugs.

Maybe he is though.

Remember, Billy, remember!

Not so easy to do, friend. Many numeros under the bridge.

He's blonde, Billy. You don't do it with blondes, remember?

Not true, amigo. I do too. Not often. Sometimes.

Remember, Billy. Remember!

Why? Because he's staring at me?

No. Because it's something to do, and you're bored to the tits! Check.

All right. Who is this number? Name? Nationality? Personality? Sex kinks? Cock size? Scars? Hot? Boring? Bad sex? Is that why I don't remember?

I decide to follow up Sam and Dave with Candi Staton's "Young Hearts Run Free." I may play it later too, when it's appreciated better. But I do a nice mix here, from the last bars of one cut to a slow fade-up on the intro of the next cut, until the next to final bar, when I suddenly turn down the mixing volume and let the intro sail out alone. Not for nothing am I known as Billy D.J., the King of Smooth.

Wait a minute! I know who the number is!

He's not German or Dutch. He's Pat Remington!

Yeah...Pat Remington...He was a D.J. too, for a while, out at the Sandpiper. He'd been a model before that. Then he began seeing Greg Durfey, who mixed two summers out there. That's when Pat got into music. Then he wrote that song for that movie. Then into production, first for Warner's and RCA, later on independently. Yeah! That's who he is!

What's Pat Remington doing at the club on a regular night? He doesn't even come for the parties.

Coming to hear me play, that's what. Maybe Herb said something to him, finally. Or Riccardo. What's Riccardo get paid to mix album cuts for him, a thousand bucks? Two thousand? Damn! I wouldn't mind mixing a couple of hits for Remington. Beats this shit! Well, well, going to have to give him something special tonight.

Maybe not. Fuck him. Ignore him. Or at least pretend to ignore him. This is a test. He's probably thinking that when I was talking to Butchie before, that I was checking out that he was Pat Remington. So, of course, I'll do something nice in recognition, like playing one of his songs, or one of his groups. No way! He's here to hear the King of Smooth. That's what he'll hear.

How about an old Beatle's number, all jazzed up. Something light and rhythmic to get these clods moving.

So I put on "Baby You Can Drive My Car," from a few years back. It's produced to the bazooms. So much brass it could be the West Point Marching Band.

A dozen horns punctuate the dancefloor, on which there are now some sixty people. Straight from the coat check counter to the dancefloor. They don't even know how they got here, it was so smooth.

Butchie tugs at my elbow.

"What?"

"I wanna go get a drink," Butchie says. "You want?"

"Now?" I ask. "I'm just getting hot!"

"Why? What's next?"

I think fast. "Working My Way Back To You," I say. "You always do something special for that cut. We should keep 'em moving for Christ's sake, now that we've got 'em."

"Okay. But after that cut, I get a drink."

The horns will all blast toot-toot, then the song is over. I put on my earphones, switch the second turntable for my ears only, and listen to the opening of "Working My Way Back To You." Terrific. But not a great rhythm mix. Should be a mite faster.

I place my pinkie really lightweight on the side of the turntable where the Beatle's cut is just about to end. Doing that slows it down a fraction. Not enough so they'll notice. Just enough so that when I mix up "Working" they'll be rhythmically identical. Some D.J.s use felt cloth. Trick of the trade.

Not bad. Smooth.

Down in the crowd in front of the booth, I see friends: Rick and Irv. They signal up to acknowledge the mix. Connoisseurs. The King of Smooth is on tonight, kids.

The dancefloor is just right now: nice crowd, not too many. Maybe a hundred, hundred and ten. Poppers are unstoppered. Two tambourines go into action on the platforms opposite me. I even see a set of sticks out. Honey, this is going to be one good set!

Didn't Irv go out with Pat Remington? Wrong! That was Mike Cohen. What did Mike say about Remington? He used to be Fashion Avenue. A little weird. Married once, to another model, right? Wrong. Rich family. Right! He was the black sheep. Dropped out of Swarthmore, where he was a Greek major. Jesus! Who'd be a Greek major? Weird. Then he hung around on the Riviera with some other rich people, began to model in France, came back here, did that toothpaste commercial. Suddenly you couldn't open GQ without seeing him. Where's the family from? Grosse Pointe? Shaker Heights? Santa Barbara! The city that declared war on Hitler in 1946. That conservative. But Pat Remington was weird, Mike said. Oh, well, that's the lemon in the honey.

...In the honey, honey! Savannah Band. That's what's next.

I find the album. Butchie looks at it, frowns. I point to the cut I'm going to play. Butchie approves. I place it on the other turntable, listen in with one earphone, checking for a harmonic mix, no sense in pretending I can mix it's speed into the last cut. Okay.

Butchie's busy doing his dark trip on the dancefloor. Lightless, except for deep red spots shooting down from the ceiling, reflected on the swing mirrors. Then he flips on a yellow and blue spot, swathing the place in orange and purple, switches off the red, so it's primary blue and yellow. Then he flips onto opposites, red and green, back and forth, so fast the dancefloor seems to vibrate. He's got a red so raspberry and a green so electric lime you want to eat them.

I segue into the intro of "Lemon in the Honey."

The dancefloor goes nuts. Shouts, screams, whistles. They seldom forget a golden oldie: a song they plotzed to, or fell in love to, or caught the clap to. The King of Smooth is on tonight, kids. You too. You there, with the cute buns.

I'll have to drop them down after this cut, make that into a little set. Not bad for early on. At the juice counters they'll be dishing my mixing. "Hot night. Billy must have done an Escatrol. What got into him so early?" Let 'em talk.

Remington has now put his feet up and crossed them guru style. There's a lot of traffic on his side of the floor. I wonder if he's wishing he were in the booth, spinning, instead of me? Who's that talking to him? A creep.

Money from typewriters, right? Wrong. Money from rifles, right? Didn't Mike Cohen say something about them going to visit some people in Pacific Palisades who had antique guns on all the walls and Pat freaked out, wouldn't stay in the house? Not money from rifles. From paper-clips, or toilet seats, or....

I think I'll really let them know the set is over. Put on something different. Van Morrison, maybe, doing his trash version of "Walk On the Wild Side."...No, better save that for later on tonight, when it gets hot, so hot me and Butchie will have to pull off our shirts, though we're not dancing, so slick with humidity down there you could slide across the middle of a packed floor on torso sweat. When the sidewall mirrors are so fogged they're opaque, and the sweat and Ethyl and poppers fill the air with a mist like hot ice. That's when! For now, I'll stay light. Something to make Remington sit up and notice, so that when he goes back to L.A. he'll remember he heard Billy D.J.

How about the Eagles? "New Kid in Town." That'll tell him something. The guys on the dancefloor too. "Wow! Billy's into Rock music! Next thing you know he'll be playing Elton John!"

And I will too. I'll curl their hair. Give them "Bennie and the Jets." Then, maybe something really old—Martha and the Vandellas, doing "Dancing in the Streets." Yeah! Don't forget the motor city.

Savannah Band ends with a thump. Butchie blacks the lights. I mix up the bass side of the Eagles, then slowly mix up the volume on the rest of it. Its intro is slow, ambiguous. The dancecrowd slows down, even stops. Tambourines drop to their sides. Everyone is half looking around. Now the high-pitched Eagle's lead voice emerges, the rhythm begins to bump and grind. Some dancers change gears right into it. Others stand still. Some leave, going onto the sidelines. Only two thirds of a dancefloor left. But they're getting off. Very smooth end of set, Billy.

Thanks.

Pat Remington is being asked to dance by a clone with a body. He refuses. The clone persists, leans forward, much tits, and begins to try to talk over my music.

"I'm going for that drink, now," Butchie says. I forgot, Butchie hates the Eagles. "I left it on a program. What are you doing next?"

I show him the album. The clone, I notice, has jumped up to sit next to Pat. Get off my fucking speaker!

"Switch on this module," Butchie points, "for a change. You want anything?"

The clone is very interested in Remington. Shit!

"Bring me a beer," I say. "And don't let them tell you they don't have. They do. I saw it come in."

Butchie leaves the booth, and I see the clone has convinced Pat to dance. Hell! I want him listening. Not dancing. Maybe I shouldn't do the Elton John next.

No, it's a good, light, hot cut. I'll segue into "Casanova Brown," then maybe something smoother—the Munich Machine. What would be fun would be those robot types singing "I Can't Get No Satisfaction." I'll bet Jagger crapped when he heard them. Then into Gloria Gaynor, LaBelle, Sister Sledge, Michael Jackson. A set, my friend.

Pat Remington dances strange. Like old times. Back to the Electric Circus or Fillmore West, but without the commitment. What's he doing in a sweater, anyway?

There it goes, off, as he looks around, holding it, then tosses it onto the speaker where he was sitting before. Just as I thought, nice body, slender, hairless, good shoulders, great definition. My type. The muscled clone seems to like it too. He looks on appreciatively, opens a bottle of Butyl. Pat takes a hit, closes his eyes, starts getting hot when the break opens on "Bennie and the Jets."

Shit! Where's that "Satisfaction?" The album isn't in the stand-up bin. Fucking Riccardo must have borrowed it to mix a listening tape at home. What's here? Philly sound. He took all my stand-bys. Jesus! What's this? "That's The Feeling." Not bad. Not bad, kids. That's next. Fuck the Munich Machine. This is a better lead into a hot soul set.

The mix is not the smoothest I am capable of, but who cares, as it's smoother than most D.J.s, and the cut is so good. The dancefloor is crowded again. More so than before. Maybe two hundred. Pat's leaving it, though. The persistent clone goes off with him. They stop to pick up Pat's sweater, then head toward the smaller lounge, out of view. I wonder if Pat will shake him. I wonder if he wants to. It's early He doesn't want to stay with one clone all night, does he?

What's it to you, Billy?

I want him to listen to my mixing, amigo. I want him to come up to the booth, hand me his card, and say, here Billy, you're as good as Herb and Riccardo said. I need a really smooth mix on a song I'm cutting. Mix it for me, will you. And if you work out, Billy, well, you know, I produce a half dozen groups, a dozen singles, as many albums a year. Big names. Hits, Billy.

I want Remington to tell me that. To tell me I'll be spending three months a year at his L.A. studio mixing. Hauling it in, then coming back here and spending it. I'll buy a summer on the Island. I'll move out of that dump walkup in Chelsea and into a loft I buy. I'll get that fur coat I saw last winter. A new mixer for home. Hell! A whole new studio set-up at home. That new Citation Power Amp. Four Hundred clean watts. A Tandberg cassette deck. Those huge speakers Ghost Music Ltd. put together. I'll buy my Quaalude by the gross. My Coke by the ounce. Go to Rio for Carnival and Key West whenever I'm fed up with slush. Cut for even bigger groups. Only spin for special parties. Be a star. And maybe, baby, I'll let you drive my car.

Hey! I have it, I'll end this set with "Rich and Famous." Yeah. I'll cut that in. I wish Butchie were back. Let me see what happens with the keyboard. How does he release it, with this switch? There it goes. Look at 'em dance down there. Man, you couldn't find room to turn around. All five platforms are filled with dancers. Let's throw them a silhouette. Nice. Now for a sweep on the keyboard. Pretty! How does he change the keyboard colors? With this? Pretty. Now for a blue spin. Now the keyboard again.

Butchie comes back into the booth with two beers. He hands me one and I back off the keyboard. He takes it over for the big finale of the cut, then stays on for "Rich and Famous," and it's as if he'd read my mind, 'cause suddenly colors erupt around us as though it were a space laser war. An inspired choice, Billy.

Merci.

I've got 'em by the nuts now. They'll only stop when they start to drop. I now give them La Belle. Butchie looks over at the album, nods, and does some fast reprogramming.

We go on a long, wild set then, and already it's feeling like a legendary night. I don't usually get high in the booth, but I take tokes on the joint Butchie hands me, and get the feeling. There's no stopping us now. Everything I select to play Butchie digs, and gives me the best possible lights for. We're in complete sync now. Good mixing. Great lights. Really together. Like in a good screwing, when you just know you're both going to come at the same time.

Butchie's completely crazed—the mad Liberace from Little Rock, I call him when he gets on the keyboard like this. In a second, he'll be asking me to play something Latin. But before that, I want to do Earth, Wind and Fire, Fairport Convention, then maybe end the set with something stratospheric—"Ain't No Mountain High Enough."

Suddenly it's five a.m. I'm spinning another classic R and B, "Pull Yourself Together," which my friend Tony calls the gay national anthem. This is going to be a funky, dirty set. And the dancecrowd looks ready for it. All shirts are off, all bodies are perspiring. Couples are body-dancing. Simulated screwing all over the place. Ditto for simulated blowjobs: a partner dips and rubs his face in his partner's denim crotch. They have definitely begun to get down. I tap Butchie and let him take over the turntable, while I sit back and have a cigarette.

"What got into you tonight?" he asks.

"Nothing, why?"

"It's like old times. Memory Lane."

"Bad?" I ask, not believing it.

"Are you kidding?"

Assuaged, I say, "I though I saw a producer here tonight. I wanted to give him what-for. Pat Remingon," I explain.

"When?"

"At the beginning of the night. The blonde number?"

Now I haven't seen Remington in a few hours, and the last time it was with another clone with tits, but with the mess on the dancefloor, it's no surprise I can't find him.

"That wasn't Pat Remington," Butchie says. "He's years older than that guy."

"How can I tell in your lights," I tease.

Butchie makes a face, then, "Besides, I met him."

"Remington?"

"I met *him* a long time ago. I mean the number. When I went to get our beer, I was talking to Timmy when he came up and talked to me."

"What did he say?"

"Nothing much. How the music and lights were really good."

"So! How do you know it wasn't Remington?"

"He had an accent," Butchie says. "German. Or Dutch or something. Wait a minute, he said he knew you. He gave me this to give you."

I flatten out the note Butchie has had balled up in his pocket most the night, and read:

> You probably don't remember me. I'm here in New York for a month. Look me up at this phone number, if you do.
>
> Jos.
>
> P.S. Remember what we did with the Anisette liqueur in the bathtub at Rick and Irv's?

Butchie looks over his shoulder at me. "What did I tell you?"

"I thought it was Pat Remington!"

"I told you he was one of your numbers. Take over here, will you. I want to do the lights."

I am blank. I have to admit I am completely shot up about Pat Remington not being here tonight.

"Come on," Butchie says, getting frantic.

I start looking for *Voyage*. That'll keep them busy until I figure out something else to play.

Voyage isn't in the stand-by bin.

Butchie gestures at me: Help. Then he picks up the Candi Staton album, slaps it on the turntable, picks a cut, and starts to mix it up.

I'm still in shock. I think about how I've mixed some good nights and some bad ones and some great ones, but how this night was special, best I can remember. Hell! For all I know the best in my life. This could be the height of my career as a D.J. Who knows, maybe next year at this time, I'll be waiting tables again. What a bringdown.

Even more of a bringdown, I suddenly realize is the cut Butchie has played: "I'm a Victim of the Very Songs I Sing." Tell 'em, Candi, baby.

Butchie's at the lights now, and he's worried about me. It's been a good night for him, for the dancers, for everyone in the club. Damn!

Then I think about Jos, who is probably somewhere on the dancefloor. No wonder he looked as though he knew me. Wants a rematch, does he?

Then I recall in vivid detail the scene in Rick and Irv's bathtub with the Anisette. Kinky!

To hell with Pat Remington! To hell with my career! This is a party isn't it? Well, Billy, party!

It's then that I get up, go to the turntables, put on "Walk on The Wild Side," and begin to mix into it.

First, they're perplexed down there. They hesitate. They listen, heads cocked to one side, as the suggestive lyrics insinuate themselves over the speakers.

I wonder if I've made a mistake with this cut.

The rhythm track slides on. It picks up, bucks, kicks, as the music gets louder, the vocal line raunchier.

They don't seem to have it. I've fucked up.

Then someone shouts "Okay!" He got it. In a far corner of the room a whistle goes off. He got it too. Then tambourines fly up over heads and are set shaking. Sticks clatter. Even a pair of Marimbas begins to spit. Another shout, then another. Jesus, that's a relief! If this didn't work I don't know what I would have done.

And suddenly I have a whole new set ready in my head for the kids. Good thing too. They dancing in every conceivable space, from the lounges to the juice bars to the check out lines.

Not for nothing am I known as the King of Smooth.

The Interrupted Recital

Nowadays, hardly anyone remembers Ken Kaufman, despite the great stir he once made and the devotion of his fans during his short-lived career.

A few still do, naturally. Connoisseurs of music and students of the violincello for the most part. Friends of the numerous Kaufman clan, of course. Strangers too: those drawn to whatever still retains its character and dignity in the vast, instant vulgarization of the arts. Or those who simply feel that delightfully icy snap of reality whenever they recall the several ironies of Kaufman's life and career.

Members of this last group are usually the quickest to pull out and play one of the rare recordings he made. As a rule, this follows an excellent, continental-style meal, one more after dinner drink, a freshly lighted cigar or cigarette, and a lapse in the conversation.

You sit back, relaxed, and listen to Kaufman playing a Bach Suite or Beethoven Sonata, and through the boxy monophony, through the cracks and hisses of the overplayed disc you can easily make out his innate musicality and utter individuality.

But as soon as the recording is over, you and your host begin to commiserate. No matter how brilliant the recordings, those who attended Ken's equally rare recitals can alone know how much excitement those events could occasion. Not all of it on the highest cultural plane, or indeed, on any recognizable cultural plane at all.

I attended but one recital: Kaufman's last: and I doubt I shall ever forget it.

"Extraordinary luck bumping into you tonight of all nights," Kaufman said, somewhat out of breath.

The most literal person I ever met, he had, in fact, just bumped into me with his large, orange, Belgian bicycle. He insisted on riding this ungainly monster everywhere in the city, despite his general abstraction most of the time he was on it, and his not so hot control of the bike itself. Our collision had taken place on Central Park South, and was only minor. I threw my newspaper in front of myself for protection, (a useless, though not unusual response) whereas Ken lost his hat and dumped a pile of published scores that had been thrown into the bike's basket.

"Why tonight, of all nights?" I couldn't help asking, as we picked up our debris and put ourselves into some order. It had been some fifteen years since I had last seen Ken: I'd only recognized him after he had spoken to me.

"Because tonight I'm giving a recital. And you must come."

I tried to beg off, pleading a pretended engagement.

"Cancel it," he said. "This is to be a rare event. You can't afford to miss it. I only play in public on a whim, you know. The tickets are sold out months in advance. It's been years since I've had a recital in the city. It may be years before I play again. As you're partially responsible for the fact that I play at all, you must come. Like it or not. However, to make it more tempting, I'll buy you dinner at _____ " (naming a quite good French restaurant in the area). There! It's settled. I really am pleased to have bumped into you," (a needless repetition, I thought: and one tinged with sarcasm). "You steered me right once. Now that I need you again, you appear. Just like that!"

"Like the tooth-fairy?" I suggested.

"God no. If anyone's a fairy, it's me. Which is part of the problem. Not all of it. I don't at all mind being comme ca. It's taken me to so many places. Allowed me to associate with so many people I'd never thought of meeting before—construction workers, office boys, salesmen, policemen, riff-raff. Like Davey. He's the one with the problem, really. Although naturally it's my problem too. Oh, but I see I'm moving along a little too quickly, aren't I? Well, let's have dinner. Then you'll hear every last word of it."

Once again I tried to get away.

But Ken ignored my protests, shoved the load of scores he'd picked up into my arms, and marched the old bicycle over to a wall with a protruding metal bar. There, he unlocked a yellow plastic covered chain he'd been wearing around his waist, and expertly chained the bike—front, side and both wheels—to the bar.

"It's only a block or two," he declared. "We'll walk."

2

Fifteen minutes later we were settled into one of the comfy booths, sipping a not at all flinty, recent Mouton-Cadet and both attacking a succulent Coq au Vin.

Ken hadn't changed much in the fifteen years I hadn't seen him. Then, he had been a tall, gawky boy with the same blandly aristocratic fair-skinned face you can see on any photo taken later on. Also as opinionated, blunt and commanding, although naturally enough, without the flamboyant manner he managed to pick up when he became a recitalist. Even the way Ken wore his thinnish blond hair didn't change over the years. He hadn't so much matured, I thought, facing him across the table in that restaurant, as he had literally grown up: gotten taller, larger, rangier.

"Hearty food in good company," he said now, between mouthfuls of the entree. "It's really necessary to me. I always dine this way before a recital. It makes having to play afterwards not merely an obligation but a pleasure. As though it were an extension of the meal. I even thought I'd keep a snifter of brandy on the stage tonight. The management will raise their eyebrows, I'm sure. But, after all, I do have a reputation for eccentricity to keep up."

I admired his sensible handling of pre-performance jitters.

"Hardly that," Ken said, waving over the waiter for the dessert menu. "If anyone has jitters tonight, it will be my fans. And, naturally, the critics, looking for new and unhackneyed adjectives with which to praise me. Don't scowl. It's not just bragging. I'm that good. Thanks to you."

"For steering you so right?"

"Exactly."

"Allow me to refresh your memory, Ken. All I really did was to gab at you so continually during that Freshman music class that we were both sent down to the Dean's office.

"Allow me to refresh your memory," Ken said. "You did a bit more than that. Weren't both of us throw out of that music class?"

"Well, yes," I admitted, having been reminded of a fault I had hidden from myself for years. "But that's even more to my point. I don't understand how that guided you. You wanted to be a virtuoso 'cellist—the new Piatigorsky—those were your very words. If anything, I steered you away from your path."

"Nonsense," he repleid airily. "The *marrons glaces*" he said to the hovering waiter, "and don't skimp on them. Now," he said, "returning to me, "exactly how many of the kids from that class today have careers in music?"

"I don't know. I haven't kept up with any of them."

"None. Not one. That's how many. The teacher was a quack. The class a farce. And I would probably be an Ad Agency account executive or petty bureaucrat in some small town social work agency myself if I too had remained. Instead I had to learn how to play the 'cello on my own—until I finally convinced my parents I was serious enough about it for them to get me an after school tutor. So, you see! It *was* all your doing.

Now this kind of illogical logic has always smacked to me of the worst metaphysical aberrations of the Far Eastern philosophies, and I quickly enough passed it over as one of the perhaps necessary delusions such an artist as Ken had had to amass over the years to rationalize his success. So I changed the subject as rapidly as I could.

"Tell me," I said. "You told me you usually dine in company before a recital. Surely you couldn't have expected to meet me tonight?"

"No. Well, tonight *was* a bit different. Someone was supposed to join me. But that didn't quite work out. We had a sort of tiff."

"Davey?" I had to ask. "The riff-raff?"

"*Quel* riff-raff!" Ken said. "But despite everything, I'm still madly in love with him."

"I hope it isn't Davey's seat I usurping this evening?"

"No. I had a spare house seat. I always keep one for the last minute. Davey has a ticket. Don't worry. He'll show up sometime during the recital. Show up, begging forgiveness. I'll hesitate, of course. I'll point up the error of his ways for the thousandth time. He'll apologize, promise me things will change. They won't. But I'll try to believe him, and I will forgive him. Noblesse oblige."

"During a gavotte?"

"Afterwards," Ken said, ignoring my remark, half-absorbed envisioning what must have been a fairly common scene between them. "Afterwards, in the green room. After everyone has come to congratulate me. That always has a way of humbling him."

"Well, if that's settled, I don't see why you need me."

"I don't. Davey does. You see, he's so undirected: he has no goals, no aspirations. If only he did have a goal, I'm sure he'd do well. Even make a name for himself. Do something extraordinary. Instead of lolling about the apartment all day, reading comic books and smoking marijuana. Not to mention his more gregarious and active pastimes. It would help keep him out of trouble, too. Not that he's ever been convicted of anything, mind you. At least not in the year or so we've been together. Why, he's never even come to trial, for that matter."

Ken grew pensive for a second, while his words slowly sunk in. Then he brightened up, and went on.

"He's such a natural, instinctive, spontaneous boy. It's really quite refreshing after all the pretentious, half-baked intellectuals I've known, with their soul searching and their psyche analyzing. Davey scarcely knows he has a soul. So full of energy though. If we could only find out what he had a ability for? Why, he could move mountains! Take my word, I wouldn't put it past Davey to do anything. Anything!"

Another five minutes of that sort of conversation—with some biographical and descriptive addenda by my host—and I had a pretty clear picture of Davey and of their relationship. The give-away had been Ken's term "riff-raff." I'd seen others beside Ken get involved with this type of hustler before. Not all of them male either: some were women on the other side of forty, just discovering sensuality after fifteen years or so of marriage. But man or woman, the boy was always the same—I call him Macon, Georgia. So much a type as to be almost archetypal.

You've seen them, I'm sure, seated, vaguely bored, next to an older, often unattractive, but obviously well-heeled man at this year's Broadway hit, or a production at the Metropolitan Opera House. They're usually dressed in a preppy, striped tie, blazer, button-down shirt, Gucci loafers, tan or grey pants pressed to a cutting edge. Groomed to a T, these lads have been groomed in more ways than one. They've come a long way, and the romance—for what it happens to be worth—usually doesn't last too long. The older man becomes demanding. The Macon, Georgia gets rip roaring soused, reveals the depth of his hatred and it's over. Either that, or he just screws around with everyone in the older man's circle, looking for a better bargain.

His name is Davey or Joe or Jeb or Reb. He is between seventeen and twenty seven years old. After that, staying in the game means he's acquired a reputation and a bit of polish, and often is willing to put up with heavy-set millionaires with heart conditions and curious propensities. But Macon, Ga. has fair looks that go quickly to pot if not taken care of, so he's usually young. His hair is longish, often fair. Sometimes when he's hit a good sugar daddy, it's bleached the way the sun can only bleach fair hair on beaches in Caribbean islands. His looks are all-American, Waspy, an ad for the Boy Scouts. He has a hard, muscular body—usually from farm work, chain gangs and reform school gymnasiums, earlier in his career. A scar somewhere on his torso, from a knife fight, he'll confess, when he was fourteen or so, back home, when the other guy got "real messed up." A tattoo on his solid, tawny upper arm that consists of a snake threading through the sockets of a skull, reading "Born to Lose" or "Leola Forever." An appetite for food, drink, drugs and sex that is as mindless and insatiable as any character out of the *Satyricon*. He still drawls, despite the fact he's been up north for a decade. He's sometimes sweet, sometimes shy, never terribly bright and often hostile, vicious and dangerous.

Like his looks, his story is invariably the same. He grew up somewhere south of the Mason Dixon Line in a large, poor family. His father was a laborer or a poor-dirt farmer. He never had enough to eat; never had toys or games to play with; sometimes didn't have shoes to wear until he was twelve. He was overworked, beaten, picked on by teachers and parents until he couldn't stand it. He spent most of his time sitting on a split rail fence watching trains headed for the big cities—sipping an RC Cola and eating a Moon Pie. His sex education was fast, unloving, and extremely varied. He had a hard life, and you could almost pity him. If you believed him.

You or I, anyone with any sense in his head, will beat a hasty retreat after the first conversation with Macon, Ga. Others don't. If, as the song goes, for every man there's a woman, well, then for every Macon Ga. there is a Park Avenue Nob.

Because the boy has a natural complement—lover, victim, whatever: the sugar daddy. Don't ever call him that, however. He thinks he's helping the boy "get on his feet." He's usually professional, well-off if not downright rich, intellectual, well-connected. He's witty, sarcastic, world weary, utterly sophisticated. He's also a sucker for Macon, Ga. I still haven't figured out whether it's just chemistry or some deeper reason—a sort of fantasy narcissism— which drives the sugar daddy into the hustler's arms, but it happens. As the night follows the day, to quote the Bard.

But wasn't Ken Kaufman—younger and more attractive than the usual sugar daddy type—too smart to get hooked up with this sort of nonsense?

"I'm deluding myself, you're thinking," Ken suddenly said.

It was precisely what I had been thinking.

"I'm not, though. I know Davey pretty well. I've seen his type before—with other men. He's different." (Here I couldn't stifle a sigh.) "Evidently you've seen the type before too. But he *is* different. Take my word for it. He's capable of anything. Anything! Look, since we have met, and since you'll be at the recital, why not give me a few minutes of your time afterwards. Join Davey and me for a drink. See him for yourself."

"But I haven't the least interest in Davey," I said.

"That's why. Your disinterest is the very thing needed. You were completely disinterested in that music class: you couldn't have cared less about me or my life. It gave a clarity, a purity even, that someone involved could never have achieved. Almost as though you were a prophet, a seer."

"I'll join you, I'll join both of you. But spare me your odious comparisons."

"Good. I'm sure you'll be good for Davey. I can't explain it. I don't know what you'll tell him. I just feel it. The same way that I feel a particular daring but absolutely appropriate modulation when I'm playing something. Oh, Christ! It's five to eight already, and I still have to stop in a liquor store to buy some brandy."

That's how I went to the recital.

3

I found my seat in the crowded hall, and quickly doffed coat and hat, scanning the program, expecting the house lights to drop any second.

"Take your time," I heard an oily, youngish voice next to me. "I have it on the best word that Kaufman was late. You have plenty of time. He never starts on time, anyway."

I turned to look at the speaker. He was a ginger haired, pale skinned, effete man of indeterminate age (but surely older than his voice by decades!) wearing what passed for a very chic suit.

Before I had a chance to respond, a mousy, grey haired woman—an expensive chinchilla draped around her shoulders—turned around from her seat in front of us to ask him if he'd been in Glasgow the year before.

"Of course," he answered. "Leeds too. Were you there? Do you remember how crowded the tram up was?"

She did. "We flew in," she proudly declared. "We're from Shaker Heights. It's a trip to keep up with Kaufman. But we haven't missed one in years. This is my husband. He's in business."

"I missed Brisbane, five years ago," my neighbor said ruefully. "But I've been to ten recitals in a row since then."

Someone else in the woman's row joined the conversation, then someone behind me. Soon everyone seemed to be discussing which of Ken's recitals they'd attended, what Ken had played, what outrageous stunt he'd performed. It was like a large party awaiting the guest of honor, like a roomful of people awaiting the announcement of the winning number at some mind-boggling lottery. The buzz was loud. Tension and anticipation sent invisible electricity throughout the rows. Snobbery—the cult of Kaufman—ran quite high. Yet for all the oneupmanship there was a sense of communication, of shared tastes. I felt as though I'd wandered by error into a lecture given to the devotees of some wonder-working Swami. If nothing else, I now understood Ken's unshakeable confidence in himself.

I managed to close off enough of the chatter to inspect the hall—it was my first time there. It was much smaller than your standard concert hall. Divided into an orchestra that held about two hundred people, (where I sat) and a balcony holding about a hundred more. That section began about halfway above the lower seats, seats that were wide, roomy, comfortably upholstered in an old fashioned velour with good sized aisles for people to pass without smashing your knees.

The hall had been built at the turn of the century. All of its touches said so: the handsome chandeliers, the plaster ornamentation on the walls, and carved woodwork that would cost a fortune to duplicate today, the high downcurving ceilings, the color—a faded, robinsegg blue. Even the stage—only thirty feet across and ten deep—with its not-quite-to-the-ceiling curtain, had a worn but handsome look.

Despite the period, it didn't look so much Art Nouveau as 18th Century. Its size, elegance, and proportions seemed those of some private opera house attached to the estate of a wealthy Hungarian land-owner of Maria Theresa's time who spent his winters in Vienna, but his summers here, having a private orchestra, and a Kapell-meister to compose and perform operas and symphonies. Haydn would have felt at home.

This effect was heightened when the lights dimmed, bringing on a hypertense hush as the curtains parted to reveal a small, Rococco harpsichord and bench, a chair and music stand.

"He's early," my neighbor complained. "He's so eccentric, isn't he?" he quickly rationalized, and began to applaud. Kaufman and the harpsichordist had just stepped onto the tiny stage.

I thought Ken took an unconsciously long time to set up his chair just so, his music stand just so, to fool around with the accompanist looking for a common tone, to search the audience—(for old faces? for Davey?) before striking the first note. He was playing an authentic 18th century 'cello with a pedigree as long as any debutante, and it had a perfect tarnished gold tone for the Bach duo sonata—the first piece on the program.

I was somewhat unnerved by the breathless hush around me, and I couldn't help but notice how red in the face Ken was— from brandy? I wondered. But it only took a few minutes for old Bach to catch me by the ears, the brain and the heart. I relaxed and enjoyed beautiful music exquisitely played.

Deafening applause followed the piece. Both players came and went offstage and on, taking bows. Then Ken came out alone, carrying his 'cello and bow which he set down. He disappeared and this time returned with the brandy snifter. He set it down on a score, which he placed on the edge of the harpsichord, then moved his chair to be near enough to sip from it. A delighted and somewhat scandalized murmur went up around me.

The next piece was a transcription Ken himself had made of a Couperin suite, originally for two *Viole da Gamba*. Utterly charmed by it, I mentally wandered through the gardens of Petit Trianon, then applauded as wildly as any Kaufmaniac (as I had at first, scornfully dubbed them). Afterwards, during the intermission, I went backstage as he had asked me to do.

He had another snifter in hand, and was looking quite glum.

"He still hasn't arrived," Ken said, swirling the brandy wildly. "Little lower class bastard!"

"Davey?"

"The white man's burden. He's never been this late before. What if…" he hesitated, and I could hear his earlier scenario creak to a stop, like a movie slowing down just before the silver acetate halts, cracks and splashes into flame.

"You're playing wonderfully," I said. "Forget about Davey."

"You will talk to him? Guide him? It would mean so much to me." He swirled the brandy and sipped. "He'll pay for this, if he doesn't show up. I swear it!"

I promised I'd talk to the boy, but I couldn't believe he could worry about such nonsense, playing for all the world like the best I'd ever heard or hoped to hear. So I refused a drink, and decided to return to my seat, leaving Ken to sulk.

My red-haired companion hadn't budged from his seat.

"I wouldn't dare," he explained. "In Salzburg last year, Kaufman waited until everyone had gone out of the hall, then he played the loveliest piece, to no one. Well, not quite no one. I was there. I'd dropped my lapel button, and had been looking for it under the row of seats when suddenly I looked up and there he was, playing to the empty hall. I wouldn't have missed that for anything. She missed it," he said, referring to the mousy haired lady from Shaker Heights, now returning to her seat. "I'll bet she can't read a note of music either," he whispered. "Sybarite! Philistine!" he hissed.

The second half of the program began with another delightful Bach sonata with the harpsichordist. They had played the first two movements, and were about to sail into the finale when Davey came in.

Burst in, rather. Like an outlaw through the swinging doors of a saloon in one of those endlessly similar made-for-TV movies, Davey kicked open both double doors to the orchestra section behind us, strode down the aisle, and shouted:

"Don't anyone make a move. It's loaded!"

He was dressed for the recital, but in much disarray. He also looked drunk. In one hand he held a revolver, pointed at Ken Kaufman's head.

Women screamed. A half dozen men stood half up in their seats only to cower back down, as Davey drunkenly revolved the pistol in wavering arcs.

Ken put his 'cello aside, stood up, and in a voice shrill with annoyance shouted back.

"When will you ever learn manners. You're late. Put down that thing and find your seat!"

Davey lurched forward a few steps, still waving the gun.

"I'm boss now," he said, his drawl enhanced by an alcoholic slur. "I've got a gun and it's loaded. I'm boss now. And you can't talk to me like that!"

Ken ignored him. Speaking to the audience, he said "Ladies and gentlemen. Please keep to your seats. I promise he'll behave himself. I'm sorry to annoy you with this example of domestic squalor."

My companion nudged me. "Isn't it perfect?" He could scarcely suppress his delight. "Just perfect? Like theater. Real theater. Leave it to Kaufman to do something no one else would do."

Davey had advanced down the aisle a bit and was shouting again. "Now I'm going to shoot you. Hold still," he said, attempting to focus on Ken. "I'll get you right between the eyes."

"Put it down, I said!"

Davey looked hurt, lurched a step back. "I'm boss now!"

"Please don't be alarmed ladies and gentlemen..."

Ken never finished the sentence. He was interrupted by a shot. The bullet missed him, but hit the side of the brandy snifter, not shattering it, but shooting it forward off the edge of the stage, spilling the brandy in a thin curtain all over Ken. The accompanist fell backwards off his bench and huddled in a corner.

"You've ruined my pants!" Ken shouted. "I'll kill you!"

Davey must have been sobered a bit by the sound of the gun. He dropped it to the floor and stepped back again.

"Wait for me!" Ken shouted. "Stay where you are!"

It happened in a second. Davey turned to run. Several men jumped out of their seats to stop him. Still purple in the face and shouting, Ken leapt off the edge of the stage into the aisle. But one foot landed on the snifter. It rolled forward with the sudden impetus, and Ken with it. He fluttered in air for a second, looking like some large, ungainly bird struck in mid-flight by a marksman's bullet. Then he fell backwards with a loud, bone-shattering thud.

All hell broke loose. Everyone—even the men who had grabbed Davey—rushed forward to their fallen idol. People shouted for an ambulance. Women screamed "Is he hurt? Is he dead?" over and over again. The center aisle was thick with heads bobbing and bodies crowding to get a glimpse. The mousy-haired lady in front of me stood up, then gracefully fainted back into her chinchilla. My companion was silent, for once, a hand over his mouth.

Stunned Davey stood suddenly abandoned at the back of the hall. Then he seemed to realize what had happened. He collapsed into the nearest seat in a monsoon of tears.

4

It was a month before I visited Ken in the hospital.

After Ken had been taken away on a stretcher, the rest of us milled about the recital hall, striking tragic postures and instant replaying every second of the absurd turn of events. The red-haired Kaufmaniac took my phone number. Somehow he had discovered I was a friend of Ken's and he wanted to keep in touch so he would have reliable information on his idol's state of health.

It was he who prodded me into going to see Ken, he who told me that visitors were being allowed in. Wouldn't I please go? The rumors circulating among the devotees were wild: Ken was totally paralyzed; he was insane; he couldn't speak, etc. etc.; it was worse than when James Dean had died, he said.

Ken could talk. "Don't tell me," he said, when I entered his private room. "I look ghastly."

He did. He was stretched out on a bed with so many side and front support bars it looked like a giant cage. His hair was longer, he looked thinner, and paler than ever.

"It's these damn flowers!" he explained. "Look at them all. Every day there seems to be another batch from Zambia or Afghanistan or Lucerne. The nurses insist on bringing them in and keeping them here for at least one day. They're sucking all the oxygen out of the room. No wonder I'm ill."

"From your fans?" I asked.

"And not only flowers. Look at that mess."

That mess was a large stack of books, greeting cards, unopened and partially opened parcels creeping up one wall of the room, tottering madly.

"It's like a monster. Every day it crawls higher. I'm beginning to have nightmares about it."

I hate to visit people in hospitals as a rule, but Ken was in good spirits, so I sat down, ate out of a box of Godiva chocolates someone had sent him, and listened to him complain for a while. Then I recalled the Kaufmaniacs. I needed some hard information.

The fall had broken a great many bones, Ken said, including twisting his spine like a rubber band. Part of it hadn't twisted back, and that was the major problem because many nerve endings just weren't connecting any more. As a result, he was paralyzed from the waist down ("except for my sex organs—Thank God," he said, "I'm on heavy saltpeter these days.") He had had a minor concussion which had left him aphasiac, but that had soon passed. But the main problem was his spine, and adjusting to his new limitations.

"Naturally, I'll never be able to play the 'cello again," he concluded very matter of factly.

"But why? You have the use of both hands."

"Scarcely. Some nerves were severed. Using them just isn't the same anymore. It's as though I've suddenly been given the hands of a brick layer. There's no sensitivity. No control anymore. And no, it's not like swimming: you don't pick up the hang of it all over again. Ah well, I'll outlive my legend."

I probed more deeply into this. Later on in my visit, when his doctor appeared briefly, I took him aside to get more information. He explained to me in horrifying detail exactly what had been damaged with the fall. Only with a miracle would Ken ever regain the ability to play the 'cello.

"There you see!" Ken said, when the doctor had left, and I stepped into his room again.

"You seem almost pleased about it," I shot back at him.

"Well, I am. Sort of," he said, then changed the subject.

I wondered about this, walking down the corridors, waiting for an elevator, riding down to the lobby. Was he relieved? Or was it all just a brave face he was putting on? Trying to deal realistically with what had to be? All that business with the fans—the annoyance, the mock indignation—seemed to support this last theory. I was both sad and very angry for Ken; so angry that I snorted into the downstairs desk telephone when the receptionist handed me the receiver and told me it was Ken:

"You will speak to Davey still? Won't you? You promised."

"I said I would, didn't I?" I told him. Of course I had no intention of doing it.

"He's been a total angel since that night," Ken said. "So remorseful and guilt-ridden, I hardly recognize him. He'll be here any minute now. He always comes after work. Oh, I didn't tell you, he's got a job now. He comes every day during his lunch hour, and again at night."

I asked myself how long all that would last, but I decided I would be a real villain to strip away Ken's last delusion now that he had so little left.

Leaving the hospital, I heard my name called in a questioning voice. I turned around to find myself facing the culprit himself. Admittedly in a far better state than the last time I had seen him— almost collegiately correct, complete with London Fog raincoat.

He blushed a little when I admitted who I was.

"How's Ken?" he asked, trying to make conversation.

"You're going up there. See for yourself."

"He wanted me to call you up," Davey said. "He said you have something to tell me. Something about my future."

Despite his conciliatory tone and humble attitude, all I thought of was that he was—intact, free, able to use all of his limbs, whereas Ken—well, there was Ken being noble and funny and brave in that hospital bed.

"Your future?" I flared up. "Your future? You ruined the future, the entire life of a great 'cellist like Ken? Snapped it right in the middle, never giving him a chance? And you have the nerve to ask about your future?"

"I...Ken said..."

"There's only one future for you," I said. "And both of us know what that is," I added, bitterly, before spinning on my heel and stalking away.

A minute later I found a cab, and passed Davey, still standing in front of the hospital doors. He seemed shocked, or maybe not, perhaps more meditative.

"Little lower class bastard," I murmured.

"Pardon?" the cabbie asked.

5

There go the house lights. No. Don't rush. We have another minute or so before we have to go in.

Yes, it is a fine recital so far. Possibly even a great one. Those solo Bach Suites were marvellous, I agree. But he's noted for them, you know. He ought to be, after winning the Casals Prize in Barcelona last year.

Yes, he deserved it. He's brilliant. I'm the first to admit it. Who would have thought him capable of it? Who would have thought that a few words, spoken in fury, fifteen years ago would have made any difference? He's been devoted to an invalid that long. It took him that long with dogged perseverance to reach this point.

I hope you won't consider me cranky, though, if I say that for all the technical perfection, the gorgeous tone, the surprising emotional maturity, that David Wrigley's playing simply lacks that inexpressibly grand style of the older masters. His recitals simply don't have that element of...well, of excitement, I suppose.

If you'd ever been at a Ken Kaufman recital, you'd know what I mean.

Shy

Everyone in New York City over thirty years old has a story about the time he went to bed with someone famous. It's almost obligatory listening. Dinner parties are suddenly hushed of dishing and chatter and laughter as the anecdote is launched. Afterwards, a few polite or even curious questions are asked, shoulders shrugged, the fact that "everyone is gay" sure to be brought up, dropped, and the conversation turns back to more fruitful topics: upcoming parties, past ones, private scandals, how so-and-so is fooling himself over what's-his-name's caring.

Of course everyone isn't gay, despite appearances, nor are the famous more prone to such escapades than say, cost systems analysts. As a result, we've heard the same tired old names, the same boring anecdotes over and over again. Nevertheless we do listen, not only politely, but attentively too: for the life of someone well-known to touch our humdrum ordinary lives is unusual enough; to have it touch as closely as sex—no matter how briefly—rubs a little glitter on us. There are other reasons for listening. I'm sure you could roll off a list of them like taffy. All of them rationalizations.

Here's another one. A new one. The story of a blowjob I got from Robertson Webb.

Of course that isn't his real name. Though he is now passed on, I still disguise the name. He was one of my gods while he lived, and the best god's names are never spoken by real devotees.

Like a deity, he swept down on me unawares. Like a god, he kept his real identity hidden from me until he couldn't anymore; and his real self hidden from me altogether.

I'd just come out of an Ingmar Bergman double feature in an upper East Side cinema. To most people, this would suggest that I was suicidally depressed when I first met him. Such was not the case.

I'd had the day off from work. The Manhattan air was swept of the ozone yellow that had gathered all humid day. The city was freshened by the sudden rain. I was twenty-three years old, naive as a racoon, and had been profoundly moved by the two symbolical films I'd watched, smoking Gitanes in the mezzanine: elated by my ability to understand their tortuous messages, to shake my head like an aged Sophocles and say, yes, God is a spider that must be crushed, indeed, Death is always playing a game with us. Etcetera.

Furthermore I was only out a year. All those unruly sex hormones that had lain dormant since puberty as I had dutifully necked and carried on with various socially acceptable young women, were now unleashed in a flood of pheromomes surrounding me in a thick though invisible ooze that sent local animals into fits of leg humping and older queens into swoons of leering. This, despite the fact that, while possibly cute, big-eyed, and curly-haired, I was pudgy, a lousy dresser, perenially sloppy and rather snotty. I *was* horny. That's all that mattered.

Webb picked up the scent a block away, and beaglelike, followed it to its source—myself, in the cinema lobby, waiting for the still dribbling rain to let up enough so I could walk the four blocks to the Lexington Avenue subway. There, I would descend to the bowels of Manhattan—Avenue B and Tenth Street—to my three room railroad flat in a sixth floor walkup, with sagging parquet living room floor, chipped, overpainted French doors to the bedroom, furniture I'd picked up on throwaway Thursdays: all for thirty-eight fifty a month. Ah youth!

Besides the sex smell, Webb was also attracted to a happy young face. I don't doubt it, knowing how screwed-up his own life was since his lover's death, that disfiguring carwreck, the pills, the operations, the fits...I needn't go on: you know the story. Yet I'm sure that what he (and probably I too, for the matter) took for content, was no more than intellectual self-satisfaction, slightly tinged with Bergmannian metaphysics. I was always influenced by a film I'd just seen. I still am.

Blissed out, I walked past my idol without seeing him, past the darkened marquee, past the flowershop, the liquor store, the card emporium. I skipped a puddle, crossed the avenue, and was off.

Webb caught up with me at the next corner. He later mentioned he'd said hello and gotten no answer.

Of course not. I wasn't there. I was mentally traversing the summery fens of Heljosfjoord, suffering in perfect backlighting with a spectacularly photographed reed forest around me that twittered nervously on the sound track: symbolical of something or other I can't just now recall.

Webb almost gave up that moment. Happily, he also caught a glimpse of my dungareed inseam, which after all was his main concern, and it so whetted his appetite for confirmation, he followed for another two blocks, now alongside me, now behind me, like a tugboat guiding a huge, daffily steered ocean liner out to sea. Oblivious, I floated on.

But not for long. I was walking under some largish trees (largish for Manhattan that is) when a vagrant breeze struck from behind, shaking a tiny shower of iced water off the leaves, down the back of my neck. Rudely awakened from my cinematographed Swedish dreams, I dashed out of the treacherous cover—right into Webb.

That's when I first noticed the dark umbrella, and the handsome vaguely familiar face.

Confused by his nearness, his surprise, and his assumption that we were to have conversation if not further contact, I stopped. I apologized for my swerve and crash. I also felt a strange hesitation in my headlong rush to the subway.

He didn't say anything immediately. I got the impression he wanted to. He certainly looked at me as though he wanted to, but didn't know what to say. That was also my first intimation that he was shy.

Baffled, I continued walking toward the subway again, but I adjusted my pace to his, allowing him to join me.

Conversation was limited and difficult. Any opening line he might have been squirrelling up to hit me with had been utterly destroyed by how we had met. Meanwhile, I wondered what exactly he meant by walking along with me. I tried sizing him up. He wore no hat, although he looked as though he ought to be wearing one. I didn't know many men like that. He was handsome, but not with the fresh ethnic handsomeness of most young men I was attracted to. His looks were a designed handsomeness: designed to be seen, to be taken for something else, for anything but streetcorner pickups. Then too, he was familiar. Not that familiar. But familiar enough that I wasn't certain if he had once taught in a high school I had visited on a track meet, or whether he was a regular habitue of one of the sawdust strewn bars I infrequently patronized, or if he simply resembled someone I used to know and hadn't seen in years.

He wore a beautifully cut dark topcoat, dark, well pressed slacks, stubbytoed brown shoes. All elegant, although slightly worn too. And he was in his forties—meaning old to me then—and so less easy to get along with. Then too, he was a stranger, a distinctly strange stranger. Bear in mind those symbol drenched spiders and chessmen—sex had been the last thing on my mind that evening.

We walked another block. The subway hove into sight. His shyness became almost painful as he tried to engage me in talk. I was full of Bergman, but all he seemed to want to know was where I lived.

When I said downtown, he stopped, folded the umbrella (needlessly open since he'd met me) and asked if I would go home with him.

If I were unsure of his intentions before, I was really unsettled now. I've given and gotten this line enough times to know it can be said in a variety of ways: seductively, secretively, openly, boyishly (no matter the age), slimily. Webb asked it a new way—the way a loyal but fatally wounded co-star in a Grade B western begs the hero to go on, please, to save himself, but to leave the revolver behind—and one bullet. He said it with that famous, inexpressible, well-documented 35 millimeter shyness.

I missed the allusion and dithered. I always dither when I can't make up my mind. Nowadays, of course, after meeting a hundred thousand men on a hundred thousand streetcorners, I either say "no" or "let's go." Then, I had the usual fears of the inexperienced: I would be drugged and forced to do repulsive things; I'd be tied up and ravaged by a dozen of his friends and several large dogs; I'd be strangled and left to molder in a cellar.

Today my worries at such times are realistic: whether the man has a penchant for, say, eating Tuna salad out of armpits, or bites when he's not supposed to, or will bore me so much I'll fall asleep. Real, live, justified fears.

Shyly, Webb rephrased his offer. He asked if I'd like a drink. I said I was still trying to make up my mind.

"Just one," he said, and was so instantly distraught by his boldness, he modified that to "only if you want to."

Let me add here that the situation was further complicated by my awareness that I suddenly had a trouser bulging hardon from the merest whisper of a suggestion of sex, one that I was certain was treacherously apparent to him.

But he was wavering, which I didn't like. Really very shy. So I said, why not.

He collected himself, reopened the umbrella (still not needed), swung it behind his shoulder, and started off in the direction we'd just come from, walking so fast I had to ask him to slow down. I had the vague feeling he was trying to lose me.

In the middle of the next block, he turned suddenly into a lower level, cast iron-grilled doorway. I almost walked past. He frowned and motioned me in.

The small, dark townhouse hallway smelled of silence. I now know from his official posthumous biography, that at least one other person lived there: his male nurse, companion, shoulder to cry on, disciplinarian. But he must have been out or sleeping because we were very hush hush in the corridor. Someone might have been dying one floor above.

Webb hung up his coat and my jacket and the umbrella (now closed) on an old wooden contraption. Slowly, because he wouldn't flick on more than a tiny night light bulb, he stumblingly led me to a doorway. A bedroom.

I wouldn't go in. He'd offered a drink. I would have a drink.

He mumbled a barely comprehensible apology, led me back through the dark hallway to an equally small room, lighted only by two fluted red-shaded lamps like those in forties nightclubs movies where beautiful women are wittily outfoxing each other over men you seldom see and who don't look worth the effort once you do see them. He pointed to a tufted leather sofa, and disappeared upstairs.

I sat on the creamily smooth sofa as if it would be electrified any second. I glanced about, saw heavy dark furnishings, tiny, thick framed rotogravure cartoons and autographs too aged and distant to be read from where I sat.

I should note that in my youth I shared the fallacy with many others equally misinformed that decoration would tell something of the man. Lies! I've been subjected to scat fetishists in spotlessly clean, crystal filled, metal and glass gleaming duplexes; gotten cautious handjobs from slavering leather covered pornographers in semi-furnished rundown sublets, had eight hour passion sessions with collectors of Pickanninniana. There's no link, believe me.

He was gone long enough for my discomfort level to rise to danger. Several times I thought I heard footsteps, conspiratorial voices, chains rattling.

I almost jumped when he finally returned. He held two water glasses and a Fifth of Bourbon. No tonic. No water. No lemon. No ice. I insisted on *something*. He got water from the sink in the next door powderroom. Webb drank his bourbon neat, keeping the bottle on the floor next to the barcolounger he sat in, his knees so close to mine they threatened to touch any moment.

Again I tried to make conversation: failed utterly, nursing the drink I'd forced him to bring me, and which I could neither drink, nor admit I loathed. I also had the feeling he'd somehow or other dishonestly gotten the liquor, making me complicit in his guilt.

There's a scene in one of his earlier films when Robertson Webb confesses a particularly gruesome and unmotivated murder. The camera zooms in front, and hovers slightly above his head. He sits in a captains chair, looking at his feet, then up again, nervously, compulsively, his face alternately swathed in shadows and lighted by the constant flickering of a neon sign outside the window. His voice in that scene is the only sound we hear: it is like millions of tiny pebbles amassing in a steady, advancing, rolling avalanche. Although he didn't say a word, that's how he struck me. As though he would explode into sudden total mania.

That, and his neurasthenic shyness.

Where do I know him from, I wondered once more. His large, bright eyes, sunken as they were in his face were recollections, the wild planes of his cheekbones and temples were memories from my childhood, the shape of his head, his gestures were utterly, fully remembered. From where?

It began to rain again. Minutes passed. I stared at him, then away from him, at a wall. My fears were slowly dissipating; but so were any ideas of having sex. I was searching for a polite lie to get out of that room.

Webb drank more bourbon neat, looked at the floor, didn't say a word. I might not have been there.

I don't know how long that went on before I decided I had to leave: now!

When I stood up, he sighed, almost as if that were exactly what he had suspected would happen when he'd first met me. He even seemed relieved. He set down his glass, and led me out into the little hall. I was glad to get out without any further embarrassment. Yet for all the relief on both sides, we were disappointed.

We reached for my worn tweed jacket at the same time. Our

hands must have brushed. I pulled back. So did he. The jacket dropped. He bent down to get it, almost fell getting up, had to hold onto my legs for support. I thought: this man is drunk and ought to be put to bed.

Though I said I would do it myself, he insisted on putting my jacket on me, mumbling all the while. I finally consented. As I turned around, lifted both arms and felt the sleeves slipped on, he sort of tumbled on me, catching himself, and turning the stumble into kissing the nape of my neck: one of my turn-on points then, as now.

Surprised, I turned around to a bourbon-scented, sloppily executed kiss on the lips, interspersed with enough garble for me to figure out I was being asked not to leave yet.

Without a further hint, he fell to his knees. I offered to help him up, and was slurringly told to "relax, just relax." He pushed me slightly, so I fell against the wall a few inches. Then he unzipped my fly.

It was awkward: unavoidable.

Then it wasn't awkward. I was horny. He was accomplished. We could have been anywhere. A dune in Autumn, windbreakers flapping, gulls mewling overhead, the surf. On a penthouse sofa, skyscraper lighting through clerestories high above, soft taped music. Under the rusted hanging spar of an abandoned river warehouse, shirtless on a July night. Or —in the dark lower corridor of an East Side townhouse.

We could have been anyone. He the next door neighbor's guest. I the teenager, home from school. We could have been lovers for the past twenty years, suddenly alone from the houseparty in the Hamptons, determined to do something lovely for each other. Or— we could have been a young man and a movie star.

You know how it can be: timeless, archetypical. We got into it.

When we had both regained our footing again, Webb smiled for the first time; a little crookedly I thought. I asked him to point me to the john.

As I was taking a leak, I noticed another autographed photo exactly at eye height. This room had better light than anywhere else in the house so far. I clearly saw this was a "still" from a movie named "Cord," a popular Western with a message from late in the fifties. The photo showed the three leads from the film, waist up, all leaning on a verandah railing, looking off-screen to what might have been a wedding party or approaching storm. You could read their love triangle from their positions, from how they looked. In the lower left-hand edge, over black, white handprinting told the film's title, the studio, and the stars. The odd man out was the man who'd just had me in the corridor: Robertson Webb.

"That's where I know him from," I thought at once, so hard I was sure it was heard all over the house.

Then the shock hit me. I had to close the toilet and sit down.

It was unprecedented. Robertson Webb, a legend since the forties, friend of Hepburn, Gable, Taylor, one of the brightest of that bright constellation of bright stars, the man who'd been my idol for decades, who'd torn my heart in film after film as the sensitive, defiant, troubled underdog—had gone down on me as though I were the best looking Third Avenue hustler.

How could I show him I wasn't? How could I explain to him what he'd meant to me? How he'd been part of my thinking, fantasizing life since before I'd had erections?

I knew chance hadn't brought us together. All my life had conspired to bring me to this moment. Hadn't I seen every one of his films—even the occasional turkey—at least twice? Hadn't I offered up secret prayers to his image, or at least to the image of the person I believed he was? Hadn't I always thought in my moments of deepest depression "If only he, Webb, were here, everything would be different, better. He'd help me, protect me." It couldn't be a chance meeting!

Then I thought of his life, of how he looked in the corridor when he'd smiled. Only half of his face had seemed mobile. The left side had no resilience, no life. I recalled the near fatal car crash, the rumors of plastic surgery, of bone rebuilding, of steel plates put inside his skin. I shivered.

This gloomy house, his furtiveness, his unhappiness—all these tugged at me. I had to convince him that I would annihilate his worries, sweep despair out of his life, obliterate pain, extinguish the depredations of his past. I would bring light and youth into his life. I'd come to love his half destroyed beauty as we come to love a shattered and imperfectly restored antique vase of great value. I'd give him new faith in himself. Revitalize his confidence, help to make him an even bigger star than before. I'd be his confidant, his friend, his brother, his son, his lover. I'd bring grams and grams of semen to his hungry mouth. Who knew, I'd probably even let him fuck me.

I didn't move from my perch on the toilet seat.

The first wave of euphoria was followed closely by one equally powerful, but more disturbing. It was ridiculous to think Webb could change so quickly, so thoroughly at his age and with his experience. I understood why it had taken him so long to get the bourbon: it had been locked away, hidden from him by someone else. He'd been an alcoholic. Probably still was. Then the pills, the other, harder drugs he'd taken that I'd heard about, counted as lies for years, knew all the while I was blinding myself to the truth because it didn't matter then. I was young, impressionable. He would love me, yes, I knew he would. But he would drag me down along with him into alcoholism, needles, mindless orgies. Not to mention his frequent bouts of depression, his stays in expensive out-of-state clinics. It would be hell.

Suddenly I felt as though I had been in the bathroom for hours. I had no idea what to do, what to say. Inside me, angels and devils, hope and reason, illusion and reality warred, and all I could think of was what to say to him when he finally got worried enough to knock on the door and ask if I'd fallen in. I had to forestall that. I flushed the toilet and looked out into the hallway.

He was gone.

I checked the two small rooms. Empty. I even thought of going upstairs, no matter what horrifying scene I might walk into between Webb and whomever had hidden the Bourbon from him.

Then the door we had come in through began to open and I almost fell down in a faint.

It was Webb, coatless, though he'd been outside. He was carrying a small plastic garbage container in one hand, saw me, put the container hastily on the side of the door.

"Almost forgot to do that," he said in a small voice. He was as uncertain what to say as I was. So shy.

Then an odd thing happened. I saw myself as Webb would see me, my pants half-zipped, my jacket still askew on me, my face reflecting that blankness that young people get when some strong emotion is passing through them. Simultaneously I was afraid of myself. What if this kid wanted money now, and would do anything to get it? What if he decided to blackmail me, knowing now who I am? He might have been playing along all this while. My trust in his large, soft brown eyes after all that time might have been displaced. How do I get him out? Worse, what if he's one of my fans and wants to stay and talk to me for hours about a life I'd rather forget, people I wished I'd never met, films I hated to make. When all I want to do is take a hot shower and go to sleep.

Then it was over. I saw once more as myself.

That was all I needed. I buttoned my jacket, zipped up my fly, feeling a tiny, post-fellatal stickiness on my upper left thigh—the only physical proof that something had indeed just happened—and went toward Webb.

He began to say something, then stopped himself. I held out my hand. "Thanks," I said. "See you later."

"Do you want to...?" he began to say, then once more stopped. "No," he added in a different tone. "You're taking the subway home, you don't need a cab, do you?"

We shook hands, the door opened, and I was out on the street again.

I don't know what got into me then, but I waited there for another minute or so. Perhaps I expected him to look out, see me, open the door and repeat the offer to see me again. I don't know for certain.

The three upper floors were dark as before. The lower windows were tiny, unalterably dim. Downstairs seemed dark too. I realized the door wasn't going to open. It was beginning to drizzle again. I'd better get to the subway before it began to pour.

§

I never saw Webb again. Oh, I could have, I suppose, if I were in that neighborhood more often, or if I were more persistent or he less shy.

I had pretty much forgotten about the incident until recently when you introduced me to that young man who vaguely reminded me of him.

Let me light a cigarette. There. Now, who's the famous person you made it with?...Who?...Darling, never heard of him.

Teddy—The Hook

Two weeks after the fall of Saigon, I received the following letter from Lt. Corporal Robert Kincannon:

As you were a great friend of Teddy's I thought you should know that he was reported shot down in action during the final airlift out of South Viet Nam. The funeral will be held in a few weeks, as soon as the casket containing his remains arrives. Call the funeral home, (card enclosed) for details. I also enclose some photos taken of Teddy not too long ago. I thought you might want to keep one or two.

The half dozen color snapshots all showed Teddy Kincannon as I'd last seen him, although in a different setting by far. His curly blonde hair was longer by inches than anyone in the Army ought to have it. He was tanned, healthy, superbly muscled beneath the flimsy sweat stained army green a-shirt. His teeth were a shocking white amidst all that dense verdant South Asian foliage, the upper half of his face shaded to obscurity by the peak of his cap.

In one photograph, Teddy was sitting in the navigator's seat of a helicopter. A white popper case hung around his neck on a leather thong. A long, loosely rolled joint of marijuana was gripped in the molars of his flashing grin. Teddy was making the peace Vee sign with one outstretched hand. His other grasped his crotch suggestively. Barely visible under the leather seat was a six-pack of Kirin beer, no doubt stashed there for coolness.

That was the photo of Teddy I kept: the one most like him.

Nor did I feel more than a passing sadness, "great friends" as his father wrote that we were. Instead, that night I went out dancing and later on trashing. Not to forget, not to throw myself into sensual oblivion. Not to celebrate either. But because I knew, without having a single fact to back me up, that when Teddy Kincannon went down in flames inside that whirlybird, he had a beer in one hand, a joint in the other, was high, happy, joking as usual, and was perhaps only for a fraction of a second surprised to realize he was about to die.

That's how Teddy was. Nothing—not danger, not death, not even the U.S. Army in the middle of one of its stupidest wars could change him. He was the Fool in the Tarot deck—a dog nipping his heels as he chased after a glittering butterfly above his head, heedlessly stepping off a cliff. The seeming fool is the wisest of men, however. Teddy at the young age of twenty-one, had found himself. And in so doing, taught me a lesson. Was the lesson, really. He was also one of the best lovers I ever had. He was six pack Teddy Kincannon, and he came to proudly call himself Teddy the Hook.

I'd better start at the beginning: in the mid-Sixties.

I was a senior in college when I first met Teddy. I'd just had mid-term exams at school and so had been away studying for a week from my father's export business where I worked a few hours a day after school, keeping his account books and generally organizing the chaos of his billing and filing systems.

About a dozen men worked there—ranging from two teen aged weekend helpers, to Jim Naylor, in his seventies, the janitor. There were six trucks, and supposedly six drivers, although we always seemed to be short a driver or two. The dispatcher, Murray, a family man in his forties who'd worked for my father for two decades held the place together, and pretty much kept the drivers in line. These guys were uneducated, wild-livers, bachelors or divorcees, mostly in their late twenties or early thirties: strong enough to be able to load and unload the trucks and drive all night without sleep. None of them took the work seriously, except on payday. Some were incipient alcoholics, weekend drug addicts and simple jerk-offs.

So, it was hardly surprising when I returned to find one driver, Alfie Chambers gone, and a new driver in his place. I first saw him at rest—also unsurprising, given the amount of goofing off Murray had to contend with. He was sitting with his feet stretched out in front of him on the elevated tailboard of an unladen, parked truck, his shirt open to the unusually strong mid-April sun, drinking a can of Rheingold. What was surprising about him was his good looks and his age—he couldn't have been more than twenty, my own age. As I passed him, I said "Hi!" and he raised the beer, toasting me or inviting me to have one, I didn't know which.

"Who's that?" I asked my father when I got into the office.

"From the neighborhood. Good-hearted kid, strong, good worker. That Alfie! You know what he did?"

I managed to escape my father's litany of complaints and went into the warehouse where I found Murray sitting on some packing cases, doing a *Daily News* crossword puzzle in ink.

"Who's the new driver?" I asked.

"Six pack Teddy," Murray said, without looking at me or lifting his pen from its progress on the page. "He puts 'em down like I never saw before. Doesn't seem to get drunk, though. I keep telling him he's going to wake up one morning and find himself with gut like mine. What's a six letter word that goes with a cold?"

"Cough," I said. "How long has he been here?"

"A few days. Damn you!" Murray said. He'd filled in "cough" and realized it only had five letters. "Get outta here!"

"Who are you?" I asked Teddy directly, a half hour later when he came into the office for me to check his lading bill.

"Theodore L. Kincannon, Sir!" he said, making an awry salute. "But my real pals call me Teddy the Hook. Want to see why?"

Now, while having a nickname, especially such an obvious one as "Six pack," wasn't rare among my friends, having two nicknames was.

Before I could respond, or Teddy do more than begin to open the brass buckle across his light colored chinos, Murray called him sharply. Teddy tipped his beer to his mouth, dumped it in my waste basket and said:

"Going to have to wait. See you."

On a scale from one to a hundred in physical beauty, Ted Kincannon was ninety-nine and fourty-four one hundredths percent perfect. That clean, that healthy. Oh, someone once said his nose was a bit too aquiline for one so young. They could already make out in it a drinker's thick red honker. And I once knew a girl who said that Ted's aqua eyes though indicative of much: passion, humor, sensuality,—never went out of their way to spotlight intelligence. What's the difference? Every other feature was unimpeachable. His skin was like that satin you used to find on the insides of expensive Valentines you bought for your mother. He had a head of hair so yellow, so curly, so fine, so abundant that every woman who saw it envied him. His smooth, hairless, perfectly proportioned body was without scar or mar. He had the complete animal health of his age, and the utter lack of absorption in his looks that often make the young so heartless.

Mind you, I didn't really appreciate him at first. I wasn't all that easy to impress, in general. I considered myself evidently superior to anyone working for my father, by virtue of my education, position and prospects. Besides, I still hadn't discovered men.

Perhaps I ought to clarify. I had intense interest and admiration for others of my sex before I met Teddy. For example, in junior high school, I was crazy about David Regen, who at thirteen years old with a perfect body and dazzling face would bound into gym class with scruffed sneakers, socks falling at his shapely ankles, shorts that fit breathtakingly too close, a four inch tear in his t-shirt. That earned him demerits from the gym instructors. It earned him silent adoration from me—and others in the class—who saw him as a sort of pre-adolescent James Dean or Marlon Brando. Not knowing any better, I was intuitively pleased to see David. His grace and swagger and skill on the track and on the basketball court were easy to admire. If I ever wondered why I liked looking at him, I usually answered myself that it was because he was aesthetically pleasing, complete, not much different say, than listening to Stravinsky's *Firebird*.

How else could I perceive David? Or Teddy? Liking boys wasn't merely unacceptable: it was beside the point. Girls were bright, sociable, verbal, far more interesting. They were also dying to try out sex. All my friends had been seduced in a park or in someone's darkened basement by the time they were fourteen. I was no exception. Our liberal, middle-class parents didn't mind. They seemed to endorse our going steady early; as though our passion would soon decline into the tedium of marriage more efficiently that way, and so make us less trouble for them. I'm not even sure they knew what going steady meant for us. I suppose they thought it meant always having someone to go with you to a movie or a dance or party. That was certainly so. But it also meant getting laid regularly in one more uncomfortable spot than the last. Later on, of course, when the girls turned seventeen and began reading *Bride* magazine, they were all suddenly virgins again: untouchable, unless you were their steady, in which case all was as before. With that much satisfaction offered to our unruly adolescent gonads, why would anyone dream of wanting a change? So, when I first met Teddy, I told myself he was like David Regen, a perfect example of a type: another aesthetic experience.

A few weeks after his arrival at my father's business I received the first glimmering of the reason behind Teddy's nickname. I came out of the office one evening to find several drivers sitting around talking, preparatory to getting their weekly paychecks. As I was pretty much accepted as a peer by them, they went on talking and joking when I sat down near them on a packing crate.

"You'll be borrowing ten dollars from me by next Wednesday," Danny, a black driver with a sweet disposition but a short temper (attested to by various pink facial scars that cut across his mahogany skin), said to Teddy. "What do you do with it all? You're just a kid."

"I don't get paid all that much," Teddy protested. He had a Schlitz in his hand, two more behind him, ready.

"It's all the beer," Vito put in.

"I buy it by the case. Cheaper."

"It's girls," Danny said. "Tell us, Theodore, how do you find all those pretty girls."

"He's pretty too. Like likes like," Murray said.

"They like to play with your hair?" Danny said.

"You got any black chicks?" Vito asked, looking to make trouble.

"What is it, Teddy," Danny went on asking in a lower voice, "all those girls—black, white and in between like so much about you?"

"Must be something special about you."

"My good looks."

"Maybe a bit more special than that. Come on. We're friends here. You can tell us. Maybe it's something you're hiding from us," Danny concluded, chuckling low.

Teddy chug-a-lugged the Schlitz, then shot-put it into a garbage can fifteen feet away. He put his hands in his pockets.

"I suppose I do have something special. I call it the hook. Once they get a little bit of the hook, no ordinary thing will do. I just can't keep them away."

"Yeah!" Danny said. "Tell us about it, Teddy."

From his swagger, Teddy changed into shyness, as though he'd been trapped into saying it, and now regretted it.

"Aint nothing else to say."

They all slapped each others palms and laughed, and kept on repeating "The hook," with lewd intonations. Teddy popped open another Schlitz and began drinking it. A few more comments were made, suggesting this was hardly a new topic with them.

I found it grotesque and vulgar: typical I thought of the entire working classes disgusting treatment of women, sex and each other. I—who studied American Literature from Freneau to Fitzgerald— felt the discussion of a physical deformity in public shameful. I'd have no part of it. So I returned to the office to see what was holding up the paychecks.

The next week, Ted did borrow money from Danny—and from Vito too. I was invited to a party. Because of that incident I'd pretty much cooled to Teddy, aesthetic experience or not. So, I hesitated.

"When is it?"

"Saturday night," he said, not affected by my lack of enthusiasm. He was clearly looking forward to it. I thought well, poor guy, he isn't that smart, what does he know?

"We'll go have dinner somewhere, then drive over. It's not too far from a friend of mine's house."

I still had no idea what to say. What would Teddy's friends be like? Did I want to know? Did I want to go around with a good looking clown who made fun of his own genitals?

"They'll be girls there," he tempted. "Girls, liquor—and pot, too."

I knew Teddy smoked grass a couple of times. So had I. We talked about it once or twice. He'd agreed it sure beat drinking beer, though he'd never give that up. My experiences had all been in an apartment on Twelfth Street and Avenue D in Manhattan, with anarchist student friends, who lived there in dark, small, elevatorless walk ups, and who got high and laughed a lot and sang songs like *La Bandera Rosa,* which they'd been taught by their socialist fathers, some of who had fought for the Republicans in Spain in the Thirties. Somehow, I couldn't picture Teddy among them. Their long scruffy afro hairdos and awful clothing—his clean, blond good looks: their verbal peregrinations in a half dozen languages—his verbal simplicity. So naturally, perversely, I decided I wanted to see Teddy high on grass. I agreed to go.

We had dinner that Saturday night in a Chinese restaurant with deep-red naughahyde booths, white formica tables, red paper lanterns and four other customers. Ted had two Budweisers before dinner, another with his Moo Goo Gai Pan, and bought another six pack for later on.

The party was held in a shabby gray frame house in a rundown area. We drove past blocks of parked cars to park. Even from that distance, we could hear the music blaring. All the houses around us were dark. Abandoned? I wondered.

The party seems to have peaked ten minutes before we arrived. Afterwards, it stumbled into a rapid decline. Not because of us: but from overuse of alcohol and perhaps sheer inertia. By the time we'd made our way through the dim foyer to the kitchen where we secreted Ted's six pack minus one beer for each of us, the party was going downhill fast. Two couples were in the living room, slowly revolving as they pretended to dance. Other couples and groups were necking in corners or shuffling up the stairs to the second floor. Another seven people were passed out, some curled around the lintels of doorways. It was far too dark to make out any of their faces. The music had been turned down to a whisper.

Ted shook one of the bodies he recognized, and asked the guy where the pot was.

"Never mind the pot," I said. "Where's the party?"

The guy mumbled something inaudible and slid back onto the floor. Persevering, Teddy tried other bodies: no luck. Then he marched through the house, snapping on lamps, despite loudly voiced complaints from couples in various states of undress and copulation, in one room after another. He reminded me of someone making a house arrest. We tripped over more bodies, bumped into tables and chairs, were struck at feebly. We finally located a large, pink, fluted-glass candy dish on a table, containing enough pot for one joint. I rolled it, and we sat forlornly in the quickly redarkened living room, hearing people panting around us, as we smoked the grass and tried to figure out what to do next.

I wanted to drive around. Ted insisted on finding another party and crashing it.

A distant siren came closer. Just as I thought it was going to arch away again, it seemed to come closer.

"Oh, boy," I teased. "They're coming here."

Then the sirens were very loud. I looked out the window behind the chair I sat in. Red lights swirling.

"It's a raid!" Teddy said, excitedly. "Hey," he said, trying to rouse some of the people in the room, "we're being raided!" They shrugged him off, or fell back onto the floor, unhearing, uncaring. I however had just gotten off on the grass, and his alarm transferred to me as full blown paranoia.

"They'll put us in jail," I said. "Throw away the key."

"We've got to get out of here," he agreed.

The two cars came to a stop outside the house. We could hear the doors slamming shut.

"How do we get out?"

Ted remembered the backdoor, leading to a backyard.

We hurried out, and just as we closed the kitchen door behind us, we could see through the hallway the front door being pushed open with no effort at all, since no one had dreamed of locking it. The flashlights swished around the walls and floors, picking out bodies.

"Let's go," I whispered. I could taste adrenalin in my mouth.

We turned to face a small fenced-in yard, surrounded on either side by dozens of seemingly identically sized, fenced-in yards. The only exit was out front, past the driveway, into the arms of policemen.

We ran to a far corner of the yard, where shelter from some bushes seemed likely protection.

"Get down," Teddy said.

I flattened myself to the ground, just in time to miss being caught in the glare of a flashlight swinging through the darkness.

"Stay down," Teddy instructed. Then, "that's all my old man would need now, is to have to come bail me out."

We lay prone for what seemed to be an hour. Then I rolled over, into a rose bush that had torn my shirt a bit when I fell, and I looked up. A clear night sky, speckled with stars. It was June, warm, the ground dry. The roses smelled heavenly. A beautiful night.

"I'm dry," Ted grumbled. "I sure could use a beer."

"Go get one."

"I could. I could be in and out of the kitchen in a second. Through the back door."

"You'd be caught," I said.

"Yeah. I would be caught. I always get caught."

A few lights had gone on in the house. We could make out shadows of people moving erratically.

At that instant, I thought about Teddy's enthusiasm for the party when he'd invited me: his high hopes for it: and how badly it had turned out. Then I remembered sitting across from him in the restaurant, carefully asking me or the waiter what each dish was, drinking his beer, and then his discussion in pidgin English with the waiter about the various brands of beer they'd tasted and which was best: a serious discussion for them both. Then I imagined Teddy sneaking over to the back door, getting in, getting a hand into the fridge, before a policeman's handcuffs descended, and how Teddy would explain he'd left the beer the day before. It was hysterical. I began to laugh.

"Shhhh," Teddy whispered.

So, of course, I had to try to tell him about it, and how funny it was. My words could barely get out through my laughter.

"C'mon," he said. "Keep it down."

Even funnier. How much further down could I go in my young life, than hiding out in a garden while a boring party was being shaken awake so it could be raided.

Ted jumped onto me and put a hand on my mouth.

"I don't want to be caught! Keep quiet!"

Now I began rocking, vibrating with laughter I couldn't stop. One hand flew up and rhythmically began hitting Ted's side. He put it down and held it. My other hand flew up to do the same, and was intercepted by his other hand holding it down too. Having nothing left to cover my mouth, he put his own mouth on it.

That was even funnier. Even so, it worked. Only a few hisses of giggles escaped from me. Finally, I settled down, my convulsions decreasing rapidly, waiting for him to get off me.

He didn't. He began to kiss me. He began to tongue kiss me.

I panicked. I struggled. He held me down even more tightly, and kissed me more lubricously.

Now at my young age I'd been kissed awfully well. At spin the bottle parties, in the back seats of cars at drive-ins, at beaches at night, even in an airplane by a stewardess on a night flight, with everyone around us asleep. The year before I'd been kissed so long and so well in the darkened kitchen of a New Years party by a Swedish exchange student named Lena, that I'd almost fainted from lack of breath and ecstasy. I'd never been kissed like this before. Nor, more importantly, by another guy. So, my first surprise was that it wasn't very different. Then, that it really was. Even the most passionate kissing girls hadn't been as forceful, as determined, as perservering as Teddy. High from the grass, and unable to do anything else, I kissed him back. I thought that suddenly finding my tongue inside his own mouth, Teddy would come to his senses, let go of me, and get up. No way. Instead, he did let go of my arms, but only because he wanted to caress me; instead he kissed me harder, and began rubbing me too. Within minutes, we were engaged in a sexual activity new to me—defined in current concerned women's magazine articles on teen-agers as "petting to orgasm." Neither of us stopped then, either. The lights had gone off in the house, the occupants had been pulled out, the police sirens had wailed off contritely into the distance before we stopped.

We finally broke away: panting.

"They're gone," Teddy finally said, his voice dropped several tones lower to what I would later recognize in other men's voices as post-coital basso.

We sat up, looked around, avoided looking at each other, then stood up, brushed ourselves and each other off, and let reality seep in again.

"Maybe we'd better jump over a few fences and go out someone else's driveway," I suggested. "Just in case."

Ted went over to the kitchen window, trying the now locked back door.

"My beer's still in there," he reported, sorrowfully.

"Jesus," I said, checking my watch. "It's almost three. I'd better get home."

Ted was jumping up now, trying to look into the window. "Four of them left," he moaned.

"I'll bet the cops swiped them."

We snaked out of the side driveway, and finding no one waiting for us, hurried to the car.

Going home in Ted's car, I felt utterly exhausted. The excitement and the grass had both worn off. I could barely stay awake. All Teddy did was talk about how after he got me home he was going to have to look around for a place to buy beer at this hour without having to pay Bar and Grill prices.

You would think that a connection that began as suddenly and passionately would soon turn into high romance with all the dressings. You'd be wrong.

The next work day, Teddy didn't show up; called in sick—a hangover it was suspected. Then it was Tuesday, and I was out. Wednesday evening he was on a trip to Connecticut and because he drove all night, he didn't come in Thursday either. By Friday, I wondered about what had happened between us, I also wondered whether or not anything at all *had* happened in that backyard. Perhaps I ought to chalk it up as another weird experience on drugs, and forget it.

"Guess what?" Teddy said the minute I saw him. "I've been greeted."

"Greeted?"

Teddy pulled out an official looking piece of stationery with a subway token taped onto its lower half and began to read, "Greetings. You have been..."

"When?" I asked, interrupting him. I knew very well what else the letter said.

"I take the physical exam tomorrow. Think I'll fail?"

If Teddy had committed suicide on the doorsteps of the Selective Service Board and then dragged in to take the physical exam, he still would have done better than some of the guys they got.

"My old man is going to bust a gut," Teddy said. "He wanted me to join up two years ago. He's been Army all his life. He said I should get special training. Officer's training. Marine Corps. Paratroopers. Anything but the infantry."

He chug-a-lugged a Schaefer, and threw it into the waste barrel.

"Isn't there anything wrong with you?" I asked.

"Hemorrhoids is the worst thing I've ever had," Teddy said, oddly nonplussed. Then he went into the office for his paycheck.

He was accepted of course, and less than a month later, he was inducted. I saw him only two times between. He quit work a week after his physical, deciding that if he had to go, he might as well party up until the day he had to report in.

It was three and a half months before I saw him again. By then, I'd argued with my parents over something trivial which nevertheless stood for everything, had moved out of their house, and was living among my college anarchist pals on East Eleventh Street and Avenue D in Manhattan. I no longer worked for my father either. I now depended on my savings from the previous three years, and on a state scholarship. I managed to live quite comfortably, although extremely economically. If I miss anything about my youth, it's how few things I seemed to need then: a suitcase of clothes, a cot, a table and chair, a few pots and dishes and glasses, a lamp, a little phonograph, a few records and paperback books. Nowadays... why go on? I was on my own, and delighted in my fifth floor studio walk-up.

One early evening I'd just gotten home from a two hour perusal of a second hand bookstore nearby ("none higher than a dollar," the sign outside read), when I got a phone call from Teddy. He must have found my name in the telephone directory.

"I need a favor," he began.

"If it's money, forget it, I've got three dollars," I replied with the casual honesty of a real friend.

"It's not money. I've got money. What I need is a place to stay tonight. I'm on leave. I'm seeing Eileen and I can't take her to my old man's place or to her parent's house. You know what I mean?"

Disappointment, but then what did I expect? At least I now had the gratification of knowing that night in the backyard meant nothing to Teddy.

"I'll buy you dinner and a movie," Teddy offered, "if you go to a double-feature."

Little as I wanted to give up my apartment that night to Teddy or to anyone, I figured he would think me not only unsophisticated, but a real prude too if I denied him a place to bring a girl he wanted to screw. So I said yes.

At eight o'clock I went downstairs and met Teddy. He pushed ten dollars on me for my trouble, and I gave him the spare key. Eileen was waiting around the corner in his car, he told me.

I got home after midnight. I expected to find them still there, or the place messed up or—I don't know—I expected some indication in my familiar, cosy place that it had been subjected to hours of wild sex.

It looked untouched. Even the bed looked as exactly made as when I had done it that morning. It was as mysterious, as baffling as that incident with Teddy after the raided party. Confused and tired, I went to sleep.

And was awakened an hour later by my buzzer ringing downstairs.

"Wha?" I mumbled into the squeaky speaker.

"It's Ted Kincannon. Can I come up?"

"Now?"

"I left some beer in the fridge."

"Oh God. All right."

Still sleeping, I managed to draw on some jeans in time to open the door to his knock.

"I still have some pot," Teddy said, holding up two joints in his hand.

"Shhh," I said, looking to see who in the hallway might be spying on us. "Come in."

"I can't sleep at home tonight. My old man kicked me out. The bastard." All of it said, good naturedly.

"Sleep here, then."

He found the Schlitz' and popped open one, offered me one, and lighted a joint. It was obvious he wasn't about to go to sleep right away.

He talked. I smoked a little grass too, sipped a cup of reheated coffee, and listened with mingled dread and fascination to his tales of the army and of basic training. It was clear that like most things in this life, Teddy got along well in the army. His good looks, general amiability, and ease in most situations helped him at Fort Dix.

"I'm shipping out this week," he told me, "right after the leave. Going to Southeast Asia. Vietnam. Ever hear of it? I hadn't until they told me."

"Oh, shit!" I said, before I could stop myself. My radical buddies— up on politics like no one else I'd ever known, had been aware for over a year about the escalation of our venture in Vietnam. It would take the American public another few years to find out how deeply in we were. But daily I received facts and figures they had somehow found out, and knew what a mess it already was. However I wasn't about to tell any of this to Teddy, who was about to see action, and so I let him talk on more, until it was clear that the grass was getting the better of me over the coffee.

I had sunk into a deep, blissful sleep, and suddenly without any reason snapped fully awake. I looked up. Five a.m. Pale light outside cigarette. An opened Schlitz was loosely held in one hand.

"Aren't you sleeping?" I asked.

He shook his head. Even through sleep-glued eyelids, I could see his tragic face.

"What's wrong?"

He shrugged. "I don't know."

"Is the bed too hard?"

"It's okay. I've slept on harder ones, you know."

"Well, then?"

"I guess I'm a big baby," he said, and I didn't interrupt so he went on. "I hear it's really rough over there. That's what the Drill Sergeant told us. I suppose I'm afraid to go."

"You could go A.W.O.L."

"I'd get caught. I always get caught." Ruefully said.

What do you do when a friend is in trouble?

"I'd be afraid too," I said. "It's natural."

"No one will care if I die. My old man hates me. Eileen doesn't care. Nobody will care if I don't come back."

"I will."

"You're okay. You're the only one who'd even do me a favor, like you did tonight. Thanks."

"Anything to help."

"It didn't help."

"It didn't?"

"No. She wouldn't go through with it. All I wanted was a little send off. You know, something to remember when I'm over there being shot at. She wouldn't."

"Why not?"

"It's the same old story. They're hot as hell. Then I unzip and swing it out, they take one look, and it's no dice. I thought Eileen would be different."

"You mean because it's…" I groped for a word.

"Older ones don't care. But I don't like them old. I thought Eileen would be different."

"But I thought you said they all liked it hooked?"

"They hate it. Won't even touch it. Here look for yourself. How could anyone like that. It's ugly. Deformed."

So saying, he pulled off the blankets and displayed a large erection. It was fine and straight right to the cockhead. But just there it bent downwards at about a sixty-five degree angle. Not unattractively so, yet distinctly so.

"It doesn't look all that bad to me," I said. After all I'd probably seen one mature cock erect in my life: my own.

"Feel it underneath," he said, taking my hand and sliding my palm along the bottom of the shaft. The bentness was much more evident this way. "They all say it hurts them. You know. Because it angles down. All I wanted was a send off: something to remember. I'll bet all the other guys in the company get one," he added, sulking.

Meanwhile I still held his erection, which seemed to remain as hard as ever. I began to play with it, while he went on complaining. I was fascinated by it. I reached down and touched his scrotum. I compared to my own. Just like a kid. Twenty odd years of my life had brought me to this minute: sleepy and confused as I might be, I wasn't going to let it just slip by. I looked at his thighs, covered with tiny golden hair, his hips that buckled and curved so delectably, his washboard tummy, his chest, his arms.

"Teddy," I finally said.

"What?"

"Remember what happened after that lousy party."

"Yeah?" His brows were furrowed: he clearly didn't remember.

"I think I'm going to start laughing," I said.

"At my cock?"

"No!"

Still perplexed. "So?"

"I think you better kiss me, Teddy."

He looked confused for a moment, then looked at his erection in one of my hands, mine in the other, and at my face. He smiled, and I didn't have to say it again.

"You are a friend," he said, and began to kiss me.

From then until that afternoon, we made love in our primitive fashion a half dozen times, breaking only for beer, breakfast and more pot.

"Now that's what I call something to remember," Teddy said, getting dressed to drive to Fort Dix. "I'll write you from Viet Nam."

Months passed and I didn't hear a word from or about Ted Kincannon. My own life became pretty active at this time, so I have to admit I gave him little thought. and whenever I did think of him, it was always with such a mixture of remembered pleasure and anxiety about his future that I would block it out quickly and go do something fast to forget him.

One day a small package arrived in my mailbox, wrapped in brown paper and so taped over I could barely read my own name, never mind that of the sender. I did make out an APO number. It came from one of the half dozen guys I knew in the armed forces.

Inside was a Marlboro cigarette pack—the hard kind—containing a letter from Teddy, and something heavily wrapped in aluminum foil. When I'd gotten the foil off I had to shake it out of a plastic baggie: inside was a blackish hard chunk.

All the letter said was that Nam was a bitch, but that Ted had tried another four or five brands of beer, and opium—which was what he sent me. The rest of his letter was instructions on how to prepare the opium for smoking.

Well, I never got too far gone on it—not really my thing, I like up drugs—but my anarchist friends went apeshit over it. In the following months, more little packages arrived. Sometimes containing opium,

sometimes a potent south East Asian grass called "Thai Stick" which
I enjoyed. Accompanying letters were brief and rare.

Then the packages stopped.

Three more months passed. Finally, I was too depressed about it
and called my father to see if he could tell me anything about Ted.

"Poor kid. I talked to his father last week. Ted's been reported
missing in action over a month."

That was all I had to hear. It had been a bad time personally for me.
In the last year I'd lost a close cousin and two schoolmates in Viet
Nam. I was pissed. That night I stayed at home drinking a half gallon
of cheap red wine and feeling miserable until I passed out.

Through the whirling, looping chasms of my hangover the next
viciously sunny morning, I heard a buzzer snarl. I stumbled out of
bed, crawled across the undulating floorboards, sidled up the
strangely tilting wall, pressed the button—and couldn't believe my
ears.

"Boy! You look like you were hit by a tank," Teddy said, when I let
him into the apartment.

"Go away. You're dead."

"Not as dead as you look," he said, with equanimity, and hauled
me into the bathroom where he stripped me, finagled me into the tub,
and held me under a ten minute icy shower. I cursed and screamed.
While I was drying off, he brewed a pot of strong coffee, popped open
a Pabst and whistled. Between forcing me to drink the coffee and
talking, he got me partially sober in almost no time.

"I thought you were missing in action." I finally was able to say
without my head ringing.

"I was. Eighteen days. Want to hear how it happened?"

How do you say no to that?

So he told me. It seems that shortly after Teddy arrived in Saigon,
he went with some others from his company to a local brothel. There
they got drunk and high on grass. The women took one look at his
hooked erection, laughed, and brought in a young boy for him.
Horny and drunk, Teddy figured what the hell, and pleasured the boy
pretty much to their mutual satisfaction all night.

Next day, however, he was disturbed by the incident and went to
the platoon Chaplain for a heart to heart talk. The Chaplain was new,
like everyone but a few officers; he was also about twenty-five years
old. Useless as he might be in ninety five out of a hundred problems
he had to face, he had the answer to Ted's problem. He carefully

explained how intercourse with a woman, given Ted's physical propensity, would be painful, possibly even dangerous to her. Intercourse, anally, however, was no problem. He added that since men had prostate glands near enough to the inner surface of their colon, Ted's hook, instead of causing pain, would cause a most pleasant massage, leading to multiple internal orgasms for Ted's partner. If Ted wanted satisfying sex, all he had to do was find a willing male. The Chaplain offered himself as a guinea pig. Dubious, Ted went ahead; and found indeed everything the Chaplain said was true. He had a good time, his partner came twice without touching himself.

Although not preternaturally bright, Ted Kincannon was realistic and a quick study, especially when it came to his pleasures. You might also recall my description of him as otherwise superbly handsome. The army life had done nothing to alter that, and in uniform, Teddy was a knockout. He continued to visit the Chaplain, and when he was transferred to another company, it didn't find him long to find another willing partner in his platoon, a guy named Drake, whom Ted graciously insisted reminded him of me.

Naturally they had to keep their liaisons pretty private. So they buddied up on bivouacs, stayed together a lot, would find abandoned caves and huts in passing villages on their longer marches. It was a bit of a nuisance, Ted admitted: but it was worth it.

While out with their platoon on a search and destroy mission, Ted and Drake decided to get it on one afternoon. They found an amenable resident with a spare house, who let them use it for a little money. When Ted and Drake were done and getting dressed, however, the farmer ran in gesticulating wildly, speaking in frantic, disjointed whispers. They finally figured out what was up: while they were making love, the Viet Cong had advanced on their platoon, and after a short battle, had retaken the territory including the abandoned farmhouse.

Teddy and Drake were hidden in a root cellar by day, where they were not only fed by the farmer and his family—American sympathizers—but also given beer and grass.

It was two and a half weeks of pure bliss, marred only by the occasional beerless stretches, and their inability to take proper showers. They were stoned and screwing, when the farmer lurched in to tell them they could come up again: the government forces had retaken the area.

They were returned to their company, treated with great respect, even given leave they hadn't earned and a medal apiece. But Drake's tour of duty was up, and so they separated. Ted managed to get transferred to the airborne division where he'd met another guy in Saigon who'd had experience with the hook and had wanted more.

"My tour was up last month," Teddy said, putting down his fourth Pabst since he'd arrived. "But I've signed up for three more years. Whenever I go into Saigon or Hue, all I have to do is snap my fingers and guys come running: sailors, soldiers, even Marines. I did it with an M.P. just before going on leave. Hell, they line up outside my room every evening. The word has gotten out, I've got something special. I love that. I don't mind the rules and regulations. I have my own cottage. I'm an N.C.O. I love whirling in the helicopters. Hell, I'd have to be a real fool to give it up."

What did I do about Teddy's new revelation, you may wonder. Exactly what you would have. I'd been out since his last stay over, so I waited for him to finish his beer, then pulled him up to his feet, and over to my bed. He never hesitated, and I would have to agree with dozens of members of the armed forces, that Teddy's hook was truly special.

After we'd made love twice, I had to get up to go to the john. Coming back into the bedroom, I looked for more grass. Ted called out he had some Thai Stick in his jacket pocket.

If I had any doubts or questions about Teddy having found success in Vietnam, they were blown away when I looked at his jacket. It was black nylon bomber, so shiny it rippled silver. On its front were various embroidered designs typical of the Far East—parrots, coral atolls, panthers, jungle foliage. Those designs continued over the shoulders and past the underarms to the back panel, where they became an entire tableau. Above them a large central design loomed. At first I took it to be a phantom jet, spewing fire at the landscape. When I stepped away from it however, I saw it wasn't an airplane at all. It was a flying penis with wings straked back; its front end hooked down unmistakably.

Underneath the embroidery design, gold lettering spelled out "Teddy the Hook."

Mr. World Buns
A Story Without a Moral

It all began on a Sunday. Larry Damrosch remembered that quite clearly because Howard found the huge ad announcing the contest in the large, multi-sectioned edition of the *Denver Post*. They were in bed, following a late night out. It was now almost three in the afternoon. Howard, as usual, was going through the entire paper before he settled on something to catch his interest. Larry was in the bookpages, deeply involved in reading a review of a controversial new biography of Sigmund Freud he'd heard mentioned at the clinic.

"Look here, Larry. Mr. World Buns Contest. All may enter."

"Terrif," Larry said. His lover's words barely made an impression. Larry turned over on the edge of the bed, searching on the carpeted floor for a ballpoint he'd dropped. He wanted to mark the review, to remind himself to pick up the book tomorrow.

"Cash prize for first place, five thousand dollars. And a two week trip to Rio de Janeiro for two, all expenses paid."

Where was that pen?

"This is just what we've been looking for, Larry. This is it!"

There it was. Larry could just make out the nub end of the pen. He stretched his fingers for it, still couldn't reach, so he stretched his entire body. He almost had it, when he felt the slap on his ass. He lost his balance and fell off the bed.

"Hey! What's that all about."

"You weren't listening," Howard said, holding up the ad. "Look! This is where you and I are going over the holidays. Without this we'll never get away, we're broke."

"Okay. Enter."

"The regional preliminary is being held right here in Denver. At the Broadway Discoteque next Friday night. All you have to do to enter is call up and appear that night."

"Great! I won't stop you," Larry said. He crawled under the bed, found the pen, then got back on top of the covers again. "Shouldn't we be getting up and having breakfast soon?"

"Think of it, Larry. Christmas in Rio. All expenses paid. We're in debt to plastic so deep we'd never be able to afford it. Not with what you earn."

"You don't earn that much yourself," Larry said. Which wasn't exactly true. As a psychiatric social worker, at least he had a future. Howard—a bartender at the Triangle—took home more, true, but he worked more sporadically too.

"Five thousand dollars," Howard mused. "We could rent a place in Breckenridge for the winter. Be right near the Bunkhouse. Ski, sled, build fires, have friends up."

"Sounds terrific," Larry said. Having marked the bookpage, he moved onto the film section.

"How about it?" Howard said, straddling Larry and taking the newspaper from him.

"Sure."

"Then you'll do it?"

"Me!? I thought you were going to enter."

"You're the one with the beautiful ass," Howard cooed. "The best in Denver. And I ought to know."

"I couldn't. I'm a psychiatrist."

"So what? You have the buns. That's all that counts."

"I can't, Howard," Larry said, and began a half dozen explanations why not. Howard seemed not to listen. Instead, he began kissing Larry's face, his shoulders, his nipples, his navel. He only looked up when Larry said it was cheap and exploitative to enter a beauty contest.

"Sexist too," Larry added. "Treating bodies like objects."

"It was all right, when *I* was going to enter," Howard said.

"That's different. You're already a sort of public figure, working at the bar and all."

Howard arched an eyebrow, then dropped his head into Howard's crotch. "Please. Pretty please."

"Stop, Howard. It's still sore from last night."

Howard got up, but rolled Larry over, and began kissing his buttocks, murmuring all the while, "This is our gold mine."

"What would Dr. Royce say if he found out," Larry protested.

"And my parents, what if they...?"

His protests diminished with every rotation of his lover's hot and probing tongue.

"I can't, Howard. I just can't."

§

Friday night Larry was standing in a fairly dark corner behind the raised platform that served as a stage at the Broadway. The place was jammed. Every square foot of the place was taken. People were three deep at the back bar, and against the walls. Not all gays either. There were students from Boulder in quilted coats and skirts, shaggy dressed straight couples up from Colorado Springs, elegant Jet set types who'd driven or flown private planes from Aspen and Vail. They all looked relatively young and hip, however, which was a relief. Not much chance of anyone from the clinic where Larry worked showing up. And, they all seemed to be having a great time. Better than Larry who was panic stricken.

"You're next," someone said to Larry.

"I can't do it, Howard."

Howard dipped a hand to pat his ass through the loose fitting grey sweat pants.

"Gene Frazer," the emcee on stage announced, "Gene is a student of archaeology at the University of Colorado. His specialty is Amerindian digs."

Gene was a six-foot-two inch blond hewn god, wearing a tiny golden bikini over his lean muscled body. He stepped up and forward, and turned slowly around in the spotlights as comfortable as though he were in front of his bedroom mirror. The crowd cheered and whistled. In one corner of the room, Larry could make out the judges—two local bar owners, both gay, a pretty woman whom he knew edited a local alternative newspaper, and another, older woman, who worked in fashion, Howard had told him.

"I'm backing out. I can't do it."

Gene crossed the stage, and stepped down in front of them.

"Break a leg," Howard said, pushing Larry forward. "And remember. Do exactly what I told you."

Larry stumbled on the step, but caught himself just as a house light came over to meet him.

"I'll get you for this, Howard," he hissed, then, rebalanced with his anger, he stepped onto the stage.

"Larry Damrosch," the announcer began. "Larry is a local boy from Denver. Twenty-four years old. Larry is a psychiatric social worker at the downtown clinic attached to..."

His words were drowned out by calls from the audience.

"Where's his ass? Buns! We want buns! We can't see them!"

Larry walked across the stage, past the emcee whose recitation was completely lost amid the continued boos and calls from men and women alike. Someone began clapping in rhythm and others took it up, chanting "Buns, Buns, Buns!"

Larry wore a close fitted black t-shirt over what he knew to be a small, but well-muscled torso. That and the grey sweat pants. And under those a small black jock strap. Nothing else. Not even shoes. He faced the audience, deafened by their noise, bowed a bit, turned to face the judges all of whom seemed a bit perplexed, then looked back at the announcer, who'd given up and just stood there, shrugging.

"We want buns," the audience chanted. "We want buns."

So Larry turned to face the emcee, then undid the ties of the sweat pants, opened the front, and dropped them to the floor.

Behind him, the audience's shouts died down to nothing.

Larry bent forward, mooning them, drew the pants off his ankles and feet, then turned to moon the judges. Behind him was a breathless, silent pause. He could feel eight hundred eyes on his back, eight hundred hands itching to reach out to him.

"Now that's what I call an ass," a woman said in a whiskey charred voice.

Some cowboy in the back of the room let out a yippee that echoed around the room. It was taken up by a few others, then by shouts and applause and whistles that rose and crested, rose, crested and rose again.

When he felt hands on him, Larry took off, running off stage to much cheering, past Howard and the others standing on the side, into the bathroom, where he locked the door and looked at himself in the mirror.

His face wasn't flushed as he'd thought, but glowing. He'd liked it.

"You idiot!" He said to his reflection. "How did a smart guy like you get talked into a performance like that?"

He changed into his denims, waited a bit, then finally slipped out. Howard grabbed him and ignoring his protests, steered Larry to the side of the stage again.

"I'm getting out of here," Larry said.

"They haven't announced the winner yet."

They had announced the second runner up; he was standing on the stage. Now the emcee called out the name of the first runner up; Gene Frazer, the archaeology student."

"Come on, Howard. I've had enough of this."

"Not yet," Howard insisted.

"And the winner, and Rocky Mountain Regional Winner for the Mr. World Buns contest"—the emcee began—"The man who will represent our area in the final contest in New York City next month, and already the winner of our special five hundred dollar prize and a weekend with all expenses paid at the Aspen Lodge...and by the way, folks, it was unanimous. Our own...

Larry never heard his name. He felt Howard and someone else propel him onto the stage. The music played a fanfare, lights crisscrossed in front of him. The emcee and male judges shook his hand, the women kissed him demurely, someone put a check in his hand, the audience jumped up and down, raising toasts with beer bottles and wineglasses.

"Now folks," the emcee said. "Let's take another look at those prize winning Rocky Mountain globes."

Still amazed, Larry had to be turned around, his denims unbuckled, and dropped. He managed to catch them just below his buttocks.

The audience cheered until it seemed bedlam was about to break loose.

"I can't believe this," Larry mouthed to Howard on the sidelines.

His lover smiled back, like a man who just heard he's discovered a mother lode.

§

Larry had just gotten the key into his hotel room door when the phone began to ring.

"Where've you been? I've been calling all day."

It was Howard—more than a little pissed off.

"At a luncheon," Larry said, dropping onto the bed and kicking off his shoes. Outside the window, he could see blocks and blocks of the Manhattan midtown skyline, building lights just going on.

"A luncheon? It's five-twenty!"

"Don't blame me. You didn't tell me I was going to have to be Miss Congeniality, Howard. It's been one meeting after another from the minute I got here and checked in. First all twenty-five finalists had a briefing with the representatives of the company backing the contest. And guess what, Howard? It's a swimsuit manufacturer. We all have to wear bathing suits in the contest. No bare buns like in Denver."

"Don't worry about that."

"I am worried. Then there was a gathering of finalists. You ought to see them. I'm certain my being here is a fluke."

"Cute?" Howard asked, although he seemed inattentive.

"Cute!? Man some of these guys ought to enter Mr. Universe competitions. And others have been posing for skin magazines all year. Half of them are professionals, I'm sure of it. They've been in a dozen contests like this one."

"Oh yes?" Howard said, seeming more far away than before.

"They're gorgeous. I don't have a snowman's chance in a furnace."

"It's about *buns*!" Howard said. "What's the difference if they have great bodies. It's the *buns* that count."

"Well, it's a good thing I found out from someone at the desk that there's a gym in the hotel. I'm going to be there every spare minute I have."

When Howard said nothing in response, Larry went on to tell him about their other activities—meeting with photographers and the photo-sessions—alone and with groups of other finalists. Then the luncheon at Joanna's. They'd had to wear ties, although luckily not jackets. He supposed the others at the big table were company executives and their wives. It was excruciating. And tonight there was to be a cocktail party where they would meet New York celebrities, underground stars like Divine, writers like Andrew Holleran, fashion designers, reporters from *Interview* and *Wet*. Tomorrow, more photos, another meeting with some other group. Then the contest—at a brand new discoteque downtown. Larry was already worn out, and he hadn't even begun.

"And the other guys," he added, "they're all right, pleasant and all. But half of them are straight."

"Oh?"

"And none of them are very bright. When they saw me reading *Freud, Biologist of the Mind,* they did everything but kick me out of the hotel. I swear, Howard, I saw one of them move his lips when he was watching TV."

"Stick it out, you'll win," Howard said. He sounded awfully unconcerned. Maybe it was the long distance?

Larry went on talking. At one point, he thought he heard his lover speak to someone else, and asked who was there.

"No one," then louder. "I don't think you know him."

They had an "open relationship," true. But Larry was both hurt and annoyed that Howard was tricking on him after only a day or so away.

He quickly admitted that he was being irrational, and dropped the subject fast. Allowing Howard to get in some pep talk before they disconnected.

The phone rang again immediately. It was Jake, one of the "chaperones" assigned to the finalists, asking about the cocktail party at ten that evening. Would Larry like to have dinner with Jake and a few other contestants before hand, he asked.

Jake was large and oily looking. Larry had already made it very clear to Jake that he had a lover back in Denver. That didn't seem to make any difference. Before hanging up, Jake unctuously told Larry he had a real chance for being this year's Mr. World Buns. "I can spot a winner."

§

The gym on the top floor was attached to a shower and sauna room, and next to an olympic-sized swimming pool. It was out of his way, hard to find, through a long, unused looking hallway. But the minute Larry opened the door, it was clear he wasn't the only one who'd asked at the desk. The place was filled with finalists for Mr. World Buns. Every Nautilus machine was in use, every weight bench occupied by groaning workouts.

"I should have known!"

A few minutes later, he found a spot in the gym not in use. One wall held calisthenic equipment: hanging rings, mats, a horse, even parallel bars.

He warmed up with push ups, sit ups and a few other light exercises. All the while, overhearing conversations around him.

"I'll never get these lats in shape by Sunday."

"Forget the lats, honey. What about your lower back. Those

dimples look a little deep to me."

"Are you saying he's fat?"

"That was the year I was Mr. Data Boy."

"I know an exercise for your lower gluteus. From ballet."

"I don't go in for ballet, I'm straight."

"Could have fooled me."

"Plenty of straight guys here. Joe there. That German guy."

"Someone was chewing on my ass last night. Think it shows?"

"I use Oil of Olay."

"Ever try Estee Lauder?"

"I don't wear makeup on my ass. I'm straight."

"You told us. You told us."

"That black guy Dwayne has the best ass of all. But he won't win. Blacks never do. He'll come in second, or third."

"It's called Callipygian."

"Cally-what?"

Larry looked up from his half minute of doing the Boat, his hip bones alone touching the mat, his hands and chest lifted up, his thighs and feet up too, feet and hands clasped in back.

"Who said callipygian?" he demanded to know, falling out of his boat position.

"I did. Why?"

The man who stepped forward looked about his own age. But tall, surfer slender, yet with huge shoulders and arms, a thick curling helmet of golden hair, and a tan that was obviously natural and could only be described as brandy-laced pumpkin pie whipped through with heavy cream. Set beneath perfectly straight, thick, sunbleached eyebrows were ice-blue eyes. His nose was slightly aquiline. His outlaw-style moustache was red and gold. He had a mouth designed for kissing, a perfect jaw with two dimples and a cleft.

"Why?" he asked again.

"Nothing," Larry said, stepping forward. "I just wanted to take a look at the intellectual of the group."

"Hal Sykes," he said, stepping forward. "That's yoga you're doing, right?"

The others went back to their workouts and talk.

"Right," Larry said. "No room at the weights."

"You're Larry Damrosch," Hal said, not asking. "How come you're always wearing loose pants, like those sweat pants? Is that supposed to mean you've got something special back there?"

"Sure does. I don't want people to take a look and lose heart, maybe even drop out of the contest," Larry said, taking up the challenge.

"Oh, yeah?" Hal stepped back. "Well, I've got my eye on you," he said, half joking, half serious, before walking away.

"Keep looking," Larry said, watching him walk away. Hal Syke's buns, like all the rest of him, were scrumptious.

§

The champagne bottles were empty, the bartenders bored, most of the party balloons deflated by now, and the big room almost empty. Larry leaned against a wall out of sight, glad to have the celebrity encounter over. He felt like an aging debutante. He was tired of smiling, tired of being nice, tired of meeting people and immediately forgetting who they were, tired of parading himself around. All he wanted was to get up to his hotel room, get into bed, and read the Sullaway book on Freud, before blissfully falling asleep.

"Hi!" a small cute blonde number said to him. "I'm Burt, from the upper midwest. Me and a few other guys are going down to the Village to play around. You care to join us?"

"Well, I don't know."

"C'mon. We'll have fun. We might even go to the Mineshaft. This is Buddy. Rory. Chuck."

"Not me," Chuck said. "The last time I went to the Mineshaft, I was crawling around on my hands and knees by morning. My ass was all scarred up, and no accounting for it."

"C'mon," Burt said. "We'll have fun."

"I don't think so," Larry said, and managed to escape past them.

"Don't run away so fast," someone said, grabbing him by the belt. It was Jake. Out of the frying pan and into the fire. "My, you were looking good tonight," Jake said, circling his shoulder with a fat arm. Larry tried not to flinch. "You've already made a big impression on several of the judges, you know."

"Were there judges here tonight?"

How could he get away from this creep?

"There were. And they liked you."

"Well...great," Larry stammered. "Thanks. See you later. I've got to go."

"You're not going out tonight, are you?"

"No. Straight to bed. My beauty sleep."

"Would you like to be tucked in?"

"I'm expecting a call from my lover tonight," Larry lied, and got away.

Hal Sykes was standing at the elevator bank.

"Where's your friend?" he asked.

"Not *my* friend!"

"He come on to you?"

"You too?" Larry asked.

"Once. I told him I was straight and I would deck him if he touched me again."

The elevator arrived and they got in. Larry had seen Hal a few times across the room at the cocktail party, "mixing." It had seemed as though he'd always been near or with a woman. And at yesterday's luncheon too. He might have known it. The best looking guy here, the only one who even vaguely interested Larry, and he turned out straight. No luck at all on this trip.

"How come you didn't go out with the others?" Hal asked.

"Guess I wasn't in the mood."

"So what now? Beddy-bye? It's only midnight."

"I thought I'd read a little."

"You play cards?" Hal asked.

"Sure."

"Poker?"

"If you remind me which is higher, a flush or a straight."

"Oh, one of *those*."

"I have a lot of beginner's luck," Larry said. "Every time."

"All right. My room or yours?"

An hour later, Larry had lost nineteen dollars and seventy five cents to Hal.

Despite the loss, he'd enjoyed the time. Hal had dynamite grass, they got beer from room service. Hal had talked a lot about himself. Larry now knew that he was as bright and personable as he was handsome. Hal was married and divorced. He worked for his father—as a partner in their Oldsmobile franchise in Laguna Beach. He could be funny, ironic, satirical. He was better looking and sexier with every passing moment.

He shuffled the deck and said, "New variation. Aces low."

"That's my mad money for the night. Count me out."

"You can still play. Don't go yet."

Larry sat down on the bed and finished the beer.

"I have an idea. Let's play for something else. Let's play for clothing," Hal said.

"Boy, you really want to see the competition bad, don't you?"

"You bet! I want to win. And—aside from you—and Dwayne who won't win anyway—I'm it. But I've got to be sure."

"All right," Larry said. He didn't care anymore.

Almost an hour and a half later, after a hard game in which both of them were reduced to their underwear, Larry put out four queens with a smile on his face. He'd been getting more and more excited by their stripping down. He wanted to see what Hal was hiding in those jockey shorts that puffed out so enticingly.

"Flush!" Hal said, laying out the royalty with a flourish.

Larry couldn't believe it. But he wasn't about to be a sore loser. So he stood up, turned around, and took off his underwear.

"There. Satisfied?" he asked.

"Come into the light. I can't see from there."

Larry stepped back, and stumbled. He was caught in Hal's hands.

"Well? How do we stack up?"

When Hal didn't answer, but kept holding onto his hips, Larry looked over his shoulder. Hal was sporting a thunderbolt erection that was trying to burst through the cloth of his jockeys. His tongue was unconsciously licking his moustache.

"Well?" Larry insisted.

"Not bad. Not bad at all. But I think they need a little loosening up," Hall said. "And I know exactly how to do it."

His last words were mumbled, as he was face deep between Larry's buttocks.

"But I thought you were straight," Larry remembered to ask him, later on, as Hal was preparing to fuck him again.

"You don't think I'm stupid enough to let a little thing like that get in the way, do you?"

§

Backstage at the Saint consisted of a large storage room filled with sound and video equipment, adjoining the runway each contestant would walk on—one third of the length of the lower level lounge—before pausing on the central section, then going off along the other ramp. Under ordinary circumstances, the room couldn't have been too orderly. Tonight, with twenty-five nervous potential Mr. World

Buns, not to mention a half-dozen chaperones, newly made friends, recent tricks, girl friends and wives, it was the absolute pits.

"You touch that phone and I'll bite a chunk out of your rear end this big," Larry said to the contestant from New England. The big, red-haired tow-headed guy looked as though he tore men Larry's size for the exercise. But he was scared off by the threat anyway.

Larry dialed again, let it ring, waited to ten, decided to try twenty rings this time, no maybe fifteen. What was that? Twelve? Or thirteen?

"Hello!" Howard. Breathless.

"Where have you been all day? I go on in ten minutes. Where's all the moral support you promised me back in Denver?"

"You'll win. Don't worry."

All said so breezily, that Larry had to ask: "Who's in the apartment with you?"

"Oh, just Andy."

"Andy?" Larry replied. "That sounds like he's pretty much of a fixture there."

"What are you wearing?" Howard said. Subtlety was never one of Howard's fortes.

"A bathing suit."

"What color?"

"Oh, sort of pale blue and sea green and pink. A little yellow too. It's sort of a seascape."

"On a bikini!"

"It's not a bikini. It's trunks. I tried on all the briefs. They didn't show me off well. These are short, square, nice fitting. You know I always wear trunks at the pool."

Howard was audibly moaning. "No one ever wins in trunks! We just blew it. Trunks always look dowdy."

"Not with this design, they don't. And they're sort of silk. They fit perfectly. You'll see in Rio. We get to keep the suit."

"We'll never get to Rio," Howard said. "Not with you wearing trunks."

So they argued. From bathing suits, the argument led to Andy, then to how terrible a time Larry claimed to be having in New York, and finally worked itself back to a month before, then three months before, then a year ago. Finally, Larry had enough and hung up, fuming.

"You look sort of uptight, kid," Jake the chaperone said. "You want a valium or something."

"I just broke up with my lover because of this rotten contest," Larry said.

"I've got to find Mr. Caribbean," the chaperone said, and beat it.

"Creep!"

Southern California was called, and Hal Sykes came by the phone.

"May the best buns win," Larry said; at least he'd be sporting.

"They won't" Hal said.

"They won't?"

"No. You've got the best buns. But I'm going to win."

§

Hal did win. Dwayne, the black, was second runner up. Larry, to his surprise, was first runner up.

"Honey," one contestant cooed after Larry had stalked onto the runway a minute after Hal had come down. "I've never seen anyone look so butch in a bathing suit in my life. You looked as though you could kill. And in those silly trunks too!"

While standing by their trophies in the center of the huge crowd, Larry happened to look down into the mass of men. He'd never seen so many drop-dead numbers in one place at the same time. To hell with Howard. True, they were mostly dark haired and he preferred surfer blondes (like Hal Sykes, now beaming, now on top of the world!). But Larry was sure their obvious adoration of him would carry through into action later on. He might even take off the whole two weeks he had coming to him as vacation time, hang around and investigate New York's fabled after hours night life.

He was interrupted briefly by the emcee, who announced that the judges had been so impressed by all three finalists that they had arranged for a second prize of a thousand dollars and a third for five hundred.

This was getting even better. Now Larry would even have spending money for his two weeks in the city.

How about that guy there, the one with the long sweaty torso, clothed only in demins and a leather thong around his neck. Or those two guys together there, both of them with close cut hair and perfume-garden eyes, cruising him rather obviously, as they felt each other up.

Ah, freedom. He forgot what it felt like. He *would* take that vacation.

But a half hour later, after he'd gotten out of the trunks and into a pair of jeans, he found none of the three men he'd considered while onstage: all were lost in the dancewhirl crowd he walked into upstairs. The lights were low in the big domed room, the music funky, the dancers into it. He was about to be very annoyed, when someone slid up behind him and put his hands on Larry's hips.

"How about a rhumba."—Hal Sykes.

"I thought you'd be with your fan club?"

"I did that already. How about a dance?"

"I don't know."

"Then how about a fuck?"

"With your pick of the crowd here, tonight. You're crazy."

Hal turned Larry around to face him. He was leaning against a section of the wall. He tucked Larry right into his legs and held him.

"No dance. No fuck. What can the man want?"

"I don't want..."

"I've got it. How about two weeks in Rio, all expenses paid."

"You're kidding."

"Who else am I going to take? My ex wife?"

On the flight down to Brazil the next morning, Hal confessed that the reason he'd taken Larry away from the Saint so fast the night before, was so that no one would come to their senses and reconsider the prize.

"No more public exhibition for those buns," Hal said. "Not while I'm around." Then he leaned back into the seat and looked out at the clouds.

Larry found his place in the Freud biography. "That's all right by me."

And Baby Makes Three

I

It all happened out at the Pines. Fire Island Pines. You've been there, haven't you? You haven't?

Well, Fire Island is a long strip of land along the southern edge of the middle of Long Island. It's several miles off the coast, and you have to take a ferry to get to most of the communities there. Just a sandbar, really, not even a quarter of a mile wide, at the widest. A good hurricane would sweep right over it.

The Pines is one of the earliest, and now one of the largest and most pretentious of the little towns. Houses there are murder to buy, out of most people's price range to build, and just to rent the place means going into hock. Still, the place is jammed. International jet-setters mix with artists and models, theater folk, lesser light movie-stars, not to mention the gays who've more or less taken over. Add any other leech, parasite, or person on the make and you have the social set up.

The physical locale is charming: simple contrasts of sky and ocean, beach, houses and trees. It's laid out clearly too: A few long boardwalks go from one end of the Pines to the other: one on the bayside, one on the oceanside, and one going right through the middle. These three are crossed by scores of smaller crosswalks, and it's off these that most of the houses are located.

But almost from the first, the Pines reveals its character. The ferry slides right into the little harbor and that is the heart of the place, as well as the hub of activity. On one side houses peep out through all of the foliage—more of any other tree than the name-giving pines. Around the other side of the bay are a few restaurants, the bars, and the little shopping center. Every inch of harbor is lined with yachts— that's another group altogether. Some of those boats dock in Mid-May and don't leave until October. The owners fly in by sea-plane every weekend to party on deck.

Well, that should be enough description. You should have the picture by now. The Pines is an imitation Antibes or Juan Les Pins, with a much better beach, mostly younger people, and a lot of smoking, drinking, partying and showing off.

It was about the middle of the summer. Aram and I were sitting on the deck of the Blue Whale one afternoon at "Tea." Naturally, no tea is served. Margaritas and Budweisers are the usual drinks. But it takes place in the afternoon, so the name.

Within the Whale is the dance floor, and on weekends it's usually jammed tight with stoned dancers, on-lookers, people cruising each other for quick sex, and others just milling about. The music is the latest—from the best discos in the city—and the dancing is hard, frantic and really superb. On any given weekend there is usually enough energy in that flashy room to launch a Titan rocket.

When not dancing or trying to make a pick-up, everyone is being their usual selves on the deck, either at the tables or in the large, open gathering space. Being themselves means being unerringly superficial, but also beautiful. Costumes are scanty, studiedly casual, with name tags from the chicest boutiques in the Village and Upper East Side. Bodies are tanned, and exquisitely developed all winter long in gyms. The level of looks—though diverse—is about as high as your best multiple-partner fantasies.

The couple with Aram and I had gone inside to stomp their asses off to the latest hit, and we were alone, just soaking up sun. It was about halfway through the summer—so far a spectacular one, not a single rainy weekend—and we were just beginning a three week vacation. Aram thought that would settle all of the little problems that had begun to creep into our two-year relationship. We would swim, sun, relax, drink, smoke, have dinner, go dancing, or just stay at home inviting another couple in for bridge, and—of course—make wild, passionate, expert love day in and day out. That was how he had advertised the vacation, and if you've ever spent the summer in New York, you'll understand why I was so ready to go along with

Aram's ideas.

He was older than I, about forty-two at the time. He'd been married several years before, and divorced when he came out. His kids used to come visit us at the triplex in the city. Polite, quiet girls, ten and fourteen years old. But they must have favored their mother, for neither of them had his Semitic dark features, his craggy face, his doe-brown eyes.

You can tell from that description that I was still very attracted to Aram. And I was. He had been my first lover, and one always remembers first lovers the longest, don't you think? We got along fabulously in and out of bed, and he had already been on the scene long enough to know what it was like having a young lover who thought himself gorgeous and who constantly had pepper in his penis, if you know what I mean.

But love and all, by that vacation I was bored. Bored of Aram. Bored of being a lover, and of being loved. Bored of the security of it all. Aram had seen this boredom coming on for a few months—perceptive thing that he was. I had started going out by myself every once in a while—hating it, missing Aram's wit, maturity and sensitivity. But I had some wild oats I was determined to sow in strange fields. And he was being an angel about it. I guess something told him there were rocks ahead. He was letting out a lot of line for me and tugging at it so gently and I scarcely noticed it.

In short, I was ripe for trouble.

Another ferry load had come in to dock, and amidst all the confusion of the disembarking, Aram noticed someone he "knew from many years back," as he put it. This was par for the relationship, and I was used to it and in no way jealous, but Aram seemed unusually abstracted and quiet. So I wondered.

It didn't take long to find out who the man from Aram's past was. About twenty minutes later—after the music and dancing, but not the cruising, had stopped—Aram looked past me, at the stairway of the deck, and stopped himself in midsentence to deliver one of those Marlboro-ad men smiles that had melted my heart years before.

In seconds, he was up and shaking the hands of a small, well-knit man about Aram's own age, but with perfectly tanned skin fitted over what might have been a sculptor's model for a head. His hair was short, prematurely bald, but very becoming, and a perfectly matched grey to his bronzed skin. He wore a brightly tie-dyed t-shirt and sailor ducks with that type of casual perfection that only models and actors can pull off.

Naturally I had seen pictures of Buddy Duvall before. Who hasn't? But I had never heard Aram mention him, so I was surprised at the warmth of the greeting between them. During the following weeks I would come across Buddy on the boardwalks, on the beach, in the aisles of the little supermarket, and I never would be able to forget that he was a great dancer and choreographer. Every step he took, every gesture he made announced the fact better than if he were wearing a sign.

That afternoon I hardly noticed him. I was a little surprised, but that's all. Why? Why, because of who was with Buddy. This younger man was introduced to me as Lee something or other, but both Buddy and Aram began calling him "Baby," a name he didn't seem to mind.

I might add he was hardly a baby. Picture someone about six-foot one, with one of those long, lean swimmer's bodies—washboard tummy and all. Add a face right off the cover of any issue of Eagle Scouts of America, and surround it all with an abundance of rich, pale yellow hair, silky fine, heavy and bleached by years of Southern California sun. In the midst of what might have been boringly regular features was the largest pair of multi-colored eyes I'd ever seen— brown and blue and speckled with yellows and greens. You know, like the Caribbean Sea at dusk.

He spoke in a slow, lazy, soft speech—not quite a drawl—but typically West Coast; every sentence seemed to intimate wells of meaning beneath the apparently simple surface of the words.

Well, I almost left my chair when he sat down. Not actually. But all the pepper got rattled about, and I had to move in closer to the table so as not to advertise to the entire deck.

Aram and Buddy forgot Baby and I existed. On and on they went, talking about people and places and events and situations I had never heard Aram talk of, but which now assumed a great and all-consuming interest. You know how it is, people catching up.

Buddy did interrupt himself long enough to mention that Baby had never been to the Pines before, and to hope that I would show him around. As far as I was concerned, that was like showing honey-suckle to a bee's nest. But it did break the ice between Baby and me, while Buddy and Aram talked on about Maggie and Bill and Ginger and Jimmy and suchlike.

To hide the embarrassment of what I was certain was the most evident case of love on first sight since Adam met Eve, I acted cynical

the Advocate

The national gay & lesbian newsmagazine. Since 1967

www.advocate.com

and funny. This is not an advisable method of coming on, I assure you. But what was I to do? So, everything in the Pines was tiny, and a little tacky. If the weather held up, I said, we might all last. Otherwise, there would be the usual quota of bad parties, drug busts, jellyfish and shark scares and local suicides.

Baby seemed amused, at first. But he seldom asked a question or made any comment of his own, and meanwhile those gorgeous eyes of his swept slowly through that deckful of glittering gym-built bodies and boutique sun-suits. I lost my hard-on, clutched an invisible hand to my aching heart, and sensed failure and despair waiting in the wings of my life. But I went on talking, joking, desperately hoping to chain him to me by an endless stream of words.

Suddenly the deck was almost cleared. Buddy said that he and Baby were having dinner with their hosts—some people Aram and I didn't know. They had better get cleaned up and changed, they suggested. They hoped they would see us again, but there was no repeat of the invitation to show Baby around, and I knew Aram well enough to know that when he met old friends once was usually enough.

I was preparing myself for a tragic goodbye, when something curious happened. A tiny, golden-orange butterfly that had been fluttering around us, suddenly ended it's aleotic flight by settling on Baby's downy blond cheek. It stepped a bit, found a comfy place and spread it's wings, nestling there, and looking like a painted ornament.

No one knew what to say.

"It thinks you're a buttercup," Buddy offered.

"Does it tickle?" I asked.

Baby didn't answer at first, delighted and half-afraid that any move would send the butterfly on its way. Then: "It's like a little piece of satin."

And the butterfly just sat there, glittering in the sunset on Baby's cheek, while we all looked on in disbelief, and Buddy told an irrelevant little story, and all of us waited four or five minutes for it to fly off.

Finally Buddy said, "This is absurd," and reached over to flick the butterfly away with a gentle fingertip. The little insect lifted, fluttered a bit in irritation, then settled deep in Baby's golden hair, right near a standing cowlick.

A waiter was passing just then. "I love you barette," he said to Baby.

Baby smiled.

"This sort of thing is always happening," Buddy said, half-apologetically. "Birds, cats, dogs. Baby's like a miniature Wildlife Preserve."

But the butterfly remained nestled in Baby's hair as we walked them along the boardwalk to the house they were staying in. I remained amazed and quiet, all the way. Symbols, after all, are all around us. But when they come that close they must mean something. Naturally, I never discovered what that symbol meant, but it seemed to sum up everything that I felt Baby was.

We shook hands, and Baby reached up and cupped the butterfly to send it into the air. I looked hard at him, trying to embed the image of him like an insect in amber. I had never seen anything like that butterfly. Never met anyone like Baby. But somehow, I was certain that was the last I would see of Baby.

So, I was silent again, as Aram and I walked to his house.

"Hey! What's up?" he finally asked.

"Nothing," I lied.

"Thinking of the butterfly?"

I didn't answer.

"That's not so strange for Baby. He's a pretty unusual kid. He and Buddy. I'll tell you all about them after dinner."

2

"How long do you think they know each other?" Aram began after dinner. We were having coffee and brandy, sitting on the second floor deck of Aram's eleven room clapboard and glass house. Ravel's piano music wafted up through the open courtyard around the pool. The night ocean thundered in the distance.

My mood hadn't changed from earlier in the day. The love of my life had come and gone, and I was feeling very sorry for myself.

"Oh, I don't know," I answered him with annoyance.

"Well, how old do you think Baby is?"

"What's with all the guessing games?"

"He's twenty-two," Aram said.

That seemed right. I figured I had a few years on him. But what difference did it make? Unless Aram was going to pull that old line about the value of different ages in love affairs.

"Buddy's known him for twenty and a half years," Aram went on.

"You're bullshitting me," I said. But I sat up and listened.

"No I'm not. That's what I meant when I said that they were unusual. Buddy first met Baby when Baby really was a baby. About eighteen months old. I know: I was there."

Aram has a way of telling a story that could charm the woodwork off the walls. For me, that was one of his strong points. He'd been everywhere, and known everyone, and done everything and could prove it. Furthermore, he could make it interesting, amusing, and instructive in the telling. I knew it would be a perfect way to pass the time until everyone else in the Pines had finished dinner and re-assembled to flaunt and dance at the Sandpiper. So, I said—"Go on, Aram. I'm listening."

"Twenty years ago—not twenty to the exact day, that would be too neat wouldn't it? It was earlier in the year. Early spring. April I think." Aram did some silent calculation. "Yes. April. I'm certain of it."

"Buddy and I were close friends then. We lived next door to each other in a recently converted brownstone in the Village. Buddy was only beginning to get some small parts in some of the off-broadway shows—they were called bistros then. He was acting a little, doing some singing and dancing. He hadn't joined the ballet yet, even though he was taking dance classes pretty regularly. I was running around town. Working for six months or so at my father's business, then just hanging around the streets and the bars and Washington Square Park, living off my savings the rest of the year.

"It was in the square that I met Debbie Redburn. She used to come to the park with her little girl in a baby stroller, and when I first met her, she was still carrying Baby. I'd noticed her before, if only because she had always given me a shy, funny look that made me wonder whether I knew her from college or someplace. Well, one day a ball was thrown between us and we both went for it—or something of the sort—and we got to talking.

"Debbie was a typically charming, too bright Brooklyn Jewish girl who'd gone to Radcliffe, met Jock Redburn and was now set up at Fifth Avenue in placid domesticity. But, all wasn't safe. Before she had married, Debbie had run around with the theater crowd at Harvard, and had desperately wanted to be an actress. She still avidly read Variety and the Drama Guild Quarterly when I first met her, and talked about new plays with a faraway look in her eyes that I've always associated with dreams that don't come true. She still had many friends in the theater—young actors, actresses, up and coming directors, and as we talked that afternoon and later, it seemed we knew many of these promising drama people in common.

Jock was Madison Ave. all the way. But he was all right too. He was a whiz-kid at his agency, making money hand over fist, and keeping his life at home quiet by developing a pre-ulcer stomach. Debbie and he threw parties at which she invited her friends, and Jock invited his friends. And, if the mixture wasn't always precise or safe, at least it made for some truly interesting parties and a few scandals. Of course I attended all of these—being in my party days— and that's when I discovered that Debbie's ability in the kitchen was next to nothing. She couldn't even put a canapes together. Soon, I was going to the Redburn's early and helping her prepare. Jock was thrilled, saw no competition, and treated me as if I were sent from heaven.

This went on for a year and a half or so, with Buddy coming out to join us every once in a while—and as he can—charming everyone. The four of us would get together very often: for bridge, for baseball over the radio, or dinner or whatever. Jock knew I was seeing another girl, and that Buddy was always seeing one or another boyfriend, and so, I suppose, it was fine with him. We kept Debbie occupied—I later discovered—made it easier for him to "stay at the office late"—that is, to have a few extra-marital flings.

One of Jock's favorite possessions—among many—was a country house way out on Long Island, in a little townlet called Moriches. At that time it was all potato farms and duck-filled marshes and little beaches. Every summer the Redburns would go out there for a month or two. Debbie and the kids stayed, and Jock came out on weekends. And, every spring, they would go out to open up the house.

That year, Debbie and Jock had been arguing a great deal, although still not ready to have it all out. Separately, each one invited me to come out to Moriches to help open up the house. I was wary of being caught in the middle of their marital squabbles. But, I said I would go it they also asked Buddy. They didn't know him well enough to scream and carry on in front of him, I figured. And Buddy had just put the finishing touches on yet another short, hot, love affair, and could use a change of scene.

Buddy and I met them outside their door, on Fifth Ave., where we helped lug boxes and suitcases out to the Chrysler station wagon.

We worked while the children directed from the car. Adele jumped around the back seat, warning that something was falling or would fall. Baby was sitting placidly in his hooked-up baby seat, playing with the plastic steering wheel attachment.

Something I dropped made a loud noise. Adele screamed and Baby turned around to look at us. When he did, he saw Buddy for the first time and smiled.

"What a beautiful baby," Buddy said. I should have realized right then from his tone of voice that Buddy wasn't being merely polite: there was a sense of awe—perhaps even of doom in how he said it.

Baby also noticed Buddy's real appreciation, and he laughed and reached for Buddy's hand.

"Haven't you ever met Baby?" Jock asked. "No. I guess not. By the time you usually come by, Baby's been asleep for a long time."

Baby had decided he liked Buddy's buttons, and he grabbed at each one with his putty little white hands, gurgling benevolently.

"I didn't even know you had another child," Buddy said.

"Lee never cries," Debbie said, pleased to talk about one of her favorite topics now that it was out in the open. "He never does anything to give me any trouble. He's always smiling, always laughing, always enjoying himself. He scarcely even wets himself and is never cross about it when he does. I don't think he cried when he was born," she added.

"Did I cry when I was a baby? Mommy?" Adele asked suddenly with the petulant understanding of a seven year old whose talents are being missed.

"I'm afraid so, Hon."

That didn't please Adele. And a minute later, she had to go back to the apartment where she had left a doll she absolutely could not go to Moriches without.

Well, that was the first meeting.

All during the ride, Baby would turn around and look at us, but focussing clearly on Buddy, and smile and laugh and reach out for Buddy's hand or lapel or something.

We stopped once—to have lunch at a little restaurant Jock had discovered the year before, half-hidden in swamp grass, but elegantly appointed within. Buddy held my arm a second before we went in.

"That child is beautiful," Buddy said.

"You've already said that."

"And he likes me, too!" Buddy insisted, as if repeating the obvious to dull, uncomprehending me.

"Here we go," I tried teasing him, "last year it was Negroes. This year it was Frenchmen. Next year it will be babies. Why don't you get one of your own?"

"I want that one."

"Ask Debbie if she'll loan him out. She must get bored of him sometimes."

"You're awful," Buddy said. "A worse cynic than Philip Wylie."

"Let's go eat, huh?"

"He's beautiful," Buddy repeated with a half-sick look on his face. "Beautiful."

Baby dominated the dinner table from one end of the room and from the heights of a high-chair. Buddy and I sat down, Buddy right across from Debbie on the other side of Baby. And they had a grand dinner together. So much so that Debbie let Buddy help feed Baby while she ate. So much so that no one paid the least bit of attention to the fact that Adele's meal was too hot, the meat cut in pieces too large for her to eat, the carrots too raw and the glass of milk she had been given too small.

As a result of their growing camaraderie and Adele's increasing whining, when we returned to the car, Adele went into the front seat, and baby's chair was hooked onto the back seat. There, while I tried to nap, Baby and Buddy commented on the passing scenery and a host of other subjects. Although Adele had the choice spot between Daddy and Mommy to herself, she evidently wasn't half so satisfied as she at first thought. For, every once in a while, she would stand up on the seat, turn around facing us, and criticize Baby for doing what any baby would do. Baby wasn't at all impressed by her sarcasm: he just laughed.

And that's how it went for the next week. We stayed at the big, rambling wooden house, unrolling rolls, unpacking boxes, repairing all the appliances, going out for long hikes along the beach or through the woods, and rides on rusted bicycles along the few paved roads in the area. Naturally, everywhere Baby went, it seemed Buddy went; and vice-versa.

"If I ever need a baby-sitter, I'm going to hire you first," Debbie said one night in the big, country style kitchen. We were having coffee and playing Clue. Buddy had just joined us downstairs after putting Baby to sleep "with a few jokes" as he cryptically informed us. When Debbie said something further about their relationship, Buddy just smiled and drank his coffee with that rosy quiet I associate with happily pregnant women and people who've just won a lottery.

"Mr. Plum did it in the Conservatory," Buddy said. "With a candlestick."

"Wrong," Jock said, and showed a Clue card to Buddy.

Debbie hid her amazement; Jock did too. Even I had given up teasing Buddy about it. But Adele saw through it all, and she was irritated at having been unable to get out of the library in the game, so she said out of nowhere, and to no one in particular, but in a loud and clear voice: "You might think it was *his* baby!"

"Adele! Don't be so fresh," Debbie said. Buddy said nothing at all.

But everywhere Buddy went, so did Baby. Even Buddy's hours changed. The first day there, we all slept until about eleven. All but Debbie and the children. She was used to getting up at seven or so, and while we men slept all morning, she and the children breakfasted and played. By the second morning, however, Buddy was up early too. As I came down for breakfast, scratching my sleep off me, Buddy charged into the kitchen door, with Baby rocking on his shoulders. Both of them were dressed and ruddy from being out in the fresh air for hours. They brought the crisp day into the room with them.

"Good God! Where have you been?" I asked trying to pour some coffee.

"Down to the beach," Buddy said, unbuttoning Baby who kept on mis-articulating one word over and over.

"Look! He's talking!" Adele said.

"He's saying 'Horse,'" Buddy explained. "We rode on a horse this morning."

"Orse. Orse," Baby said with great pleasure until silenced by his own absorption in the nipple of a warmed bottle.

"We met a fellow on a wonderful stallion riding along the beach," Buddy went on to Debbie and me. "A Forest Ranger or something like that on his way to work. And he asked if we'd like a ride."

"Orse. Orse," Baby said, spilling his formula.

"It's Horse, stupid," Adele said.

"Of course, we only walked on the horse," Buddy said, trying to mollify Debbie.

But she wasn't at all frightened. More pensive.

"God, eighteen months old and he's riding on a horse," she said. "I'm thirty next month and I still haven't."

"I did. I did, Mommy," Adele piped. "A pony. Remember?"

"Yes, dear. Well, Alina was right. She said he'd have an interesting life."

"Alina Zeka?" Buddy asked.

"You know her too? She cast a horoscope for Baby when he was born. As a gift. She told me Baby was a child of love, a man of love, living a life filled with love. But she also said he would have a strange, unusual life. Fortune's child she called him: someone with a strange destiny. He's a Libra you know. I have his chart at home somewhere."

"I'd like to see it sometime," Buddy said, eagerly.

"You know how to do all that?" Debbie asked.

"Not very well. I fool around with it. You know how superstitious all show people are. Everyone uses Alina."

Baby was done feeding, and the courtship went on.

And the courtship continued right up until we returned to the city, and Buddy had seen Baby to bed. As we walked away from the Redburn's apartment building, Buddy seemed springier, cheerier.

I was pleased. The week had rested me, had cheered up Buddy, and had never developed into an out and out fight between Jock and Debbie.

"With new faith, the great Buddy Duvall goes into the world...." I began.

"What a beautiful child," Buddy said with real determination.

"Inspired by the love of an innocent Babe..." I went on.

"Go on, laugh," Buddy said.

The next day the Ballet company Buddy was interested in joining called him, and I scarcely saw him for a month. When I did finally bump into him outside our building, Buddy went on about how hard he was working, and how his career suddenly looked as if it were going in some direction. Baby had been a distraction I thought.

But I was wrong. Later that week, Buddy and I met again at a local dinner place, and Buddy took me aside and said, "We fit, you know." Seeing I had no idea of what he was talking about, Buddy explained, "Baby and I. We fit. Alina says she's never seen such a good fit in two charts. It's called synastry or something."

That type of comment can leave even someone like me pretty speechless. But Buddy dropped the subject quickly enough.

A few months later I realized why I wasn't seeing so much of Jock and Debbie. They were fighting again. This time badly. When I did call, one day, Adele answered the phone blandly with scarcely any

recognition of my voice or name. Buddy might never forget Baby, I
remember thinking; but with children it was different. Adele said she
would "get Mommy" for me.

Debbie was to the point. "I'm getting a divorce. I'm going to
California. I'm taking the children."

"Whoa. Whoa," I said. "I'm not Jock, remember?"

"I'm sorry, dear. I'm just reminding myself to steel my determination," she explained.

Thereafter followed fifteen minutes of conversation which only a
good friend would tolerate. The main topics—to no one's surprise—
were Jock's failures as a husband and a father, and specific
infidelities in some detail. Debbie added another five minutes of pep
talk about how terrific it would be for her and the children living in
sun and surf and mountains and country.

When she was quite done rhapsodizing a rather confused
geography of California, I asked if she had told all of this to Jock yet.

"Just yesterday. Buddy and I did."

"Buddy!" I couldn't believe it.

"It was his suggestion that we go out West. I couldn't stand being in
the same city with *him*, anyway. Buddy's gotten a job out there. And
the kids are crazy about him. It'll be nice to have a man around
without being tied down to a man and all his dumb ideas. You
understand, don't you?"

I didn't but said I did. Buddy? I couldn't believe it.

Jock didn't contest, and in a short while I saw Debbie and Buddy
and Adele and Baby off to Los Angeles. And that was the last I saw of
them for another ten years or so.

I heard plenty. Every time a mutual friend of ours came back from
the Coast one of my first questions would be had they seen Buddy.
Invariably, they had. And everyone was eager to talk about it. Some
were amazed. Some worldly-wise. Everyone suspected it couldn't
last.

This is more or less what I heard.

Buddy had bloomed. He had gone from the Ballet company into
films and was hoofing it or choreographing every major musical out
of a major studio. All of this had brought financial success, and a
comfortable home life for Debbie and the children in a large house in
Bel-Air. The children were growing fast, were beautiful, even-
tempered and happy. Debbie was into crafts and exploratory extra-
marital affairs. She seemed fine, had opened up a great deal more, all

of my informers said, had let her hair grow long, was wearing longish, country style dresses, was very close to nature and animals and plants and to several young men whom she drove miles to visit. Evidently, Buddy didn't have a beau himself—to everyone's surprise: he had always had a beau back in New York. But, they supposed he had completely settled down into family life, and that and his work kept him too busy for extracurricular affairs. Whether he and Debbie—well, they had gotten married after all. And who knew, one misogynist friend of Buddy's said, what a man could or would do once he was domesticated.

I heard all, sifted all the information continually, adding a piece here, another there, but could not reach any real conclusion. Perhaps all his life this was exactly what Buddy had always wanted: a wife and family. And now that he had it, he was fulfilled. Perhaps that infatuation with Baby had been Buddy's first, tentative step toward it all.

It couldn't last. I was certain of it.

Scarcely six months after the latest report from the coast, I decided I had been justified in my doubts. I had changed my life completely, after all—leaving Jeanette and the kids. So, it was with little real surprise that I heard that Buddy was back in New York. Not for a visit: he had taken a large apartment in Murray Hill, and was now choreographing a show on Broadway. Buddy had gotten quite a reputation from the film work that he had done, and "Fair Day" was going to be a very contemporary musical, with real people and real problems and terrific music and stupendous dancing. It would be just the beginning of Buddy's meteoric success in the theater, and everyone knew it.

As for Debbie and the children, who knew?

Getting hold of Buddy before "Fair Day" opened proved to be next to impossible—so I bided my time. And was rewarded. For he contacted me—or sort of did. He sent two tickets to opening night.

I was still trying to talk to him at Sardis that premiere night when the reviews came in. Buddy had no doubts. He had been like a live wire all evening—making certain everyone else from the cast and theater were up too. But with the rave reviews, Buddy settled down, became almost pensive: as if his life were now out of his control, he admitted, and he wasn't so sure he liked it that way. Of course, his future was spread out in front of him like a picnic. Even he could see that. His choreography had made such a hit that he had gotten offers weeks before from other producers, as a result of rehearsal leaks in the business. I was glad to share in a friend's success, and did so with a great deal of champagne. But I remembered why I was there—at one point I asked Buddy about Debbie.

"She's fine. Going out West was the best thing that ever happened to her. She met this guy last year, a sculptor—does things with boles of redwoods and suchlike. A real mountains and woods type. She's crazy about him. They're living together up in Marin County. The show came just in time for me. We got a quick divorce in Mexico, and kissed goodbye at the airport. No hard feelings or anything. Debbie said she thought it was the best marriage any two people ever had."

I wasn't surprised to hear Buddy being philosophical about it, even if no real reasons were being offered. "How about the kids?" I asked.

"Fantastic. Adele's in high-school. Calmed down a lot. Very grown up. She'll graduate next year."

"And Baby?"

"He's beautiful. Big now. About twelve, but already as tall as I am. He's really one of the best tempered children. He really may be too good for this world."

And that was that. No faraway look or anything. The kids were grown. Debbie was married off. And Buddy was successful in the theater. Was life that simple? Had Buddy married Debbie just to make sure they would all work out well? I couldn't really believe it. I kept thinking that there really had been some sort of love affair—no matter how curious—between Baby and Buddy. And that ten years of teething, and spanking, and report cards and bruises had been to much for it. So I probed more. How could Buddy leave the children, just like that.

He shrugged, but assumed a very serious demeanor. "It had to be done."

"For their sakes?" I asked.

"For my sake," he shot back. "Mine and Baby's sake." But he refused to elaborate. "The heart has its reasons, as Pascal says," Buddy muttered.

"Whenever you quote someone it means the topic is closed," I said.

And it was.

Well, I've always been suspicious about Pascal and his lucid sounding ambiguities, and it wasn't for another five or six years that I would know the truth about Buddy and Baby.

I had finally settled down into trying to work at my father's clothing business, determined now to make money if not a name like so many of my friends. And Buddy was now running in very different crowds: with the theater set, and later on with the ballet people over at Lincoln Center after he made his well-publicized return to ballet. So, we seldom saw one another. And the answer waited.

When it came it was all the more a surprise. One morning, my secretary said she had a personal call on the line for me. It was Buddy. He asked if I would do him a really large favor. I immediately assumed it was money. He denied this, but the way he kept on hesitating made me uncertain. Finally he let it out:

"Baby's coming to New York. He'll be going to Columbia. He's arriving tomorrow morning at La Guardia. Debbie called and asked me to meet him there, and to look after him a bit until he finds a dorm and settles down."

"Why so depressed?" I asked. "It sounds like fun."

"Well, maybe. But we've become such strangers lately. You know Baby's been away at school. I haven't seen him since I left the Coast. And we don't write. I haven't talked to him over the telephone for three years."

Well, that was surprising. I had assumed they were in some contact. "Sure, if you want," I said. "I'll go along with you. When's the flight due in?"

"We'll probably be like strangers to each other," Buddy re-iterated nervously in the waiting room at the air terminal. "He may not even recognize me. You'll get him for me if that happens, won't you."

I said I would, although I couldn't see how Buddy had changed much over the years. His body was a bit trimmer than before. His hair grayer. But he was agitated as hell. And I was supposed to be there to calm him down. I wondered if he was feeling guilty—just a little guilty—about abandoning Baby so suddenly and completely, and if that wasn't what was playing on his nerves.

"Don't worry, Buddy. You two will hit it off. You always did."

"I hope so. I hope that..." but Buddy didn't finish his sentence. The passengers were disembarking, and he was straining forward to catch a glimpse of Baby.

"There!" I said pointing. But Buddy had already sprinted away and jeted right into the midst of the crowd.

When the commotion Buddy made had cleared a bit, he was shaking hands rather formally with a tall, rangy blonde boy in denim jeans and jacket, with an open necked shirt, and toting two huge canvas bags: Baby at seventeen: as usual, smiling for all he was worth.

By the time I joined them, everything seemed to be smoothed over. At least there was an aura of great friendliness. Baby was better close up—especially as by then I was into younger men myself. Of course he was tired and toussled from the trip, but as Buddy had always said, Baby was beautiful.

He had no idea who I was, although he politely enough said he had heard a great deal about me, and knew I was his mom's friend. Buddy and I waited in the airport lounge while Baby went to talk to another boy who had been on the plane and who would also be at Columbia that year.

All of Buddy's nervousness had disappeared. He had that same, placid composure he had had years before in the Redburn's country kitchen out at Moriches.

"You see," I said. "You had nothing to worry about."

"He's fine," was all that Buddy said.

"Beautiful too," I teased.

"We're not out of the woods yet," Buddy said cryptically.

And before I could even begin to think that one out, Baby had returned, all smiles and California sunshine. We all ordered something to drink, and Baby answered all of Buddy's questions about the family and school with gentleness and a good word for just about everyone and everything. Generally, this makes me believe a person's a fool. In Baby it was not only tolerable, but completely in character.

Only one cloud seemed to pass over our conversation. Suddenly, and as if I weren't even there, Baby asked Buddy a question with that breathtaking honesty of the very young: "Why did you go away, Bud?"

I thought that lightning was about to crackle. I was wrong. Buddy didn't answer, but asked Baby a question in turn. "Tell me, truly, how did you and Bailey get along?" Bailey was the outdoorsy sculptor Debbie had married.

Baby looked sad. "Not very well. That's why I went off to school in Santa Barbara. I tried, really I did. But somehow he always got on my nerves, and I always seemed to get in his way." I could tell from the way he said it, that Baby considered this a great defeat in his battle to wage love on the world.

"If it weren't Bailey, it would have been me," Buddy said. "There's always a point when fathers and sons . . . well, it happens. I didn't want it to happen to us."

I was beginning to have a glimmer of understanding.

Buddy continued. "You see I didn't want you to grow up thinking of me as Daddy. As a not very well liked Daddy. Because that would happen. You would see every fault of mine, and not be able to feel the same about me. Besides, I never wanted to be your father. That's too limiting. Can you understand that?"

"You mean this way we can be friends?" Baby tried.

"Well, . . . yes," Buddy said; but I suspected he wasn't saying everything. "At least it'll be easy for us to stay together until you move into your dorm."

"I'm not all that crazy for living in a dorm," Baby said. "I've done that trip for the last four years. Why can't I stay with you. I'll go up to school every day."

"You're certainly welcome to," Buddy said, guardedly. "But I don't know if you'll like it. People coming and going all the time. Weird people. Freaks really. Your mother might not think it was a good influence on you."

I knew what Buddy was trying to say. But I couldn't help. We got into my car in embarrassed silence, with everything unresolved. About a mile or so into the drive, Baby suddenly said, "Oh, by the way, did mom tell you—I'm gay now."

Buddy almost hit the next car, swerving so wildly.

"That's all right, isn't it?" Baby asked, hesitantly.

Buddy left me off at my office, and got out to walk me into the lobby. He repeated his thanks to me, pumping my hand furiously. "I just couldn't be sure," Buddy said. "But I just had to take the risk."

"The risk?"

"Well, it was twenty years of planning. Of waiting. Any gamble that goes on for that long would make anyone nervous. But we'll be fine. Baby and I. He'll be a perfect lover."

3

"A perfect lover," Aram repeated, as if unwilling to let the words go, to let them speak for themselves.

"And they've been together ever since?" I asked stupidly, already knowing the answer.

"Ever since."

"Hmmm," was all I answered. And then I noticed it was about time to go out to the Sandpiper. Aram didn't complain, didn't take a half an hour choosing what he should wear, didn't lose his house keys, or anything. We got up and went.

I didn't bring the subject up again after that. But I didn't have to. That very night Buddy and Baby were at the Sandpiper too. Buddy sitting with some older friends in one of those booths that define one side of the lightshow smash of dancefloor, Baby dancing in jeans and t-shirt, until even the t-shirt went in his exertion. I separated from Aram as soon as I had gotten my Bourbon and Soda at the bar, and I sat brooding behind a mirrored pillar, hidden in the middle of everything.

I resented Aram for telling the story. It made even the slightest interest I might have in Baby make me feel like a truly destructive character. If I so much as talked to Baby after what Aram had told me, it would confirm all of Aram's worst complaints about me: I was selfish, inconsiderate of others, bent on my own pleasure, unthinking of any consequences. I was incensed at Aram, and even somewhat annoyed at Baby.

What made it worse was that everyone on the dance floor—male or female, old or young—were at that moment busy falling all over themselves to get near Baby. Especially after the t-shirt flew off in a slow arc. I couldn't really blame them; anyone in their right mind would do the same. But I couldn't.

I had to get away; to get away from Baby altogether, and to be able to mope. I decided to go out onto the deck, but as I got up, Aram—who must have been watching me—got up too. I motioned him to sit back down. I wanted to be alone.

Well, the deck was no better. Although Baby wasn't out there himself, his reputation was. It only took me a minute or so of sitting in a photogenically sulky position to realize that everyone out there was talking about him. No one knew his name, of course, But there were enough references to "that new blonde number," and "Mr. San Diego Bay," and "Golden Boy" for me to know whom they all meant.

Driven from the deck, I wandered out onto the paved section of the landing dock, and finally way over to the curved wooden section. There I sat down with my legs over the side railing and counted slowly to one hundred. When I was done, I felt better. There were no yachts tied to this part of the dock, but others lined the half-moon of the other side and floated in the dark water of the bay; electrically lighted within, they seemed like so many Japanese lanterns. I tried to picture the entire scene flattened in perspective—as it would be in a Japanese print by Hokusai or Hiroshige, and I had just succeeded when there was a pad of footsteps near me, and a shadow standing there.

"How come you came out here?"

No need to look up: it was Baby, pulling on his t-shirt now in the cool of the outdoors.

I didn't answer, so he tried again: "I love the night on the water, like this. Don't you?"

"Sometimes," I said, in a voice as icy as Ida Lupino in that movie where she played the cruel, girl's reformatory warden.

"Don't you dance?" Baby asked.

"Sometimes," even colder.

"How come you didn't dance with me. I waved you over the minute I saw you."

"You didn't look as if you needed any help."

"Are you angry with me?" he asked.

"No."

"Well, you sure act like it."

He sounded half-hurt, half confused. He was trying to be sweet and kind, and I was being a complete bastard. But I couldn't help it. Earlier I might have been able to. But not now. I suddenly realized what it meant to lose innocence and I shivered.

"Why don't you come back with me and dance?"

"Why don't you just go away," I said, harder than I meant to.

Baby had hunkered down to talk to me. Now he stood right up.

"I'm not angry with you," I said quickly. "Why should I be?"

"I don't know," he said, very quietly. Now he really was hurt, and I was annoyed with myself.

"Well, I just want to be alone, right now."

"All right. All right."

And that was his goodbye. I watched his intensely desirable body as he walked away from me, along the curve of the slatted pier, over the concrete, then onto the steps of the Sandpiper. He turned to look back at me, and I was so anxious not to let him see me seeing him, that I half fell over, looking away just in time.

But I felt better already. And, after a half-hour pep talk to myself about how I was being so mature, I felt considerably better. Aram came out to find me, and found me in much better spirits. We didn't return to the Sandpiper. But we took a long walk along the beach, and had a really good night together.

So Aram's story had worked: I had renounced Baby. Or—I have to say it—Aram's story would have worked, if it weren't for that curious factor in life that the ancients revered and called Destiny or chance.

Destiny had something completely different in mind for me and Baby. And it didn't take long for me to see that renunciation had nothing to do with it. For the next two weeks, every time I took more than five steps out of Aram's house, I was pushed, bumped, collided up against Baby. On the boardwalk, he would be pulling a wagon load of groceries. On the beach, he would be rushing out of the surf directly toward me. At Tea, every afternoon, Baby seemed to be everywhere I turned. He might have been triplets. Not to mention at the Sandpiper, dancing every night, at the liquor or ice-cream or grocery store, anytime I went into them. Even at the little post-office, the one day I went there to mail a letter. Everywhere and anywhere I went, Baby seemed to be too: smiling, waving, always about to come up to talk to me, but always just far enough away that I could get away with nodding "hello" and getting out of there.

I had never understood before what temptation meant. Now I lived a life that Dante could have envisaged in some tawdry, but sandy lower circle of Hell. Baby was intensely desirable to me, and completely out of the question. However, he was always there—if not in direct line, then somewhere within the periphery of my life—to remind me, to goad me with what I had renounced.

And, what was the clincher, wherever Baby wasn't—and there were two or more other people I knew well enough to stop and talk to—Baby was the central topic of conversation. His beauty, his sweetness, his swimming and gymnastic abilities. His aloofness. His complete unavailability to anyone else in the Pines.

I thought I would go crazy. I knew that if this went on I would break down completely; throw over my maturity, my grown-up renunciation, and someday, suddenly, attack Baby and ball him in broad daylight in full view of Tea-dance.

I decided on a drastic plan.

"Oakleyville!" Aram shouted. "You're nuts! That's an hour and a half away!"

"Forty-five minutes," I corrected, "at a steady clip." Naturally, I had been prepared for some initial resistance. "Anyway, Ar, you could use some exercise." This, I knew would hit Aram below the belt, where most of his vanity was located. "Besides, if we stayed for a week or so, on Friday afternoon we could catch the ferry back from Point of Woods."

"Oakleyville?" Aram did nothing to hide his disbelief. "But why? Why?"

"Billy Jameson said we could have his house."

"We already *have* a house," Aram reasoned. "A far better house than Billy Jameson's. We don't have to borrow his. And what would we do in Oakleyville that we can't do here?"

"Oh, I don't know. Go fishing. Visit Peter." Peter was an artist friend of ours who lived nearby in Point of Woods. "We could always collect specimens. And the Sunken Forest is right there. We could be there every afternoon."

"Collect specimens! When the hell did you ever collect specimens?"

I tried to point out how charming it would be with only one or two other houses nearby on the thinnest part of the island.

"We'd be completely isolated," Aram answered. "No one to play bridge with or have dinner with."

I attempted pointing out the enchantments of Billy's turn of the century house, mostly restored but unmodernized.

"Mosquitoes. No electricity. No tap water. No showers. Outhouses," Aram shot back at me. And then went on to ask me why I would want to give up sun-decks, beach front, martinis, a swimming pool, house-boys, continental cooking every night. How, he wanted to know, could anyone give up this luxurious, sun-drenched life to go *au primitif* at Oakleyville. "Only someone who is completely psychotic or desperate," Aram answered himself.

Well, he was close. I was one and on the way to being the other. I thought fast. "I'm sick of all this. Sick of all this disgusting, pampered, namby-pamby, sissy life. I've had enough of the Pines. You can have it. All of it. I'm going to rough it at Oakleyville. And I'm going to love it!"

Aram saw I was determined, and he was silent. I was still hoping he would offer to go along with me. If only for a day or two. I felt I had made a major concession to our continuing relationship by renouncing Baby, and the least Aram could do was humor me in this. Besides, the idea of being all alone at night in Oakleyville, miles away from anyone else, was more than I could think of.

I must have looked as if I were wavering, because Aram finally said. "We'll talk about it after dinner. Let's go get dressed. You know how Bobby and Sam kvetch if anyone is too late."

"I'm not going to dinner. I'm going to Oakleyville," I declared. I knew to put it off until after dinner meant the end of it, and the continuation of my torment about Baby.

"At night? You'll never find it from the beach."

"I'll go inland. Through the forest."

"You'll get lost. You've never been there."

"I'll find it."

"They'll find your bleached bones in the sand, months from now. And they'll blame me!" Aram said.

That did it. I hated Aram when he was smug like that. I went upstairs, locked myself in the study, and called Billy Jameson in the city. I needed directions.

Meanwhile, I could hear that Aram had also come upstairs and was taking a shower. Getting ready to go to dinner. He would leave the house, arrive at Bobby and Sam's and tell everyone at dinner how I was being difficult, that I would show up a little late, and would they all not pay any attention to me. They would listen sympathetically, and agree to be very cool about it, when I finally arrived. No sir!

Billy was home, but was stoned on downs. So I copied down a pretty confusing pageful of instructions about how to get to Oakleyville via the inland route, and how to recognize the house when I got there. These instructions included a yellow brick road through the Sunken Forest, a high fence along one side, some telephone wires, and a lot of "turn sharp theres." In short, nothing that would help me to find the place on a moonless night. But I was determined to go; trusting to my unerring intuition in a tight spot and among unknown locations.

As soon as Aram had left the house, I put a few extra clothes and some toiletries and a paperback novel into my little canvas rucksack and went out. I walked along the beach toward Cherry Grove, hoping to avoid metting anyone I knew who might be curious about where I was going. Whatever else happened, one thing was certain— I would finally be free of temptation. I could reflect on Baby from a distance, meditate upon him until he was nothing but a half-remembered image. This brought me up a lot, and I trudged through the cool sand like a real soldier.

Almost at the Grove, I reflected that without Aram, my chances of sex for the next week or so at Oakleyville were admittedly slim. So, while I was passing through, I decided I would sashay through that open area of bushes and forest between the Pines and the Grove known affectionately as the "Meat Rack," where I was certain I could find some last minute passion before my enforced chastity.

I hit the place at the worst time: dinner time. I hung around for a half an hour seeing no one, then walked more and more frantically until I was finally chasing my own shadow on well worn paths. Then I gave it up.

The Grove seemed closed up. The bars weren't open and going yet. Everyone must have been home. The boardwalks were deserted. I walked through the little town with growing unease, then followed the boardwalk Billy had mentioned and found myself on the crest of a hill, but squarely on the brick pathway that would lead me through the Sunken Forest and to Oakleyville. This achievement made me feel so secure, that I stopped, sat down, smoked a joint of potent grass, and ate one of the sesame chewies I had brought with me. Then I went on until, looking back, the Grove was merely a dim phosphorescence above the tops of the trees behind me. The path curved down and around, and I enjoyed myself immensely.

Then the concrete path ended. And everything around me was sand.

I won't go into many further details about that terrible journey. I only note that I never found the slatted fences, that I walked on and on, so deserted, and with so little in sight beside sand dunes, that I might have been trekking across the Gobi. I could hear the ocean on one side. But I knew that any beach walking would be more tiring, and that only a little path led between the dune walls into Oakleyville. I came upon a Coast Guard station Billy hadn't said anything about. I saw the telephone wires stretching into infinity. Could find no one around to ask any directions from. Came upon signs that said "Private Property. Trespassers will be Dealt With," and I wondered how. I must have shot right past Oakleyville, missing all of those sharp turns Billy had warned me about, because when I finally—after two hours or so—reached a tiny hamlet of houses, no one was there.

Could this be the place? None of the houses looked in the least bit charming or old fashioned. All small, ugly, clapboard cottages. But, perhaps someone would direct me. No one answered my knocking, and as I had lost all sense of time and was certain it was past midnight,

I was afraid to awaken anyone. One house door was open, and I pushed in, hoping it was Billy's left open for me. I had a minute to flick on a hall light and to notice three rubber slickers hung on the pegboard, then a huge German shepherd stood sleepily in the doorway, and growled.

Well, I just managed to close the front door on him, and to run fast, tripping over myself, back in the direction I had come. After a half hour or so, I did see a slatted fence, and it did curve around. And there was a house. Too densely covered by trees and the night to tell if it was Billy's. As I approached, however I heard voices. Closer, I heard soft moans, and a little whine. I stepped to the screen door, and tried to look in.

Something moved within, and I jumped back. "Who's there?" a man asked.

"Uh. I'm lost?" I barely answered.

"Is it Karen?" a young girl answered from deeper inside. "Karen!"

"What do you want?" the man asked me in a very unfriendly tone of voice.

"Karen," the girl insisted. "C'mon in. We're having such a good time."

"Shut up," he said.

"I'm looking for Billy Jameson's house," I said. "This is Oakleyville, isn't it?"

"Karen? C'mon in. We'll have a good time."

"Shut up, I said," he repeated. I could hear him slap her flesh. She giggled. "It's not Karen. It's some guy."

I was already backing away from the door. "This is Oakleyville?" I asked.

Then she was up too. They were interlaced shadows through the screen door. "Why don't you invite him in," she suggested.

"You like to hit chicks?" he asked me, then pushed her down on the bed, and gave her another slap to illustrate.

"Uh, no thanks. I'm supposed to be at Billy Jameson's house. But I'm lost. Could you tell me..."

"Turn around, take the left bend of the path," he said indifferently, "it's near—Ow! You bitch! I'll get you good for that!"

Well, I got away from there, and tried to follow his directions. By then the mosquitos had discovered me, and I was being eaten alive. Slapping myself, flailing my arms to ward them off, I finally spotted the screened in porch Billy had talked about. I was bitten all over my face and hands, tattered, disheartened, weary, terrified, and totally brought down from my high.

But, I was in Oakleyville. I was safe.

I pushed in quietly, and stood in the screened-off room, trying to get my bearings. To one side was a hammock slung across the porch. I could make out several small pieces of furniture, and my knee crashed into a table. Feeling around, I found a kerosene hurricane lamp. Another minute or two to find matches. Then trying to light the thing. Every match seemed to go out in the dampness. But I finally turned up the wick and got it going, if so faintly all I could see was a foot around the lamp.

I put down my knapsack on the table, and reached for the glass bell to cover the lamp. It skidded out of my reach, and over the edge of the table, crashing onto the floor. Then the lamp went out.

"Shit!" I shouted. "Shit! Shit! Shit!" I think I even stamped my foot.

Then I re-lighted the damned lamp, and bent down to pick up the shards from the glass bell. I had accumulated about a dozen of these in my cupped hands, and was rising to set them on the table, when I stopped in mid-rise. Someone was standing in the doorway that led from the porch into the house. I gasped, the lamp went out, my blood froze, and all the glass fell out of my hands back onto the floor.

"What are you doing here?"

Before I could recognize his voice, a flashlight was turned on, onto my face then turned up to the face of the man standing in the doorway. It was Baby.

"Oh, No!" I couldn't believe it. "What are you doing here?"

"Billy said I could come here," Baby said, so defensively, that I was immediately ashamed of myself.

"But why?" I asked.

"I don't know. I wanted to get away from the Pines for a while." He was still unsure of me. "I can go back though, if you're staying here. I'll go back in the morning."

"Don't bother," I said. "You just scared me that's all." I went back to picking up the shards in my hands. "Is Buddy here too?"

"Are you kidding? He told me I was crazy to come stay out here. There's a broom and dustpan inside for that, you know."

"I've got it," I said, proudly. It was all busywork of course; I was still trying to get over the fact of his being in Oakleyville. After all that! Finally, I laughed.

Baby laughed too. "You know, it really is funny," he said.

By then other lamps were lighted, and a few candles. And we went inside. Baby had put on socks and a shirt—I had gotten him out of bed with my cursing—and we were sitting in the little Victorian parlor drinking tea. Outside, crickets chirped, and the surf hummed. Inside, we were two feet away from each other, inhaling incense, and talking quietly and guardedly. I knew my temptation had reached its apogee, and I gave in. It was like a chiropractor giving you a back crack: all that tension, then a sudden release. I yawned.

"There's another bed in that room," Baby said. "It's smaller. I'll sleep in there, if you want?"

"I'm afraid of the dark," I answered.

Baby laughed, took my hand, led me to bed, and it was Paolo and Francesca all over again.

Six days of brilliant sex, wonderful weather, delightful meals, quiet and deliciously warm companionship went by like that. Really. I was so busy being content, I couldn't take time out to wonder why it was so idyllic.

On Friday morning, we were planning our last day so we could do everything we had been doing—swimming, sunning, making love, and just hanging around talking or listening to music on his portable cassette player and yet have enough time to get to the six p.m. Point of Woods ferry back to the Pines.

We were up early, having breakfast of his making, when Baby suddenly asked me the question he must have wondered about from the minute I stumbled onto the front porch.

"What I'll never understand," he began through mouthfuls of homemade blueberry pancakes—"is why it happened out here. I mean why did you avoid me for two weeks out at the Pines?"

I had long gotten past my humiliation in failing to resist the temptation that Baby had represented to me: I was so somewhere else, that I could look back on those weeks with amused indifference—and so answer honestly.

"Well, after what Aram told me about you and Buddy, I didn't want to get in the way."

"Aram? What does he know about me and Buddy?"

"Oh, everything," I said casually. "He was there when you and Buddy first met."

"Aram?"

"Surely you know that?" Then a thought came to me. Maybe Baby didn't know. "It has been a long time ago," I added.

"It has?"

Was he teasing me? "Well, hasn't it?" I had to know.

"Four or five years. Not longer than that. But I really don't think Aram was there."

"He was—with Buddy. At the airport."

"The airport?" and now Baby seemed really confused. "Gee. I don't remember any airport. We met at a party in Fairfax. That's a little town north of San Francisco. I remember Buddy was there with two or three other dancers…"

I let him go on for a while, still unsure of whether or not he was putting me on. Maybe he didn't want to talk about the relationship. Fine. I wouldn't go on about it. Everyone has their quirks. They're entitled to them. I would drop the subject. But then Baby asked:

"Why? What did Aram say?"

"Oh, nothing much."

"C'mon. Tell me."

"All right. He said that you and Buddy had met some twenty years ago. When you were still a baby. He married your mother right after she divorced your father, and you and your sister and he lived together in Los Angeles…" the way he looked at me, made me pause.

"Go on. Go on. I'm fascinated."

"Well. That's why. Aram has always complained about me being destructive. And it would be an especially destructive act to break into such a long term relationship: especially when it seemed to be fated and all that."

"I see," Baby said, with emphasis on the second word.

I saw too. I immediately started to feel that spot right next to my solar plexus that must have something to do with the adrenalin. Then I got all hot, and began to blush. But I held back my anger, while I probed Baby about every detail of Aram's story, point by point, being very calm, almost too calm.

Baby had been born in California. His parents—still wed—had lived around the Bay all their lives. He had first met Buddy—as he had said before—several years ago in Fairfax. He had no sister Adele. And he had met Aram only two weeks ago for the first time. No—that wasn't true. He had met Aram—although not with Buddy, at a party several years before. Also—his relationship with Buddy was much looser than anything I had thought, and certainly not what Aram had said.

When every detail was certified, Baby started to laugh. No doubt at the look on my face. Then he said,

"You know, Buddy did the same thing to me once, a couple of years ago. I was interested in some guy in his company, and Buddy..."

Baby stopped. He could see I was not amused. Not at all amused.

"Aram would never do a thing like that," I said in a tight little voice. "He's got too much integrity. He'd never lie to me. Whatever the reason."

"Well, look. I'm sorry," Baby said very gently, but very firmly. "but he did."

"I'll kill him!" I said, standing up so fast I knocked my coffee over.

"Sit down. Sit down. Let me clean that up."

Images of how I could get Aram passed in front of me one after the other, faster than the speed of a speeded up film. In every one of them, just as he was at his last breath, and could only manage to gasp "But why?" I whispered like a cobra into his half-hearing ear, "Because you lied to me."

"I was angry too," Baby was saying, as I tuned back to him. "But that'll pass too. I'm still with Buddy. Even you can see that. It took a while to understand why he did it. But when I did understand I was very touched. That Buddy would do something so different from himself just to hold on to me—just because he was afraid of losing me. Well, it was really very flattering. Not terribly mature, I have to agree. But it was the only way he knew of showing me how much he did care. And, in such a way that I would have to understand. You can see that, can't you. I'm certain it's the same with Aram. It'll change your relationship. It changed mine with Buddy. We're a lot more open now, a lot more free. It was the first time he had to be forgiven by me. You'll see. It'll be much better now. Much more open."

It was the first time I had heard Baby really concerned. And as he talked, I could understand exactly what he was saying. I had half-forgiven Aram already.

"And besides. I'm going to be in New York all this fall and winter. And we'll have a great time together."

Well, Aram couldn't have had a better spokesman. After a little more of that, I bought it. We went out to the beach and played with the big rubber raft that Billy keeps at the house, then returned to the house to make love and take a nap. We just made it to Point of

Woods in time for the ferry.

Aram and Buddy were both at the dock at the Pines waiting for us. I later found out they had both attended that dinner the night I made my great trek to Oakleyville. It hadn't taken very long for them to compare notes on where Baby and I were, and Aram had been living through a week of sure torture.

He looked it. In fact, he looked so pale and humiliated standing there at the dock, that I forgave him all over again. Poor thing. I leapt up the steps of the boat, sidestepped some laundry bags being unloaded, wound my way through people and a pair of large, nervous Afghans, ran up to Aram and hugged him.

"Oakleyville was paradise," I said. And without letting him get in another word, I went on. "You missed a wonderful week. You really should have come."

Aram was looking past me, at Baby who had just stepped up.

"We had the best time," I said, watching Aram's reactions.

"What's in there," Aram asked, pointing to my bulging knapsack.

"Some dirty laundry." Everything but the sneakers, tank top shirt and shorts I was wearing. "And, I could really go for a hot shower."

"At least I was right about that?" Aram said, half-defiantly, but half-nervously too.

"Stupid," I said in a low voice. "Very stupid. But I understand."

Aram looked a little surprised, but also relieved. His forehead unwrinkled, and he even managed a little smile.

Buddy joined us, and all four of us said hello and then a quick goodbye. They walked off to the grocery store, and Aram and I headed toward his house.

"You know, Baby and I really had a terrific time this past week. We really got to know each other well." That last sentence so that Aram would have no illusions about what I knew and didn't know. Then, to be certain our relationship would be more open in the future: "We're going to see each other in the city, after this. You don't mind, do you?"

"No, why should I?" Aram answered, not missing a beat, "you should have some friends your own age. My friends are far too settled down for you. I should have realized that before."

And that was how he rationalized it.

4

"Is that all?"

"That's all," I said. "I rest my case."

I sat back and watched for Tim's reaction. When I had first begun talking, he had been fidgety, lighting one cigarette after another, crossing and re-crossing his legs, occasionally taking a sip of Budweiser, and all the time looking hopefully toward the telephone. He was waiting for a call, I knew. When he got it, he would be going out for the evening. I knew. I had seen his restlessness coming on for weeks now. This would be only the beginning. Everything would be downhill from here. Unless I could do something to stop it. Now. Before it was too late.

"And you stayed with Aram?" he asked now, almost indifferently. At least he had followed it. Closely enough. I had hoped he would.

"Until two years ago, when he died. And right after that I met you."

"Yeah, right. And Baby? What about you and him?"

"During that fall I saw him several times. But he didn't really like the winter in the city. Too cold and grey. So he went back to California. I haven't seen him since. He did send a card last Christmas. Remember?"

"No," Tim said. He seemed so precious to me, because I was afraid I was losing him. All his habits—his way of not seeming to pay attention to me or any of my friends was typical—all of his gestures seemed so strong, so much him that they might have served as archetypes.

"Well," he said finally, "I think it's a stupid story." He got up and went into the kitchen. Probably to get another beer.

Well, I tried, I thought. Maybe I had been wrong. As reserved and cool as Tim was, maybe I should have just let him know where I was. Too late now.

While he was in the kitchen, the phone rang. Just once. Tim must have picked it up on the kitchen extension. Well, this was what he was waiting for. I got up and went closer. I could hear him talking to someone.

I couldn't resist listening in. I went right up to the louvered doors that separate the kitchen and the dining room—Tim had pushed them almost closed. I felt like a man about to be guillotined whose fascination with his fate is so intense that he has to inspect the blade beforehand to see exactly how sharp it will be.

"No, don't worry," Tim was saying in a curious—almost congested voice—"I'll be allright. It's only the flu or something. Yeah. Maybe next week sometime... Yeah. I have your number. I'll call. No, that's all right. I have it written down in my telephone book."

His last words surprised me: Tim had no telephone book. He always had to hunt up a telephone number he needed. Or ask me.

"Sure. Sure," he went on, making a bored face in the little mirror above the shelf. "Don't worry. I'll be ok. I'll call. Unless it's something worse... I don't know. There's a lot of hepatitis going around."

Then Tim looked intently in the mirror and turned around to face me through the opening in the louvered door.

"Yeah. Yeah. Bye," he said, and hung up the receiver. Then in a louder voice. "You can come out now. What a schmuck that guy was. He wanted to come over here with chicken soup for Chrissakes. Too dumb to know when he's getting the brushoff. Well. What are we doing tonight?"

"There's a double bill at the Elgin, *Duck Soup* and *Coconuts,* I said. I had been planning to go alone.

"I never saw them. Let's get ripped first."

And we did.

Tim referred to the whole business only once, about a week later, late at night, in bed.

"You didn't expect me to believe that stupid story, did you?" he asked.

"Which one?"

"Oh, forget it!"

Soon afterwards, I sent out my set of the Burton translation to be bound in Morocco with gold tooling. It was the least I could do to show my appreciation. Before I had read it, I was certain that storytelling was a waste of time, and, completely impractical in daily affairs. Of course one story usually is. But a story within a story... well, that's another matter altogether.

Scheherezade would understand.

Xmas in the Apple

The electric blue of the juke box is the same flashing cobalt of the spotlighted metallic wreath hanging over the head of the bartender at the Eagle's Nest. It is also the same neon blue of the tight-fitting t-shirt on the raven-haired number Ned Hausmann has been cruising for the last hour and a half. It is 2:15 a.m., Christmas Day: and Ned doesn't want to go home alone.

It doesn't seem as though the number is ready however. Now he's talking to friends who've just come into the Nest. The bar is otherwise pretty empty: or just as bad as empty as far as Ned is concerned, since he's either balled with, rejected, or been rejected by everyone else in the place who even vaguely interests him. Ned's a little high from the six Budweisers he's put down since his arrival— with help from two quarters of a Quaalude in between to keep his act calm.

Ned Hausmann is twenty six years old and has been living in New York City for two years. He works for a paperback reprint house, where he's somewhere in middle management, doing marketing—a job he doesn't like and wasn't hired for originally back in St. Louis. There, when he signed a contract with the employment scout for the publishing house, he thought he'd finally be getting to do something his graduate studies had prepared him for: editing books. Like everything else in his recent life, the job turned out to be delusory and disappointing. He's found it hard meeting people in New York; found it equally hard making friends, found it especially difficult getting used to the high energy activity level and inbred elitist social life of the gays he's met so far. But here at the Nest—at least—he can be more himself: more relaxed, slower, more mellow; even if he has to calm himself down with a Q now and then. Not that it seems to be helping tonight.

The number's friends go to the pool table, chalking their names up on the board for what will probably be the last game of the night. The number looks toward Ned, and Ned makes his move.

His opening line is banal, but so what? The guy responds with an equally banal follow-up. They stare at each other, then away again. Ned asks how the number's drink is, (fine!); says it's slow in the Nest tonight (the number agrees); even goes so far as to compare the number's shirt to the wreath—an off hand compliment that seems to take nicely (at least he doesn't move away). But the chemistry is off between them, and they both know it. So after a few minutes of conversational leads from both ends that go nowhere, the number says "See you!" and saunters over to the pool table to his friends. And that's that.

Ned splits the place. Not even anyone out on the street in front of the Nest. Cabs waiting however. A line of them. They know the place will close in twenty minutes. Ned stands for a minute, wondering whether he ought to check out the Spike on the next block, or even the Ramrod, downtown in the Village. There's always the baths, or the Mineshaft: they'll go on all night. But it isn't sex Ned really wants tonight, but companionship. And the chances of finding that in the tubs or down on his hands and knees on a urine stained floor aren't too promising.

He gets into the first cab in the line, doesn't even see the driver until he's halfway home, uptown, along deserted Tenth Avenue. That's when the cabbie slides open the little window separating driver and passenger and says something. Ned has to lean forward to make out. The driver, he sees, is fiftyish, middle-aged, gone to fat, with a scruffy black beard and glasses.

"No luck tonight in the Nest?" the driver asks.

Ned thinks he's just making conversation. "No," he answers.

The driver, flips on the inside lights so Ned can see the front seat better, sees the driver is holding a considerably fat hardon in his free hand, slapping it against the lower rim of the steering wheel.

"You wanna swing on this for a while. I'll pull over into a side street."

Before Ned can even realize what the driver said, the cabbie adds: "It'll pay for your ride home."

"No thanks," Ned manages to say, and falls back in the seat. He wonders if the cabbie is a nutcase, and should he get out right here. What's the chances of finding a cab on Tenth Avenue and Forty-ninth street at this hour? Ned pops the other half of the Quaalude into his mouth. It tastes awful without something to wash it down.

"Hey man, no hard feelings," the cabbie says when they arrive at Ned's address.

"No hard feelings," Ned says hurriedly stuffing the fare and a tip into the change box between them.

"I'll go back down to the Nest, now," the driver says in what Ned would have to call a leering whisper. "I'll find me a taker there tonight, you'll see. Hey. Thanks. Merry Christmas!"

Ned gets into the building foyer just as the Quaalude really hits him. He gets through the glass doors in time to see the cab turn around and drive off. He drags himself over to the elevator, spaces out waiting for it to arrive, finally climbs in, gets out at his floor, manages to get the keys to turn into this apartment, and falls on his bed, fully clothed.

Better than last year, Ned thinks. He passed out at an orgy at a complete stranger's house last Christmas. Jesus! How he hates the holidays in New York. Maybe with the Q he'll be able to sleep right through this one.

§

Just before the alarm goes off, there is a slight click. That is the sound Gregg D'Amato has been waiting for, lying in bed next to his lover, Steve Lange, smoking a cigarette. He leaps out of bed and shuts off the alarm before it can begin its harsh buzz. It's only nine a.m. No sense in waking Steve this early.

Gregg dresses fast in baggy grey cordorouys, an old cashmere pullover sweater and the deerhide slippers he received last night; an early Christmas gift from Steve. The floors are wood parquet, but cold nonetheless. He has to turn up the thermostat ten degrees to even begin to warm up the huge loft. The heat is kept at 65 degrees all night: it's a rule of the Co-op voted on at their last meeting to save fuel.

It's warmer in the kitchen as he stands close to the range, boiling water for the Melita: he'll only drink drip coffee nowadays. Then

Gregg goes to the toilet and takes a piss. Coming out of the bathroom he stops to admire the enormous Blue Spruce tree he and Steve put up last night in the center of the large living area. They'll decorate it this afternoon, leaving some ornaments out for the eight dinner guests who've been asked to bring a special decoration for the tree. Gregg is still knocked out by how large and handsomely furnished his lover's Soho loft—his now too—is. Three months ago when Steve asked him to move in, Gregg was unsure. He's thirty-two years old, and has had more than one lover since he came out at the age of eighteen in the Merchant Marine; but this was a step he had never taken before. He always prized his independence—his ability to come and go where and when he wanted. Probably the result of growing up in a large, overly interfering Italian family in Scranton, Pennsylvania.

The tea kettle begins to whistle, and Gregg runs to shut it off. He makes a pot of coffee for three then sits at the big built-in table against the enormous window looking down on Greene Street. He's brought out a half dozen cookbooks, looking for some new ideas. This will be his and Steve's first Christmas together—with both of their closest friends visiting—and Gregg wants it to be special.

Outside, the street is empty. When he opens the window a crack, he is surprised by how warm it it: he opens it more. It's still quiet out: not even the usual hum of traffic a block down on Canal Street. Opposite him are rows of cast-iron buildings identical to this one— with large inset windows. Gregg still hasn't gotten used to living in Soho. He misses trees, parks, people walking the street day, noon, and night, as it was in the Village where he rented a succession of overpriced two room apartments. But he knows he'll never leave this place voluntarily.

The Joy of Cooking has an oyster-chestnut dressing that looks festive and should taste great. He bought fresh chestnuts last night, preparing to serve them roasted. The oysters will have to be canned ones: unless Steve is willing to join his trek to the Fulton Fish Market to see if any shops are open there.

Gregg finishes his coffee, goes to the refrigerator and pulls out the plastic wrapped twenty-two pound turkey. It looks bare and cold and rather sad. But he can already visualize it golden brown with an apple in its neck and browned stuffing pouring out of its plump rump.

Just thinking that reminds him of how much he disliked Christmases in Scranton in the past six or seven years. His large family: his brothers and sisters with their wives and husbands and kids. His mother working away in the kitchen from dawn on. His father holding court in the big chair in the living room, surrounding himself with his grandchildren. The T.V. set going full blast from the den. The kids chasing each other around and being yelled at by their parents. His father's snide comments on every subject Gregg ever brought up. The arguments that invariably erupted just before dinner was served. The kissing and making up. Or yelling and stomping out. The noise.

Gregg is planning to make a Christmas dinner as rich, as enormous, as delicious as the one he would have at home. Only this dinner will be civilized.

He has gotten the big bird washed when he hears singing outside. He wipes his hands and goes to the window. Greene Street is as empty as before except for about ten carolers—all bundled up with colorful scarves trailing and brightly knit wool hats.

"God Bless You Merry Gentlemen," they sing, and they sound much younger and cheerier than they look.

Another dozen or so tenants across the street open their windows and look out. Many of them are dressed in robes or pajamas, just awakened, but not upset.

Then, magically, it begins to snow. Big flat flakes shimmer down on them.

Gregg feels the brush of lips against the nape of his neck and then the encircling warm arms and familiar smell of his lover.

§

"That was a beautiful service, wasn't it, Walter?" Mrs. de Nathan asks, as they step out of the vestry of St. Thomas' Episcopal Church on Fifth Avenue and Fifty-Third Street.

Walter Meredith agrees that it was a lovely service altogether. The boy's choir has been giving concerts all year round and are now quite professional: their Victoria motets were wonderful. The decorations around the chapel were seasonal without being vulgar. The sermon was lovely and brief. The congregation was well dressed and remained mostly awake.

Walter is more concerned with getting the frail old lady down the slippery dozen or so stone steps without her falling. Mrs. de Nathan is Walter's great-aunt, his only relative in New York, and is close to ninety-three years old. It has become a tradition for them to see each other every Christmas. To attend St. Thomas', then to retire around the corner, to her sixth floor duplex, overlooking the garden of the Museum of Modern Art where they will sip sherry and talk until the old woman begins to doze.

It's not really a holiday charity—although Richard, Walter's lover of seven years, always called it that. He resented the few mornings a year Walter gave to her. But he never understood how much Walter likes Mrs. de Nathan. He likes her peppery monologues and unconventional opinions on subjects culled from the *New York Times*. He likes her anciently decorated oversized apartment. He likes her insistence on applying the most discriminating tastes to every subject that passes her view. He likes her money—old New York money—although since Richard's accident and the insurance money coming through, Walter is certain he's better off now than she is. He even likes the fact that she is so old. Perhaps that means that it runs in the family; that he too may live to be...

Walter isn't obsessed with age so much as he is *interested* in it. He's only thirty-nine years old and looks five years younger, but he has recently acquired a taste for younger men—from nineteen to twenty-three. Richard was a contemporary: born a month before Walter. But ever since his death, and more importantly, since Walter's beard and moustache became salt and pepper, he's found younger men looking at him in the streets, coming up to him at bars, allowing themselves to be approached, talked to, easily persuaded to come home with him. At first, Walter's vanity was wounded. He had always been the sought after one: the hot number of his set. But after only a few encounters with younger guys, he's come to enjoy their freshness, their unrelenting sexuality, their easy-come easy-go attitude. They all seem so accomplished in bed—certainly more so than he was at their age. And none of them want a relationship other than "fuck-buddy", a term Walter just learned and loves to say.

Mrs. de Nathan does the steps gracefully, even without the rubber tipped cane she left in her apartment foyer; and waves goodbye to some other ancient ladies gathered on the sidewalk in front of St. Thomas. She then allows herself to be guided home.

At her apartment, she throws open the window because of the stuffiness of steam heat. Walter turns on the big old Zenith console. Corelli's *Christmas Concerto* has just begun. The dark-hued strings slide from theme to exposition as though covered with fine oil.

Mrs. de Nathan pours the sherry—Jerez for her, Bristol Cream for Walter,—and they sit down in her newly recovered Windsor chairs looking out onto the raked grey garden of the Museum with its giant Mailol women. This view always excites Walter and makes him feel he did well to leave Sacramento and come to New York—almost twenty years ago.

The old lady begins to talk about the tower that will be built atop the Museum. The city has just approved the plan and she is certain someone was bribed.

Walter finishes his drink and pours himself another. He thinks vaguely about tonight—and of his special Christmas gift to himself. Then he listens to Mrs. de Nathan's protests more closely.

What an amazing old thing she is! At the rate things are done in New York, it will be a good six to eight years before the tower across the street it done. How sure she is she'll still be around to be annoyed by it!

§

The phone has been ringing for a very long time.

Still mostly asleep, Ned reaches across the bed to get it. He is foggy from last night. The few visible objects in his sparsely furnished, recently decontrolled studio apartment blur in his vision. Even the muscleman riding atop the mythical beast in the New St. Marks' Baths poster opposite his bed looks like hell today. As Ned's hand grasps to lift the receiver out of its cradle, he wonders who in the world it could be. Isn't today Christmas? He falls back onto the mattress and lets out a muffled hello.

"Is that you, Edward?"

His mother. The last caller he expected.

It comes out sounding wrong—and he's immediately aware that she knows it too.

He can hear his father in the background asking what's wrong. He can hear others in the room too—his sister Nan, her husband Tom, their two kids. Ned is suddenly filled with hatred and nostalgia for Kentucky family Christmas.

He manages to convince his mother that he has a cold to explain his sleepiness at eleven-thirty in the morning. It's the antihistamine pills he's taking, he says. She shouldn't worry. Once more he repeats how sorry he was he couldn't get away from work to fly down to be with them this year: although he never even tried to get the days off.

Then his father is on the line, cheery and filled with Yuletide spirit and perhaps an early laced eggnog or two. Next is Nan, then little Eddie, supposedly his favorite nephew, though Ned doesn't even really remember which child he is.

As he talks, Ned lights the long roach of a joint of Acapulco Gold he'd left in an ashtray by the bed. One hand reaches over to lift the greyed window shade to look out the grimy window to the small patch of street. Grey. Still warmish. It still might snow. Might even have snowed before. The sidewalk's damp. Even if it does snow it will probably be dirty, wet snow, quickly melted or turned to slush.

Ned promises to be home for his birthday in late March, then has to say goodbye to all of the speakers again.

When he drops the telephone onto the receiver, he turns the bell to "low" so he won't be bothered by it again. He goes to the bathroom, finds a blue Valium 10 in the medicine cabinet, pops it into his mouth, and drinks water off the faucet to wash it down.

In the few minutes he lies awake in bed before the pill slides over his consciousness, Ned thinks about what it would be like having Christmas with his folks. Probably not half bad. But he's planning on taking his winter vacation in San Juan. He doubts he'll even pay the extra fare to stop by on his way back.

§

Snow is still falling—or falling again—Steve isn't sure which, at one o'clock in the afternoon; although it doesn't look as though it will stick. Steve and Gregg are just getting out of a taxicab at Fifth Avenue and Forty-Second Street. Steve is surprised to see the avenue hasn't been closed off to cars as it was for Easter Day this past year. Evidently a lot of other New Yorker's beside them had the same idea in mind today: a stroll down the avenue, checking out windows on that famous stretch of street.

Steve Lange used to do this once a month when he first came to the city, eight years ago. Now his interest is only partly that innocent excitement. At thirty-three years old, Steve is one of the country's up and coming designers—and some of his best work is in window display. When the big names in display are mentioned—Bob Curry, Candy Pratt, etc. Steve's is always included in the top half dozen. So, naturally their walk today is professional too. Steve wants to check out the competition. He also has a surprise for Gregg. He wonders if Gregg will see it right away in the north corner window of Saks, or whether he'll have to stand there and point it out. Gregg is sometimes dense about visuals, like most people involved in words—like most advertising copywriters.

They pass various stores, crossing and recrossing the avenue— Takashimaya, Wallachs, the airline offices from all over the world, then the bookstores, Brentanos, Barnes and Noble, Scribners. Gregg is in a great mood today, like a kid, grabbing Steve's arm to point out this or that, someone passing by.

Their straight neighbor on Greene Street, Al Clifton, a sculptor in sheets of acrylic, and Al's older ladyfriend, Mara, who calls herself Al's patroness (for which read: she owns the co-op and pays the bills) are at Steve's and Gregg's loft right now, watching the Browns-Giants game on the TV, making certain the kitchen doesn't blow up or anything else weird happen.

Before leaving the loft, Gregg checked the turkey and pulled out of the top oven three sumptuous looking pies—apple, mince and pumpkin—he'd baked that morning. He also chilled the dozen bottles of Perrier and half dozen of Piper-Heidseck. Steve's convinced they'll all be looped on the champagne by midnight. Gregg also prepared an enormous platter of antipasto, and went around the dining room changing candles. Steve counted thirty-four of them.

He's still amazed that Gregg D'Amato is his lover. Gregg had the reputation of being the hottest and the most promiscuous man in the city when Steve first met him at the Ice Palace last July out at Fire Island. Steve can remember sunning on the beach the next afternoon with his housemates—friends for years—after Gregg had left, and how they very seriously warned Steve not to get too involved unless he wanted a summer heartburn. That same afternoon Steve went for cocktails at Jeremy's house. Jeremy is his oldest friend in the city; a decorator in his fifties who conquered and tamed a famous stud in his own time and domesticated him very nicely. Steve asked Jeremy what he should do about Gregg.

"Either forget him, or really set your mind to it," Jeremy had instructed. "By which I mean milk him in the morning, milk him in the afternoon, and fuck him to the wall at night: *every* night."

Since Gregg was the most attractive guy Steve had ever seen and was easy, Steve had no trouble following Jeremy's advice. And to everyone's surprise—not the least Steve and Gregg—they soon fell in love.

They are now at the north east corner of Fifth Avenue and Forty-Seventh Street. A skinny Santa in an outfit two sizes too big is ringing a big brass bell, holding out a small basket. Chestnut and pretzel vendors are sending up gusts of aromatic smoke every time they uncover the tin foil keeping their comestibles hot. On the next corner a doorway is open in St. Patrick's Cathedral, a choir singing distantly, sure sign of the last high mass of the day. Steve was brought up a Catholic and assumes Gregg was too: he wonders whether he ought to suggest they drop in for a minute or two.

"Well?" Steve says. "What do you think?"

The big store window has a half dozen female mannequins in casual attire in a winter setting, chatting busily as they paint the dark grey clapboard house wall a bright white. One of them is apart—on the far left—where the wall is still mostly unpainted. She has a brush in her hand too, and is just pulling back from the wall, where she has painted a circle and written inside "I love Gregg D'Amato."

Gregg shouts so loud in his delight that people turn to stare. Then he grabs Steve, hugs him, swings him around, kisses him, and dances around him.

Steve's trying to think how he can get the message on a Billboard in Times Square for Gregg's birthday.

§

It's finally really snowing when Ned gets out of the shower. Big fat shapeless flakes that melt before they can reach the sidewalk and spot it. It is colder outside; he had to shut the window when he awakened; the snow might stick.

Ned thought he heard the telephone ring while he was scouring; but now he sees the bell has been turned down. He has been in the shower a long time; under the most vigorous ministrations of the massage nozzle of steaming water. He still doesn't feel completely together yet.

He makes a cup of instant coffee and sips it without the sugar he forgot to replenish for the third straight week. Sitting down, he tries to remember what if anything happened last night in the Nest. All he can recall is the dark haired shithead in the neon blue t-shirt who turned out so ditzy he didn't know a good fuck when he met one. Then Ned recalls the cabdriver who wanted a blowjob and had the cheese to come onto him. Ned doesn't think he'll go back to the Nest for a while. He ought to cool it for a bit. Stay home. Watch TV. Read that bestseller sitting on his bedtable for months.

It's already getting dark slowly and greyly outside his window. He puts on a disco music cassette by last year's hot DJ at Fire Island Pines that Ned ripped-off a kid he tricked with one night in September—the only night he was at the Island that summer.

Then Ned sees the rectangle of white under his door, bright against the sooty color of his industrial carpeting.

It turns out to be an invitation with a designer's Christmassy motif—sort of abstract Mistletoe and Bell, obviously bought at Greetings or some uptown version of the shop. It's from two guys who live down the hall, lovers, in their mid-forties. Jose and John are asking him to come by for "Xmas Cheer: light supper and who knows?"

Ned knows. Ever since he moved into the building they've been making goo-goo eyes at him in the elevator, whenever they've met downstairs at the mailboxes, or on the street where they constantly seem to be walking their Afghans, pulling the poor beasts through the cold block after block, shit-scooper in hand. One of them is fat and one is thin. Ned doesn't know which is which. Nor does he care. They're both nelly and obvious. Light supper, his eye. He's probably going to be the main course.

Ned opens the blinds all the way, but he doesn't put on a lamp yet. He considers making himself a quick dinner, then wonders where he could go eat something outside the apartment. Will everyone be in groups and families? Or, worse, will there only be single persons, loners, the abandoned, like himself?

Instead, Ned rolls himself another joint of grass then makes himself another cup of coffee which is so bitter he only drinks a sip.

As he smokes, he wonders if he shouldn't have sucked off Fattie last night for the hell of it. The cock was thick and red looking, just like Ned likes them. Give the old fart a real treat if he's used to getting head from those dirty whores who hang out in the Meat Packing area. Nah! Let the creep beat off until he has a stroke!

Ned sits smoking in his bed, the pillows propped up behind his head, listening to the disco tape until it is dark. And continues sitting there long after.

§

The fireplace is crackling, four large logs burning; another dozen on the side of the brickwall. The dining room table is set, the living area cleaned up and ready for guests. After passing around a joint of Thai Stick, Al Clifton and Mara have gone back to their loft, to get dressed for the dinner party they will be going to uptown.

Steve and Gregg are stretched out on the big, pillow covered, backless divan in the middle of the loft, looking at the lights on the Christmas tree: tiny gold and silver lights Steve ordered from Japan in mid-summer. Music is softly emanating from the four ceiling-hung Bose 901 speakers strategically placed around the room: Peggy Lee's *Mirrors* album, one of their favorites.

Gregg is wondering what he has to do in the remaining half hour or so until their first guests arrive. He really ought to call his folks in Scranton to say hello. Steve's parents called an hour ago, just as he and Gregg got in the door; and they all had a good talk and were warmly polite to Gregg. He probably ought to check the turkey: he removed the aluminum foil he cooked it in so the outside would brown: he hopes it won't brown too fast. He also hopes he hasn't forgotten something minor but all-important—the cranberry sauce, or olives. That would be awful. His ankles are still throbbing a bit from the workout they got from the hour and a half of ice skating he and Steve did in Central Park. Steve is rubbing his legs gently. They are intertwined: denim and socks and flannel shirts.

Gregg expresses all these minor anxieties to Steve, who has become his other self and will never laugh at him.

"I have a better idea," Steve says, and slides down Gregg's body until his head is over Gregg's crotch. Softly biting the denim, Steve looks up at Gregg. Greggs gets hard instantly, long before Steve opens the button-fly.

Gregg shoots his load in his lover's mouth, just as the doorbell rings.

§

The only concession Walter Meredith has made to the holiday in his handsome federal-style Grammercy Park duplex is a huge basket of red pointsettias that he has set atop the Pace glass coffee table in his study. More than a dozen plants almost cover the table, hanging over three sides. They are bright and festive and look just right, picking out the reds and oranges in his matched cloisonne ashtray and candy dish, and on the covers of *Gentleman's Quarterly* and *The New Yorker.*

Outside it is night and snowing heavily. The snow has stuck to the macadam of the street, muffling even further the little bit of traffic on Park Avenue. One of the advantages of living in this area is how quiet it is, especially on weekends and holidays.

Walter has just awakened from a late afternoon nap and made himself some coffee. The three sherrys he drank with Mrs. de Nathan put him out long before she was ready for him to leave. At least he managed to get into a cab and safely home. The coffee has completely revived him. Now he goes downstairs to the kitchenette and fixes himself a light dinner: always aware of his thickening waistline: scrambled eggs with a touch of Cognac, link sausages, toasted English muffin, watercress salad, no dessert, but accompanied by a 1975 *Pouilly Fuisse* he has been storing for just such an occasion.

Walter has had several offers for passing Christmas day with friends. Jean and Harv Toomey—old buddies of his and Richard's for years—invited him to dinner uptown. Billy Donath invited him to a large, noisy party he and his two roommates will be having. But Walter has gone to Christmas dinners with friends and to Christmas parties with friends in the last three holiday seasons he's been on his own. He discovered last year he would rather not be with people at all—except of course for his great aunt in the morning.

After supper, Walter takes the still half full *Pouilly Fuisse* upstairs to his study. Here, with an infrequent foray to the kitchen or bathroom, he will spend the rest of the evening. He will be by himself, with his phone shut off, doing what he wants to do, what he can't do with others. He will listen to a new recording he recently bought of Bach's *Christmas Oratorio,* and he will go to the side table and blindly select a book from the previously selected half dozen titles he has put there. He will listen to music, read his book, sip his wine, and toast himself for his good sense.

The opening of the Oratorio begins—all trumpets and drums—original instruments from the middle of the Eighteenth Century. Walter leans over and shuffles the books—chosen for brevity and previous pleasure giving—then closes his eyes and picks one up. With his eyes still closed, he opens it to the first few pages, sits down in his Brazilian leather chair, and begins to read: "The story held us, round the fire, sufficiently breathless..."

Walter's surprised. He doesn't even recall including *The Turn of the Screw*. But it's short, and compelling, so why not. The Regensburg Boy's Choir begins the first long, celestial chorus: "Rejoice, be glad. Praise Thy Days."

§

The disc jockey is in the little booth in the second room of the Eagle's Nest tonight, playing "You're No Good," when Ned enters the bar through the swinging doors. The place is more crowded than last night, less macho wear on display than usual, more people in casual clothing. There are even a couple of guys in tuxedos and white scarves. Evidently they've been somewhere fancier early.

The singer repeats the song's title over and over again "You're No Good, You're No Good, You're No Good!" and Ned snaps his fingers to the beat, not really even listening, but enjoying it nonetheless. And the Nest too. Lot's of people here tonight. A good mood in the place. The guys must have had a good day—or a troubled, tense day requiring release. That's more likely. There will probably be some really wild fucking and sucking tonight. Maybe he ought to go right to the Mineshaft. No. It's *friendly* here tonight: people being festive. That's a break.

Ned's still not certain he ought to have come. He found himself getting dressed for the place at eleven-thirty tonight without even giving it a thought. So, it's either habitual, or good intuition at work.

The wreath hanging over the bartender is now spotlighted a deep scarlet—metallic and glittering. The checked flannel shirt opened to the waist of the blond number opposite Ned is more of a strawberry hue; as is the light bathing the guy's arms and hairy chest and moustached face. The jukebox is still neon blue—as is the black tenor on the record the DJ is now playing. He couldn't have had too terrific a holiday. Why doesn't somebody tell him his music is too down?

Surprisingly, the blond number smiles at Ned, then does so again, and finally as Ned returns a half smile, makes room next to himself for Ned to join him. He really is a hot looking guy. Could be a porno star or something with that body, the jeans molding his calves and thighs!

Hiding his nervousness and awe Ned joins him. They talk about the music, about the lousy weather which has finally turned to snow for a white Christmas, talk about other bars and even other parties—most of which Ned has heard of but wasn't invited to.

The number suggests they have another drink, and they do. After that, the number suggests they step outside to get high. They cross Twenty-First Street and huddle in a doorway smoking grass and watch taxis pull up to the Nest, and take off again usually with a passenger. Somehow that irritates Ned: maybe that fat guy will be there and recognize him. He hopes not.

But Rob—the blond—is getting hotter. He has his hands all over Ned on one pretext or another before they've finished the joint, and is soon rubbing Ned's crotch, admiring the erection he has produced.

Ned's expectations grow too. He kisses Rob hard, deeply, getting off on the fact that passers-by and car passengers see them doing this: two hot guys making it in a doorway. Ned feels as much of Rob's body as he can through the Wranglers and the fur-lined brown leather bomber jacket he's wearing, and he likes what he's found. He's beginning to think this may make up for last night's bomb-out.

Suddenly Rob stops and pulls away, adjusting his clothing. He explains that he thought he saw some friends go by. Ned thinks that it's unlikely Rob's friends would recognize him, and he gets up the courage to suggest that they'd be better off doing this more privately, say at Ned's apartment. He has to repeat his offer. They are out of the doorway now and in the middle of the sidewalk. Ned has one hand on the handle of a taxi door. Rob pulls away.

"No. No thanks," Rob says.

Confusion and impending disappointment take over Ned's usual reticence. He asks why not.

But Rob won't or can't explain why not, is vague, weird, and he even takes Ned's hand and shakes it limply before backing off. Then he breaks away, turns and almost runs around the corner back through the doors of the Eagle's Nest.

Ned remains where he is a long time. He can't go back in and he doesn't want to go anywhere else. He's pissed off: he'd like to smash Rob's face in. Finally, he jumps into a cab at the head of the line and mumbles out his address. Two blocks later, he changes his mind and tells the driver to go downtown, to the Mineshaft.

Sitting back in the cab seat, Ned pops a whole Quaalude into his mouth, chews on it, washes out the taste with a stick of Dentyne. He checks his pill box—two joints—both Dusted—another Quaalude, and half a Tuinal. He just might get through tonight.

§

Gregg seems dead to the world as Steve tiptoes into the room. Slowly, quietly, he slips off the new robe and slides beneath the warm down comforter. The fragrance of pine fills the loft; the odors of dinner, burnt out candles, fireplace logs all mixing into a fragrance that is almost as delicious as the musk that surrounds his lover's sleeping body.

He kisses Gregg lightly on the forehead, thinking this is the best Christmas he's ever had, then he rolls over and settles onto his own pillow, and stares at the dimness around him, wondering if he is extra alert right now just so he can remember this moment in years to come. Could this be the apex of his life? Will everything be downhill from now on? Will Gregg still be here next Christmas? Or will...?

Before he can begin to panic, his lover rolls over, seemingly still asleep, and slides a hand onto Steve's chest. The hand slowly drops until it cups Steve's genitals.

"You awake?" he whispers.

But Gregg keeps on snoring lightly.

"Goodnight," Steve says, "Merry Christmas."

Just before he too falls off, Steve thinks, "God, but this must look beautiful. I wonder if I can get it into a window."

Slashed To Ribbons In Defense Of Love

"It's about time you decided to wake up! We have a brunch at one o'clock, as you very well know."

Gary was up, dressed, sitting across the room sipping coffee and smoking a cigarillo. He'd been out: the Sunday *Times* sat unopened on a nearby chair.

"It's almost twelve now. A cab will take at least fifteen minutes. If we can find one. Go shower. You know you take forever in there."

Behind Gary's head, sunlight came in through the skylighted dressing room and pushed through the flecked fibers of the shoji-screen. Spence could see the gold flecking on the rice paper very clearly today. The undulating fields of lacquered flowers were backlighted—bright as persimmons. Gary's face was in shadow.

"I want you to know beforehand that this brunch is extremely important to me. Arnie has invited Seitelman, the Oriental Art expert. I've been trying to get near him for months. I want him to come look at those *Monoyama* scrolls I picked up last month."

Gary exhaled blue smoke. It floated into the sunlight, turned grey then yellow then grey again. He exhaled again and a second cloud rose to meet the first in a billow. It spread thinly, forming a tiny tornado around the head of the smiling Shinto statue precariously perched on a wall shelf. The Shinto idol kept smiling; it never seemed to notice the smoke descend again and form a flat halo directly over Gary's head. Spence noticed though. He laughed.

"I'm not kidding, Spence. Arnie's gone to a lot of trouble to get Seitelman. And it will take a lot of tact to keep him there. So I don't want any interference from you. Is that clear?"

Gary exhaled forcefully and broke the halo. He began picking at the edge of the cup he was drinking from, as though it were crusted with something. It was his favorite china—from the Northern Sung—and invaluable. Spence never touched it. He only used china that could be dropped: or thrown. Gary frowned. Spence turned over in bed.

"As soon as you've met him, go to the other end of the room or table or wherever we are. And stay there. And, Spence, do try to keep your pin-sized knowledge of art to yourself. No one is interested, I assure you."

If Gary weren't dressed, if he were still in bed, he'd be vulnerable. Spence was bigger, stronger. He'd roll Gary over, pin him down, wrestle with him: anything to make him shut up. Sometimes fucking helped. But Gary wouldn't fuck now. He was dressed already. He'd been up for hours. Up, smoking one cigarillo after another. Up, drinking one cup of coffee after another. Up, scheming about the art and Seitelman. Up, thinking, thinking, thinking.

"I don't even know why Arnie and Rise invited you. I suppose as a compliment to me. Either that, or they think it's the enlightened thing to do."

Enlightened, my ass! Spence thought. Ah, enlightenment. Spence could see it all. He and Gary were on the Johnny Carson Show. Johnny was asking Gary about his career as New York's most successful male model in decades. Gary was saying how boring it all was—boring and superficial. The only real benefits, he would admit, were the money he made, the investments—the hotel in the Colorado Rockies', the model agency he owned on the Coast—and the freedom it gave him. He was such a prig he wouldn't realize Johnny was looking for a sensational expose, hinting at it with all those sly innuendoes and lousy one-liners. Gary would begin talking about Oriental Art, detailing the difference between *Kano* and *Genre,* and those with *Ukiyo-E.* Johnny and his audience would be bored stiff. In desperation, the talk show host would turn to Spence and ask if he shared Gary's interests. "Only fucking," Spence would answer. Tumult. Delight. The camera would remain on Spence, as he went on, describing the last orgy he attended, holding Johnny and the audience rapt. Enlightenment ruled all!

"Don't think I'm going to ask you to behave at this brunch. I know that will only incite you to turn it into a three-ring circus."

Spence turned over again. The sunlight was above the Shoji-screen now, creeping towards him along the arabesques of the Shiraz carpet. More sun came in through the side windows, lightening up the dark corner where Gary sat in his Regency wing-tipped chair, next to the little Hepplewhite table. Everything Gary had was either antique or invaluable. Everything but Spence.

"Seitelman doesn't socialize much. Arnie says he's very sensitive. So even you can fathom that this brunch ought to be as pleasant as possible."

Gary's head was in the light now. He shaded his eyes. His arms, neck and face were a perfect tan from Long Island summers and Caribbean winters: so evenly tan he could be a Coppertone advertisement. Spence was tan too. Spence also passed his summers at Amagansett, his winters in Dominique or Palm Springs or St. Thomas: they were all interchangeable by now.

"The other guests either know you already, or have been warned. Try not to lecture Kate Halliday about Jung today. She's the psychoanalyst. Not you."

Spence leaned over the bed, opened one of the drawers built into the bedboard, and lifted out a flowered *Cloisonne* box. A gift from Gary. Everything was a gift from Gary. A tiny silver spoon was attached to the side of the box by a silver turnaway hasp. Spence removed the spoon, opened the box, dipped the spoon and lifted away a tiny mountain of snow white powder. Gary always kept cocaine in the house. He said it was the only civilized drug: it cost an arm and a leg, and you needed a bushel basket of it to get hooked. Spence propped himself up against the pillows, held a finger to one nostril, inhaled through the other one; then reversed the process.

"Christ! Spence! You're not even awake, and you're already into that!"

Spence had closed the box. Reconsidering, he reopened it and snorted twice more. Then, carefully—he was already feeling the rush—he closed the box, and replaced it in the drawer. Then he slumped back.

"Didn't you have enough last night? You were like a maniac. Chasing that dark little number around with your spoon all night. He was covered with it when he left."

Wasn't it Beckett who said that a light wasn't necessary, that a taper would do to live in strangeness, if it burned faithfully? Yes.

Beckett. A taper, and Spence added, a spoon of coke.

The sun was playing hide-and-go-seek in the infrequent gray hairs among the chestnut brown of Gary's head. They would glint for an instant, then die away, then glint somewhere else, and die away. Little signals. Maybe a glint was all you needed. And a spoon of coke, of course.

"I hope you're not going to wear these filthy denims again?"

Gary threw the pants at Spence. They hit the side of the bed and fell. Motes of dust had shaken off them: the motes rose in the air and performed an intricate ballet to a silent score.

"When was the last time you washed them? People know you're coming a hundred yards away. You have so many new, clean slacks in the closet, Spence. Why do you insist on wearing these?"

Spence wondered if dust motes had senses of perception.

"I don't care if you make a good impression today. I would rather you made no impression at all. But there are certain rules of hygiene. I'm surprised you don't have lice. And those people you call your friends are no better. God what a bunch! The Allies' liberation of Bergen-Belsen couldn't have been more unsavory than that party you took me to last week."

Could dust motes be sentient? Even intelligent? Look how they danced! Spence shook the denims once more. More dust motes flew up into the sunlight. God they were lovely when they danced. Stately.

"While Seitelman and I are discussing our business, why not talk to Rise. She always asks about you. She wants to help you. She really does know a lot of useful people."

Could man communicate with dust motes? They had to be intelligent to dance like that. So organized!

"Rise thinks I'm holding you back from doing something wonderful. Me?! If they only knew how shiftless you are. Someone who needs an hour just to get out of bed."

Spence would ask the dust motes to dance for Gary.

"You have to begin to do something with your life. You can't just hang around here and party all the time."

No. Gary wouldn't recognize a million dust motes dancing for him.

"I'm not saying you have to be a great success. You don't even have to earn a lot of money. But just do something!"

If communicable, and friendly, the dust motes might be persuaded to dance around Gary's head. Then, one by one, without his noticing it, they could enter his ears, his nose, his mouth. One by one. Little by little. So subtly Gary wouldn't notice a thing, until it was too late. At first he would cough a little. Then he'd begin to gag. His multicolored eyes would begin to fill up with tears. Then he'd really begin choking. His handsome, craggy features would be distorted in agony. It would be a sad struggle.

"If you weren't bright, it would be different. But you are. Imaginative too. Why I've never met anyone with so many crazy ideas as you have. Write them down. Draw them up. Make them work for you."

No finger prints on the throat. No murder weapon at all. Spence wouldn't even have to get out of bed. The perfect murder. He could see the headlines already: "Wealthy Male Model Dies Mysteriously in Uptown Triplex. No Clues!"

Spence would confess, naturally. He'd call the press and explain how he'd entered into a conspiracy with the dust motes. How they'd waited patiently for his signal to attack. He'd explain that dust motes are not only sentient, but intelligent too. He'd reveal their highly organized cultural heritage—based on their major pastime, the art of the sunlight dance.

"We could turn the greenhouse into a studio for you. We hardly ever use it. And that big closet, that could be used as a darkroom. Arnie would help find you a distributor. He knows everyone."

At first his confession would be ignored. Spence might be asked to take a lie-detector test, a mental examination even. He'd pass it with flying colors, return to the triplex—his, now that Gary was gone— he'd have almost unlimited resources. Once home, he'd contact the dust motes again. He'd study their dance patterns, draw diagrams— he could see them as variations of the double helix already. It would take years of study to get to understand their habits, their customs. But it would be worth it.

"You know I'll pay for whatever lessons or extra equipment you need. It's just that you have to do something, Spence. Man cannot live by partying alone."

He'd compile his findings, edit them carefully and send an article to *Scientific American*. They'd be impressed. They'd print it with four-color diagrams and half-page photographs he'd taken of the dances. In an editorial, he'd be hailed as a pioneer. He'd call his new science Motology.

"Jack and I talked about you last week at Ron's. He thinks this crazy life you're leading is simply compensation for having no real motivation. Everyone needs a goal."

Spence would go beyond science. He'd wait until his work was fully accepted. Then he'd reveal the true meaning of the dust mote's dance—how it embodied their philosophy of life: endless flowing, total dance. He'd try to show how this could be of supreme advantage to people too. He'd be the first and foremost Theomotologist in history.

"Without a goal, you're working against yourself all the time. Kate said so, too. And she ought to know."

Naturally, Theomotology would attract many others. To stay ahead, Spence would specialize. He was certain the dust motes held the secret of levitation. He'd learn it from their elders, and apply it. N.A.S.A. would approach him. Imagine floating immense spacecraft on molecular motology. "Man Flies to Pluto on Dust!" the headline would read in the *New York Times*.

"You don't have to be self-defeating, you know. You and I aren't in competition. I'm done now. Retired. It's your turn, Spence."

On Pluto, Spence would make his greatest discoveries: he'd find out how dust motes propagate. Beginning as non-essential carbon crystals from pollution, they develop externally—like all crystalline forms—by simple geometric accretion. On Pluto, of course, there would be no pollution. The motes would have to evolve along other lines to survive.

"What kind of life is this for you, Spence? I have my friends, my businesses, my collections. What do you have?"

At first the adjustment would be difficult—all selective evolution was. Millions, perhaps trillions of them would fail to develop and perish. But one day it would just happen. One mote would make the changeover, and discover how simple it was. The others would follow. Spence would be hailed as a new Darwin.

"Spence, are you listening to me? I asked you a question."

Spence would remain on Pluto. He'd crystallize himself.

"Spence? You haven't fallen asleep again?"

He already suspected the miniscule viruses found in every living body were crystal compounds. He would use them as a point of focus for the process.

"I see you moving. You're awake. Are you getting up today?"

It would take years, possibly decades for the process of autocrystallization to work. Meanwhile he would derive nourishment from air-tight gardens in which only nitrogen-high greens were grown. He suspected the crystallization would require absolute stillness.

"It's ten minutes to one, Spence. I'm going. If you aren't getting up, I'm going alone."

Spence might be four hundred years old when his last remaining living tissue—the stomach lining—crystallized.

"And when I get home, you and I are going to fill out that application for registration on the back of the Film School catalogue. If you insist on acting like a child, you'll be treated like one."

On Earth, Spence would be a legend.

"Since classes won't begin for another month or two, you'll have time to get a job. I know plenty of people who need work done in their gardens, or in their apartments. That'll keep you busy."

On Pluto, Spence would be metamorphosized as pure crystal. He'd be immortal.

"I've put up with your nonsense long enough. I will not have you laying around the house stoned all day. And, if you don't care for my plans, you know where the door is."

Spence would disperse into many smaller crystals: all of them immortal.

"That's it. Either go to work, or get out!"

Millions of crystals levitating around the universe.

"Spence! Are you listening? Are you?"

"Fuck you!" Spence said.

"I see it's clear, then. I'll be back by four. You have three hours to make up your mind. And make up that bed when you decide to get out of it."

Gary left the room. A few minutes later, Spence heard closet doors crack open and shut downstairs. Then the front door slammed.

Gary had never talked like that before—never about going to work, or leaving. He must be nervous as hell about meeting this Seitelman. Perhaps if their meeting worked out all right at brunch, Gary would forget what he said, forget this morning's hysteria. Fat chance! That would probably only convince him he was right. Gary was so terrified of being thought inconsistent, he always did precisely what he said he would do: even if it went against his best interest. Ah, well, Spence thought. He'd at least have three more hours of peace. He'd make breakfast, listen to some music, enjoy himself while he still could—until the axe fell.

The sun had already reached halfway up the sheets. Spence threw them off onto the floor. It was warm, hot really. Hot as Mexico. The way the sun advanced along the room, it would take another hour for him to be completely bathed in sunlight. He wouldn't even have to go out on to the terrace to sun today.

It was hot as Mexico.

He could feel the rough stone surface of the ceremonial altar cool against his back. It almost made him forget the itching hemp he'd been tied with, hand and foot, to the altar. He was atop the highest pyramid in Xochomilcho. Above him, the sky was clear blue, cloudless. Below him, invisible, but known from previous occasions when he'd merely witnessed, the immense stone-flagged plaza was filled with people decked out in holiday finery, covered in flowers, chanting. Pennants flew from poles and towers. Children danced in imitation of old legends. Instruments of all sorts whistled, chimed, clacked and stuttered.

His body was the focal point of twenty thousand eyes, of ten thousand minds. He knew, as they knew, that when the sun had completely illuminated his figure through the astronomically precise arch above him, that everyone would suddenly go quiet in the plaza. Everyone would know that the Vernal Equinox had arrived, bringing life again, and once more demanding its payment from them. He would be the absolute beginning of their year: a dot on their calendar: the focus of their collective soul. When the sunlight reached his eyes, the new chant would begin: the people's plea for the sun to accept their votive.

Amidst the hypnotic droning voices, the Priests would gather around him, their gilded masks blinding him with reflections. They too would begin their guttural prayers to the Solar Deity, asking for blessings, good harvest, victory in battle.

When the sunlight had warmed to tips of his long hair, he would know the time was fulfilled. He would be the center of the people, the nation, the world, the universe. He would see the primitive obsidian knife raised in the air, see its final fatal glitter, see it descend and tear out his bowels.

Expertise

When his third lover walked out the door, Alex decided he'd had just about enough of gay romance.

Bradley had been as beautiful as an old Arrow Shirt ad model, as delicious as Entenmann's chocolate-chip cookies, and alas! in the final evaluation, about as nourishing. How long could love go on with the perpetually wounded vanity of one partner and the adoring selflessness of the other? Yet it had happened to Alex before: with Tim, with Lenny, and now—most disastrously—with Brad. Enough times, Alex concluded, to qualify as a bona-fide self destructive syndrome.

What he needed was to look after himself for once in his life. Yes, to cultivate selfishness: an enlightened selfishness.

So, after the requisite day and a half of tears, the usual two weeks of increasingly bored sympathy from friends, and the necessary month of depression and self recrimination, Alex decided to turn a new leaf.

He would transform himself into a sex object; and as this sex object, he would seek out none but other sex objects. They at least would have the realistic insecurities of their humble origins, the confidence of their developed narcissism, and a healthy respect for anyone who'd accomplished as much.

In a city like New York, Alex knew that taking this step would soon assure him of: 1) innumerable one night stands, 2) invitations to all the hot parties in town and on Fire Island, 3) as a result of those parties, more one night stands of even higher quality than before, 4) memberships in private discos, discriminating baths and sex clubs, 5) as a result of those, invitations to even hotter parties in the city and even more distant—to Los Angeles and San Francisco, and 6) as a result of all that, extreme, intense, non-stop, mindless self-gratification.

Alex inspected himself in the full length mirror hanging in his bedroom and thought, well, it's worked for people with far less raw material than I have to start with.

His evaluation was born in that total objectivity that often follows despair. His face was attractive enough—although scarcely magazine handsome. At least it had the character that accompanied ethnicity (Greek-American) without a hint of immigrant to it. Large, light colored eyes that some had called hypnotic. Dark, straight hair that required little care. An obvious but rather nice nose. Cheekbones that could only become more prominent with age. Of course his body could use some work, he thought. But mostly detail work. Five-ten, fairly lean and well proportioned, his limbs weren't apelike like some porno-stars people jerked off to, not cutsey doll short either. His back was straight, his posture and walk fine. Detail work: a few months swimming and playing on the rings at some gym: a touch of weights to build up his pecs, laterals and deltoids. As for dress—that all important system of codes and invitations to the knowing—Alex already knew what he would need to buy, what he would have to discard, what he would have to pre-age and partially destroy to achieve that particularly casual look. True, Alex wasn't a natural knockout beauty. But then, how many current Living Legends around him had been before they went to work on themselves?

He began the next day so that he wouldn't have time to find excuses. He phoned Jim Maddox who cut all the hottest and most highly paid models in town and set up an appointment. He joined a local health club with a great pool, extensive athletic equipment and few sisters to distract him. He went through his closets and cut his wardrobe in half, then shopped in the Village, blowing about six hundred dollars in plastic that he would be sorry about next month.

He could already picture himself, eleven-thirty on a Sunday morning, his lean, tanned body half wrapped around some dropdead number he'd picked up at the Ice Palace and necked with at the afterhours party at a Bayside poolhouse, sweeping down the boardwalk at the Pines, past an astonished Bradley.

It would be heaven!

§

And, six months later, it was heaven. But for one, tiny, yet all important fact he hadn't taken into consideration months before when he'd begun his transformation plans—a fact that provided Alex with a rather icy awakening.

Henrik turned over on the double bed and seemed to brood. Brooding, Henrik looked as breathtakingly handsome as Henrik seductive, or Henrik comical or Henrik intensely following the progress of a spotted beetle across a beach blanket. His golden blonde hair shimmered in the champagne haze of the ocean afternoon. His skin glimmered in the venetian blinds' mottled light, now red, now pale blue, now the faintest hint of green against his deep tan, and against the striking diamond white on white pattern of the designer sheets.

Henrik had gone limp once more, however, which was why he was brooding; and all of Alex's tactics to revive the flagging erection proved failures. Alex knew it was his fault without being able to say exactly why it was his fault. They'd started off so well on the beach, doing a *From Here to Eternity* number in the swirling surf, despite the passers by, despite the critical commentary from surrounding beach blanket occupants, even despite the two little tots who insisted on playing with beach pails only three or four feet away. Started off so well, so hot, so frantic, Alex and Henrik had finally stood up, rearranged their hardons in their tiny Speedo bathing suits and trekked back to the house. Where they had continued hot—until they'd fizzled.

"I guess I turned you off?" Alex said, knowing it wasn't a question at all.

"Oh, no," the gloomy, polite, deep voiced bed lie.

"What was it I did wrong?" Alex persisted. "What didn't you like?"

"Nothing. Nothing at all," Henrik insisted, looking at Alex with eyes of the bluest depths of a fjord in summertime. Then those eyes seemed to widen and narrow, as though Henrik were trying to gauge Alex's capacity for truth, vulnerability, and all the connecting links between. He must have decided Alex could stand more truth than flattery, because in the next minute he slowly said, "I suppose my problem is that I'm more used to—well—to experts."

"Experts?" Alex asked, then realized what exactly was being said;

he became embarrassed.

"It's what American men are best at, you know," Henrik said, gently, firmly, decisively. "All over the world it's known. I have a Finnish friend, Ole, who comes to America two weeks a year on vacation just to get American blowjobs. He saves up all year for it. He hasn't missed a vacation here in eleven years."

Alex surveyed Henrik's pale, long, flaccid cock and thought, well, I did the best I know how; no one else ever complained. Not good enough, the little voice within him replied. Not good enough for beautiful Henrik. Not good enough for the other beautiful men you want. Not even good enough for your goddamn country! What kind of patriot are you, anyway?

Because Alex was silent, listening to the little voice, Henrik took this as encouragement to go on. He described the five best blowjobs he'd received: their circumstances, setting, the other person, the techniques employed, any other interesting little details. Then Henrik described Ole's travels across the country by train, plane, car and Trailways Bus in search of the perfect blowjob. He mentioned the small, out of the way towns where Ole had been astounded; the times he found himself suddenly surprised by luck on the backseats of buses, in the lavatories of jets, at truck stops, at public toilets—places he'd returned to again and again.

Every phrase reproached Alex; reproached and shamed him. They also excited him. He wondered if this was because it was Henrik, beautiful, sexy Henrik telling it, or if it was because such anonymous, mechanical sex must of necessity be more exciting.

"Here," Henrik said in conclusion, reaching for Alex, "let me show you how it should be done."

The neighbors two houses down the beach must have heard Alex when he arrived at that orgasm.

"Now that," Henrik said proudly, "was what Ole would have called a blowjob."

Alex too. But he was afraid to try it himself, fearing his lack of expertise would cause yet another, and even more embarrassing failure. Handling the Swedish Adonis' now own splendid erection, he asked in what he hoped was him most enticing tone of voice:

"How would you like to fuck?"

§

It was a turning point. For the next few months, Alex continued to go to Fire Island, to parties, to the baths, to bars and orgies. He continued to meet handsome men anywhere and everywhere, and to get them into bed with little or no trouble just about whenever he wanted to. And, though it was all undoubtedly more satisfying than having to put up with Brad's moods or Tim's tantrums or Lenny's falling asleep on him whenever he wanted them to make love—something was missing. As though for all his new rugged looks, his posed stances, his rehearsed words of seduction, he'd still not made that last final step in his planned transformation.

During these months however, he began to realize that one group of men completely eluded him. Not a real group, more like an amorphous assemblage; but a distinct one. They weren't the best looking, nor the best connected, not the most talented or talked about—but they were the most desirable. Alex seldom saw them at bars or baths or orgies, and whenever he did see them they were always with each other, always being private, obviously together, without any attempt to hide it, or more to the point, to include anyone else in. They dressed no differently than Alex or thousands of others, yet they had an altogether distinctive aura. Their flanks looked longer and flatter, their asses more delectable in denims or bathing suits, although they wore the same button-fly Levi's and Speedo's he wore. Their chests seemed more defined, less pumped, more natural. Their mouths looked more sensuous, their hands more eager and experienced, their crotches more...more everything! Alex didn't know what it was they had, but they knew they had it. And they knew he didn't. He never once received even a half curious look from one of the group, never mind a cruise, never mind the hint of a pick-up.

§

"It's really only a matter of expertise," Jeff said. He and Alex were sitting at a formica-topped table in a booth in a coffee shop of utterly no distinction across the street from a shoddy, abandoned gas station bathroom where Alex had followed Jeff's offhand cruise a half hour before and where Alex had gotten the best blowjob of his life.

"You simply have to be committed," Jeff went on, "to want the best, and then to practice until you are."

Jeff—no last name offered—was about ten pounds overweight—around his waist where it showed even in a loose t-shirt. He was balding at the back of his curly haired head. He was prematurely grey in his beard, at his temples and on what Alex could see of his chest. He didn't dress well, nor was he more than ordinarily good looking (certainly not in Alex's class!); yet Jeff was one of that group Alex lusted after. He was always among those seen sleazily grinding their hips into each other at eight-thirty in the morning at Flamingo, and always amid those seen leaving the Ice Palace for a private morning party where who was excluded was more important than who was invited. So, when Jeff cruised Alex on the street, Alex knew he would be late for the movie date he had with a woman friend: he couldn't pass this up. He followed Jeff into the bathroom, and gave himself up to Jeff's expert hands.

Now, however, Alex had to know why he and so many others desired Jeff or his ilk so much, so hopelessly. That was why, after the blowjob, he'd talked to Jeff, asked him to this hepatitis dispensary, why he made himself completely miss the film he was supposed to see, why he sat here with Jeff, why he could bring himself to ask the embarrassing question Jeff had answered so succinctly.

"Practice!" Alex said. "I practice all the time."

"Where?"

"The backroom bars, the clubs, the orgies, the parties, the bushes, the baths, at home, in bed. Everywhere!"

"Too many distractions," Jeff said, all-knowing. "What you have to do is find a place where distractions are at a minimum, where you can concentrate on what you're doing, where face, body, personality, character, past history, social connections, none of it can get in the way. You need a still, intense focus. It's an art, you know, and like all arts must be practiced purely!"

When Alex paid for the coffee and pastry, Jeff reached into his own wallet and pulled out a tattered, yellowing card.

"Go here. Use my card until they get to know your face. It's very private. Not anyone is allowed in."

Alex stared at the card, defaced by wear to a few lines and cracks. "What is it?"

"Blowjob palace. Two fifty and all you want."

Alex thanked him, wishing he could bring himself to say something about seeing Jeff again. After that lecture, it seemed entirely out of the question, unless Jeff brought it up.

"I hope this works," Alex said.

"It will. Oh, take my phone number. When you think you're really ready, give me a call."

§

Alex waited a month before going to the place. He put off going week after week, telling himself he wanted to be certain he would go there in the right frame of mind—horny, experimental, perhaps slightly frustrated, perhaps somewhat detached.

Even so, when he did finally go to the club it was more by chance than by design. He'd had dinner with some old friends in the neighborhood, had drank a bit more than usual, had smoked more grass than he usually did and was feeling—if not all he wished to feel—at least horny and bored with the prospect of trying to pick up someone in one of his usual haunts this late on a weeknight.

The club was two floors of what had once been a storefront years ago. A small foyer led to a large, high ceilinged room, surrounded on three sides by small, closet sized rooms, divided by wood planking. In the middle was another free standing series of closets. Each one locked on the inside by a simple latch and was unfurnished except for a low, rough-hewn stool. All very ordinary, except for the obvious irregularity of large holes at lower torso level in each partition: more oval than round: not big enough to put your head through, but sufficient for most genitalia. Alex supposed they were made that way to accommodate men of differing heights.

Inspecting the almost empty club, he discoverd that most of the closets had similar layouts except those located on corners, which only had two holes. Later, he would discover that the two middle rooms within the free standing group were large enough to hold two or three people, with six, seven and even more holes hewn out of their partitions. Evidently these rooms were favored by couples, groups, teams and insatiable singles.

Aside from the closets were only the most primitive amenities: a sort of waiting room with two benches and floor ashtrays, a cigarette and soda machine, a small bathroom. It was all moderately lighted— not as dark as most of the discos and backroom places he frequented. Disco music of the funkier sort was played over six speakers on each floor, the records spun by the same guy (youngish, cutish) who took your money at the door and gave you a coat check.

As Alex wandered exploring several men came in, making him feel more cautious. He went into a booth, locked the door, sat down on the stool, and lighted a joint. He smoked, hearing the sound of doors opening and closing around him. None of the three booths that opened up to his were occupied. It must be too early in the evening. Here I am, Alex said to himself, all ready to practice. He didn't feel drunk, or woozy, or overstuffed from the meal, nor even sodden from the grass, but as he always felt while cruising, oddly extra alert. He tapped his feet lightly on the wooden plank floor to the beat of the music, leaning back against the door.

Before the song was over or the joint in his hand half smoked, the door in the booth to his right opened and Alex made out someone come in and saw the figure turn to lock the door. Now something Jeff had said before was clarified: unless the other man bent down, Alex couldn't see who he was, could only see part of him, certainly not his face. Alex leaned forward to get a better look and a longish semi-erection was immediately pushed through the hole in his direction. Alex took a final toke of the grass, smashed its embers out on the floor and began to idly fondle the erection.

Practice time, Alex said to himself. No fooling around tonight.

The guy must have been really horny—he got stiff instantly and came in about three minutes flat. Hardly enough time to be considered anything but a warm-up, Alex thought, turning away to find that roach he'd dropped and relight it. He was somewhat pleased with himself, even though he knew this had been too simple to be any different from his past experiences—certainly not different enough to place him on Jeff's level of expertise. By the time Alex had located the small piece of joint and lighted it, he found two more erections facing him from the previously unoccupied booths. One was olive skinned and thick with a fat head, the other smaller and red on top as though bruised. Choices, choices, he thought, playing with both of them for a minute. Then he decided to take turns, jerking off one while blowing the other and then switching it around. He got two more rather quick orgasms, and was soon facing another erection from the other hole. Was this beginner's luck, or was it like this every night, he wondered.

When Alex emerged from the booth some two hours later for a soda and a rest he'd given more blow jobs than he could keep count of. He'd also received the third and fourth (after Jeff and Henrik) most spectacular orgasms of his life, thanks to guys on the other side of the partitions.

He still had a long way to go before he could attain Jeff's seemingly effortless degree of expertise, he felt, a lot more practice before he could begin to be comfortable with Jeff and his group.

§

Having found his first experience painless and fun, Alex began going to the club more often: first a night a week, then two nights a week, then three nights a week, clear weather or foul, from midnight to three in the morning, sometimes staying later.

He also began to experiment with moods and mood altering agents to see if they helped or hindered him. Some nights he'd merely have a vodka or smoke some grass before going: that always made him horny and seemed to turn on the other men. Sometimes, if he were feeling a bit tired, he'd sniff a bit of coke before leaving his apartment. Other times, he'd drop half a Quaalude, which definitely made him feel looser, sleazier. But that could also prove counter-productive to practicing, as he would be swinging on a really nice large cock while high on a down and decide he'd really rather take it up the ass, which was cheating. He almost always supplemented whatever mood he had designed with poppers. So did everyone else. He tried heavier drugs once—Mescaline—but it wasn't as good: he became too distracted by the music, lacked alertness, forgot what he was doing, got overly imaginative about the man attached to the cock.

In less than a month, Alex encountered more different cocks than he'd ever imagined existing, even though he'd had his share before. Maybe it was because they were so emphasized here. In one night at the club, he would bring off long ones, thin ones, thick ones, lilly-white ones, flaring purples-headed ones, angry red ones, black ones, tan ones, fat ones, flattened ones, bent ones, squarish ones: some with tiny little pointed heads, others consisting of almost nothing but head: several had a network of bulging veins, some had no apparent veins on the shaft at all: some smelled of colognes and powders, others of wintergreen, (athletes?) some of urine, others of perspiration—ranging from metallically acrid to sweeter-than-butterscotch: most smelled of nothing at all.

In those early months, Alex practiced on each one that came his way. Even if it were small and thin, even if it were so large he could scarcely encompass it with a hand, never mind get his lips around it. He made it a point with each to find the right angle of approach, much as one does when first meeting a person socially, as though the cock were the entire individual encapsulated, personified. Some were to be handled gently, others more roughly. For some, he had to drop onto his knees, squat and angle up; others had to be gotten at from the left side, or the top.

Alex naturally also observed others: the holes in the partition provided enough room to view. Between increased practice and observation, he learned how not to gag, how to use the top of his palette, how to tongue the sensitive vein-rich shaft bottom, how to titillate the area beneath the head. He learned how to stroke, caress, lick, grasp, grip and fondle each scrotum. He even learned how to hold both genitals—if they weren't too large—together in such a way that he could blow both cock and balls simultaneously.

These technical matters aside, Alex also discoverd there was a right attitude and a wrong attitude to take in sucking a cock. Demanding orgasm was meaningless—even wrong-headed. If he were relaxed, in time with the music, and thoughtlessly sucking away, he became nothing but an internal muscle—the ideal state. Often, he'd be without a thought in his mind, almost oblivious of where he was, what he was doing or how much time had passed, when the telltale sign of a sudden new thickening in the head told him he was about to get another little explosion.

One night, he stood up from one of the larger, center booths and saw a handwritten scrawl that read:

BROUGHT OFF TWENTY GUYS HERE TONIGHT

Alex laughed. Only a tyro would bother to keep count—or to crow about it.

He'd become comfortable in the club. He got to be known to the two guys who alternated at the door and spinning records. He started to know almost instinctively the minute a man walked into the foyer whether he'd be good for one orgasm or more. He even began to size up cocks from how their owners walked, from how they played with themselves through their pants.

Soon, men were flinging their bodies against the partitions, moaning and calling out in orgasm when Alex had hold of them. One night someone fell backwards against the door of the booth. Another forgot to lock his booth and fell right out—into someone passing by.

Alex became sought after in the club. Booths on either side of his were seldom empty. He began to feel easy, casual, confident, effective.

After not too long, he felt ready for anyone: anyone.

§

When Jeff walked into the club, he must have been stoned: he walked right past where Alex was sitting on the waiting room bench without noticing him.

Jeff had lost weight and his grey hair had spread to an even salt-and-pepper over his beard and curly head. He looked terrific.

Alex followed him around a bit, trying to get his attention, but Jeff still didn't recognize him, and finally entered a booth flanked by two occupied ones. Alex stood against the wall, lighted a joint and waited until one of them emptied or Jeff came out again.

Alex had progressed from being completely promiscuous to being utterly selective. He didn't need practice anymore. Now, whenever he stepped into a booth, it was to give someone he'd chosen a special treat. He usually stayed out in the waiting area until someone exceptional arrived—someone attractive, well remembered, or simply new to him. He would then follow the man around, cruise him, watch until his intention was clear. Most guys he cruised, cruised back pretty fast, picking up on his supercharged sexuality. Most of them remained outside a booth until they could find one adjoining to his. But there were times when the place was so crowded only one booth was available. Alex would open the door, and invite the guy in. All of them entered, and all of them stayed.

Afterwards, sitting on the front benches sharing a Seven-Up, a cigarette and a desultory chat, most of the men offered Alex their phone numbers and a few asked for his. It didn't take him long to make a good sized collection. But the few times he called up guys he'd met at the club, there always seemed to be a lot of talk, and endless grass smoking and interminably long foreplay before they got down to what interested him. After a few turn-offs like this, Alex still took phone numbers and said he would call, but he never did.

But he was known now. Whenever he went out to parties or bars or discos—all the most attractive, most desirable men knew him. Some fondled his nipples as he passed, others groped him or patted his ass. All at least nodded or said hello; including most of the men in that group he wanted to know so badly before. Especially them.

Finally a booth next to where Jeff had entered flew open and a tall, good looking guy stepped out. Alex went in, sat down and looked. Jeff was sitting down too. He needed a little motivation.

Alex had evolved a little ritual which seldom failed to interest. He would walk into a booth, lock the door, play with himself through his denims until he was hard, slowly unbutton his fly, open up, draw it out hard, play with it a little, take out his balls, rub them a little, unloosen his belt, slowly push his pants down to his knees, all the while turning his cock to various angles for differing views, then he would unbutton his shirt, pull off his t-shirt, let them look at his lean, muscled abdomen, then kneel down and present his face. It was as certain as a spider web: and most guys stayed not only to reciprocate, but often for a second blowjob.

It worked with Jeff too. It took Jeff a while to extricate his cock from his shorts and then a bit longer to get the studded cockring untangled, but finally it was free—still flaccid, but large, with exactly the right sized balls, exactly the right color, the head just thick enough, the cockshaft exactly the right degree of veininess. His lower torso was perfectly muscled. Even Jeff's pubic hair had a shape that excited Alex.

It took Alex a while to get the thing stiff, but when it was, it felt so right in his mouth and hand, that he gave it the benefit of every trick he had learned: the palette rub, the hand slide, the ball tug, the sideways shaft lick—he pulled out all the stops. When Jeff finally came, he lunged against the divider so hard, he even banged his head. He emitted a low guttural sound and spurted a long time. Then he staggered back, dropping onto the stool like a bag of beans.

Alex had caught the substantial load straight down his throat—no more messy moustaches for him anymore—and it still tingled with heat and a slightly alkaline taste. He stared at Jeff, hoping he wasn't having a heart attack.

Jeff's stunned look met his, and there was a momentary smile and mumbled thanks. Jeff still didn't recall him. It must have been over a year ago they'd met. Then Alex was hard and pushing himself through the hole. After a few minutes of that, he asked Jeff to join him in his booth.

There, Alex stripped Jeff, necked with him, sucked him hard again, turned him around, and fucked him. All the while, hands from other booths were sticking out, caressing them. Mouths, faces, eyes were pushed up against them through the holes, wanting to share. When Alex came inside Jeff, it was a moment of total triumph. He'd never felt so good in his life. He'd outdone an expert.

§

On the bench in the waiting room, Jeff put him arm around Alex's shoulders.

"I was pretty downed out when I came in. I'd only come an hour before too. I sure didn't expect to find anyone like you here tonight."

Alex smiled. Then he reminded Jeff of their meeting in the gas station bathroom and their conversation in the coffee shop. He enjoyed Jeff's surprise, the grey eyes narrowing in sudden recognition, then widening is satisfaction.

"Well, I'll be damned," Jeff said, and pulled Alex closer.

People came and went around them. They could hear doors opening and closing in the large room.

"Tomorrow's Saturday," Jeff said. "You don't have to work, do you?"

"No, why?"

"Why not come home with me. We'll get some shut-eye, then take up where we left off tonight. All day tomorrow if you want."

Alex suddenly didn't want to. He felt cold, distant. A year before this would have been perfect. But now . . . well things had changed in a year: he had changed.

Jeff went on to talk about the big disco party the next night. He and Alex would fuck and sleep, fuck and then go out to the party, dance sleazily, make out, get each other and others hot too, then go home and do it all again on Sunday. Jeff was amusing, offhand about it. All Alex could read was Jeff's eagerness: his uncool eagerness: his desire to possess Alex alone because he was just as good.

"Well, how about it?" Jeff asked.

"Maybe another time," Alex said, trying to soften it. "I have to see some friends tomorrow night."

"Well, how about tonight then?"

Alex read even more eagerness in Jeff's eyes.

"Don't think so," Alex mumbled. "I'm sort of beat. Got a dog to walk when I get back. Dishes in the sink . . ."

He felt Jeff's arm slide off his shoulder. They sat next to each other for another awkward minute or two.

"I sort of like you," Jeff offered: all casualness gone.

"Me too," Alex said. It came out wrong, hard, wrong. Alex decided to let it pass. He didn't care.

After another few minutes during which he was afraid Jeff would do or say something even more tactless, Jeff stood up, straightened out his pants and said, "Okay. Another time."

That was better. "See you," Alex said.

The minute Jeff left the club, Alex realized he hadn't even offered Alex his phone number.

What a phony, Alex thought. All he wanted was a one night stand. All he wanted was me fucking his tired old ass.

He angrily lighted a cigarette and smoked it, thinking what a phony shit Jeff was. It was three-thirty now. He ought to go home. Why stick around. Nothing but pigs here.

He was just getting up to go to the coatcheck when someone walked in: a lanky blonde with full, darker beard and denims molded so that every inch of his heavy headed cock could be made out.

Alex exchanged a cruise with him, then a heavier one, and watched his sultry, slightly bowlegged walk to the booths. His jeans were so rubbed around his ass, they looked white. They looked as though they needed spreading.

Alex could probably get him off by eating through the denims.

He got up, went into the room, cruised him again, then found a booth next to another empty one. Inside, he went through his ritual body showing. His cock never looked as ready, his rippled stomach more touchable. He knelt and faced the open hole, and saw the erection push its head at him. He began to fondle it till it was really stiff.

He suddenly remembered Jeff walking out of the place after the best fuck of his life without even offering his goddamned phone number. Fucking phony!

Then a fat, warm cockhead was brushing against his lips. Alex opened his mouth. And was pacified.

Hunter

It was sunset when Ben Apres drove up to the hanging shingle that read "Sagoponauk Rock Writers Colony," and, on a smaller, added-on shingle, "Visitors see Dr. Ormond." An oddly Autumnal sunset, despite the early summer date and no hint of dropping temperature, as Ben stepped out of the ten-year-old Volvo that hadn't given him a bit of its usual temperament on the long trip, as he urinated on a clump of poison ivy until it was shiny wet, as he surveyed what appeared to be yet another rolling succession of green humped New England hills.

The muted colors of the sunset fitted Ben's own fatigued calm following weeks of torment, his final uncertain decision to come, and his more recent anxieties since the turn off the main road that he'd never find the place, that he'd driven past it several times already, the directions had seemed so sketchy.

He found himself gaping at the sky as though it would tell him something essential, or as though he'd never see one like it again. Then he made out some houses nestled in a ravine: the colony. He'd made it!

§

Dr. Ormond was easy to find. The paved road that dipped down into the colony ended at his front door in a shallow oval parking lot, radiating dirt roads in several directions. Two cars with out-of-state-plates were parked next to a locally licensed beat-up baby-blue pickup.

The active, middle-aged man who stepped out of the house chomping an apple introduced himself, then looked vaguely upset when Ben introduced himself and asked where he would be staying.

There appeared to be a mix-up, Dr. Ormond said. Another guest—and here Ormond threw the apple down—and went on to mention a woman writer of some repute—had unexpectedly accepted the colony's earlier invitations, thought by them to have been forgotten. She had taken the last available studio. They hadn't been certain Ben was coming this season either. Victor Giove hadn't heard from Ben in weeks. Of course, Victor hadn't heard from Joan Sampson either, and she'd come too, though naturally, they were all delighted she was here.

Ormond motioned behind him vaguely. Ben saw a white clapboard, pitched-roof house standing alone on a patch of grassy land. He supposed that was her studio: the one he was to have lived in.

Before he could ask, a plump middle-aged woman—her apron fluttering, her hair in disarray—was waving to them from the doorway. She'd already telephoned Victor, she called out. He was on his way. Mrs. Ormond, Ben guessed.

He leaned against the Volvo. Darkness was quietly dropping into the ravine. One or two lights were turned on in the Ormonds' house, other lights appeared suddenly in more distant studios. Ben wanted to wake up tomorrow morning in this enchanted glade, to spend sunny and rainy days here, long afternoons, crisp mornings, steamy nights. He would not allow the mix-up to affect his decision. After all the inner turmoil he was glad he'd come. He wasn't leaving.

Above all, he was grateful to Victor Giove, who was jogging toward them now, accompanied by a large, taffy-colored Irish Hound, the two racing, skirting the big oak, circling Ben and Dr. Ormond, the dog barking then nuzzling Ben's hand for a caress; Giove hardly out of breath, glad to see Ben. He took Ben's hand, clasped his shoulder, smiled, and was as openly welcoming as Ormond hadn't been.

Victor was tan already. His curly dark head already sparkled with sunreddened hair. He looked healthier and more virile than he'd ever looked in the city: an advertisement for country living with his handsome, open-featured face, his generous, beautifully muscled body that loose clothing like the old t-shirt and cordorouys he was wearing couldn't disguise. Ben felt Victor's warmth charge into his own body as they touched, and he knew that all things were possible this summer: even the impossible: even Victor.

"There's no place for Ben to stay here," Dr. Ormond protested once they'd gotten inside the Ormonds' living room.

"What about the little cottage," Victor said. "That's empty."

"What little cottage?"

"By the pond. I passed it today. It's all closed up. You don't need a full studio, do you Ben? Of course, he doesn't. He'd love the little cottage."

"It's a fifteen minute walk from here," Ormond, unpersuaded.

Ben suspected he'd be crazy about the little cottage.

"He's young." Victor said. "It's not far for him."

"But it isn't ready for him."

"Sure it is. You helped clean it up yourself. Remember? It can't have gotten more than a little musty in the meanwhile. Besides, he can't go all the way back now, can he?"

Ben told them he'd already sublet his apartment in the city. He had nowhere else to go.

"You see!" Victor said. "Come on, Ben, dinner's ready. I'll take you to the little cottage after."

"Victor!" Ormond said in a strange tone of voice. "That cottage was Hunter's."

"It belongs to the colony."

"You know what I mean."

"Ben's here," Giove said firmly. "Hunter isn't."

"No. I guess you're right."

"Then it's settled."

§

Four of them ate dinner. Joan Sampson was to have joined them but she called to cancel, saying she had work to do.

Ben did know they had no such thing as community dining at the colony, didn't he, Frances Ormond asked. Everyone took care of themselves. Except of course everyone dined with whomever they wanted to. She hoped that Ben would feel as welcome at her table as Dr. Giove was. It was impossible for Ben to not like the transplanted urban woman who'd evidently found peace in Sagoponauk Rock. Like Victor, she radiated health and happiness. Ben would later discover that was a rare quality at the colony. Others had brought their sufferings and neuroses, unable or unwilling to let them go. They argued around kitchen tables just as badly as they had in

Manhattan bars. They outraged and scandalized each other in country bedrooms with infidelities and treacheries as though they still lived in West Side apartment complexes. Over the following week, Ben sized up the colony members quickly. Only Mrs. Ormond was judged to be sound.

And Victor, of course. Victor, who was the reason Ben had come to Sagoponauk Rock, and the reason he had almost not come. Even after Ben had sublet his apartment. Even after Ben had turned off the exit from the New England Thruway and had driven north for what seemed hours.

After dinner, Victor got into the Volvo's driver's seat and drove through the dark, rutted road to the little cottage. Ben held an extra kerosene can Frances Ormond had given him—unsure whether the electricity was turned on.

It was, they discovered after a long, silent ride through the deep darkness of the country, passing what would later become landmarks to Ben on his night walks and night drives: the community house, the first two studios, then Victor's, the apple orchard, then the fork past the pond.

The cottage was L-shaped: a large, bare bedroom separated by a small bathroom and cavernous storage closet from a good sized study area, which opened onto a small one-wall kitchen with a long dining counter.

Victor built a fire to help clear out the unseasonable chill. Ben went through the kitchen cabinets and found a bottle half full of *Fundador*. They sipped the brandy, talking about the program they'd tentatively set up the past April at school, which Ben as an apprentice writer would follow at the colony. He was only to show Victor a piece of writing when he was satisfied with it, or unable to find satisfaction in it. Some of the others at the colony never shared their work with each other. Victor and Joan had agreed to meet regularly to read to each other. Ben could join them.

Although it was only a three and a half month stay, Ben had decided he would write day and night. Not only the few short stories Victor asked for, but a novel too: *the* novel, the one he'd planned, the one he believed he'd been born to write. Free here of most distractions, he felt certain he'd get much of it done before the last school year rolled around again. He already loved the cottage.

Only the bedroom—after a second look—didn't seem as cozy as the rest of the house. Ben thought the bedroom's coldness was due

to its appearance: low ceilings, uncarpeted dull wood floor, only a few
pieces of furniture: hardly inviting. Perhaps a single night's sleep
would warm it up. The double bed—higher and wider than the one
he was used to, was firm yet comfortable when he tried it out.

Victor had gone into the bathroom. He found Ben stretched out
on the big high bed, and stopped, lingering on the threshold.

For a long minute they looked at each other. Ben—his hands
under his head for a pillow—felt suddenly exposed, then seductively
positioned, inviting. Giove seemed suddenly bereft of his usual
composure, uncertain, fragile, even frightened. Neither of them
moved: Ben could feel the tension of the possible and the impossible
filling the room like a thick mist.

"It's getting late," Victor said, his voice subdued, his hands
suddenly gesturing as though controlled by someone else. "I'll come
by in the morning to show you around the colony."

Ben was embarrassed now too and quickly sat up and got off the
bed to see the older man out. In an attempt to cover over the shame
he felt he asked: "Who had this cottage before me?"

"Stephen Hunter, the poet," Giove said, looking out into darkness.

"You're kidding! I didn't know he stayed here at the colony."

"Oh, everyone important comes to Sagoponauk sooner or later."

Ben was about to say something about how happy he was that the
cottage had a literary past, but Giove said good-bye and was gone.

Ben settled into the dank chill of the sheets they'd found in the big
closet and thought of that moment in the bedroom, of Victor's
suddenly coming upon him, his hesitation, his distracted gestures,
the quiet tone of his voice and his sudden decision to leave. If he had
remained another minute, come into the bedroom, come closer to
Ben: the impossible would have been possible, in this very room.

Ben climaxed with a sharpness he hadn't experienced masturbating in years, not since he was an adolescent. Wiping his abdomen
with a handtowel, he wondered whether it was the fresh country air
or seeing Victor Giove again after so long.

§

Victor didn't come by in the morning to show Ben around; Ben
didn't see him until dinner time. But that was only the beginning of
Victor's fluctuations of intense consideration and total aloofness that

finally formed itself into an inescapable pattern.

That first morning Ben didn't care. The bedroom faced east and he awoke to a sunny splendor of nearby trees and bright clear sunlight flooding every inch of what seemed to be a really handsome, though sparsely furnished room.

After a breakfast of bread and honey provided by Mrs. Ormond the night before, Ben wandered around the colony. He was still too awed to closely approach any studios, believing the other colony members would be intensely concentrating on their writing, and thus not to be disturbed. But he had enough to look at: the pond, surprisingly large, still and lovely, quite close to his cottage; the apple orchard stretching miles; the lively stream that formed a tiny marsh at the pond; the large old trees, many varieties he'd never seen before; the young saplings everywhere; the fruit and berry bushes in demure blossom; the wildflowers surrounding the house; the cottage itself, beautifully crafted of fine woods, so that built-in tables, drawers, and cabinetry were perfectly integrated by color and grain, all of a piece.

Following Frances Ormond's instructions, he skirted the colony later on, driving up to and along the two-laned highway, locating in one direction a truckstop all-night diner, a gas station and after another five or six miles, the tiny hamlet of Sagoponauk—where he purchased a backseat full of groceries and supplies. Driving in the other direction past the colony Ben found another gas station and an old clapboard roadhouse containing a saloon and an Italian restaurant.

The peace that had settled on him momentarily the dusk before, returned when he drove back to the colony and arrived to see the little cottage—highest of the houses on the property—aglow with fuschia and orange, it's western windows reflecting a brilliant summer sunset.

Victor apologized when he saw Ben. Besides doing some writing that day, he said he'd fixed a propane gas line to Joan Sampson's oven and hot water heater and had helped Mrs. Ormond pick early apples for saucing.

Ben was embarrassed by the apology. He could spend all day with Victor. That was why he had come to the colony. But now that he was here, he could not justify deserving Giove's attention. Victor wasn't merely gorgeously un-selfconscious, he was altruistic, giving his time and energy to anyone who needed it. Obviously there were others in the colony who needed it as much as Ben.

So Ben contented himself. Especially after the first few weeks, when he began to realize the impossible love between them could only occur suddenly, impulsively, unforgettably: like any other miracle.

Victor's comings and goings appeared to fit some obscure plan. Ben wouldn't see him for days, only come upon him mowing a shaggy patch of lawn, or wrapping heavy black tape around a split waterpipe of one of the studios. Then Victor would come by the little cottage early one afternoon, spend all day, remain for a hastily concocted dinner, talk about people and writing and books until midnight. Only to disappear for days. Only to reappear again as suddenly, stretched out on the yellow plastic lawnchair at midday as Ben returned home from a walk, or suddenly diving past Ben's surprised face into the clear water of the pond and swimming to the other shore. His appearances were unpredictable; the hours he spent with Ben so full of talk, of intense attention that Ben would be charmed into persuading himself that Giove was merely being careful: getting to know Ben better: making sure of him before he would suddenly turn to Ben, put his arms around him, and....

That was when Ben would feel frustrated all over again, full of lust, and he would have to go into the bedroom, to lay down, to picture how it would be, sometimes mastubating two or three times after Victor had been with him, feeling his fantasies becoming so real that the impossible *had* to happen.

Once, Victor came by after dinner when Ben was writing. Giove lay down quietly on the sofa, began to read a magazine and fell asleep. When Ben realized that, he couldn't concentrate. Even sleeping, Victor was too disturbing. Ben wandered around the cottage, trying to wake the older man by the noise he made. He even tried to fall asleep himself, but it was an absurd attempt—the bedroom felt as cold, as uninviting as the first night he'd spent there.

He finally decided to wake Victor—he was so tall, he had to sleep bent up; he'd awaken with cramps and pains. Ben didn't say it to himself, but he suspected that once they were in bed together, Giove would relent.

Victor stretched, got up, looked once at the bedroom hallway as though trying to make up his mind whether to stay, then said he wouldn't hear of it.

It was hours before Ben could fall asleep, even after he'd taken a mild sedative.

He had purposely not touched himself during those tormenting hours of unrest. During the night, however, half-awakened, he felt heat emanating from his genitals, couldn't fight it away, and worked groggily but efficiently to bring himself to orgasm. Dazed, exhausted, he sank back into slumber.

The following afternoon, Victor was at the pond again when Ben arrived for his daily swim. With Victor, sitting on the tiny dark sand beach, wearing a huge sunhat, was a chaperone: Joan Sampson. Ben remained with them only long enough to be polite.

After that day, Victor and Joan were always together: Victor seldom alone.

Even without her interference, Ben thought she was the least sympathetic person he'd met in the colony. She epitomized all he disliked in the others: their utter sophistication and real provinciality; their brusqueness, their bad manners, their absorption with themselves and lack of interest in anyone else except as reflections of themselves. Her frail child's underdeveloped body and the expensively casual clothing she wore, her bird-like unpretty face and unfocussed blue eyes that seemed to look only with disdain, her arrogance, her instant judgements and devastating condemnations of matters she couldn't possibly know, her artificial laugh, her arch gestures and awkward mannerisms—she might have been a wind-up toy. Next to her, large, naturally graceful, athletically handsome Victor, his Victor, looked bumbling. Together, they were grotesque.

Ben made certain he wouldn't see them together. He pleaded work when they asked him to join them for dinner, didn't show up for readings of their work, never went where they were likely to be.

The impossible, he began to see, was impossible. He had to forget Victor, to forget him, and above all to stop fantasizing about him.

§

When the cold showers and manual work he made for himself around the cottage no longer served to keep his mind off Victor Giove, Ben began to run miles every day along the two-lane road, to swim hours at a time in another, larger pond he'd discovered a short drive away. When he realized these methods were not working either, Ben got into the Volvo late one night and drove to the all-night truckstop diner.

Two cars—one he recognized as belonging to the owner—and a large red Semi, were parked in the gravel lot. Ben pulled up close to the truck, hidden from both the diner and the road and waited. When the truck driver finally came out of the diner, Ben rolled down his car window and asked for a light for his cigarette.

The trucker was close to middle-aged and heavyset, but he had kind brown eyes and an engaging grin. He lighted Ben's cigarette. When he asked if Ben weren't a little young to be doing this sort of thing, Ben shrugged, then leaned back in the carseat with a loud sigh. A second later, the trucker's lower torso filled the car window frame, the worn denims were unzipped, not another word said. Ben sucked him off and came without touching himself.

The following night, Ben stopped at the roadhouse and struck up a conversation with a travelling salesman who had a suitcase full of encyclopaedias. After a few drinks, Ben was able to convince the man he wanted something other than books. The salesman was younger than the trucker, thinner, better looking, just as obliging. They drove separately away from the roadhouse, met a mile further at a turn off, and made love in the backseat of the saleman's car for over an hour.

Ben drove out late every night. One time he picked up a long-haired hitchhiker who offered him grass. They smoked and Ben drove twenty-five miles before he got up the courage to ask if he could blow the kid. Sure, the hitchhiker said, unzipping, I was wondering when you were going to ask.

Several times he repeated his first night's success at the diner. He also discovered the Esso station outside of Sagoponauk had a removable plank at exactly the right height between the two booths in the men's room. High school boys came there after unsuccessful weekend night petting sessions with their girls; and local older men furtively used his services at various odd hours. Ben became bolder, picking up strangers leaving the roadhouse. He was often misunderstood, sometimes threatened. The bartender, a married partner in the place, offered to guide likely men Ben's way in return for occasional favors. A week later he took his first payment sodomizing Ben on a shiny leather sofa in an office after the roadhouse had closed.

During all of these experiences, Ben never felt less frustrated, less craving of sex, or less in love with Victor Giove. But he told himself that whatever else he was doing, at least it was better than fantasizing about Victor and masturbating. That seemed to help.

§

Although he had gone to sleep very late, and was even a little drunk when he'd finally gotten back to the cottage, Ben awakened instantly, fully, as soon as he thought he heard the footpads in the darkened room. Fully alert, tensed, he kept his eyes closed, pretending to be asleep. Whoever had stopped at the foot of the bed was looking down at Ben.

Despite his terror, Ben didn't panic. Then, oddly, he felt a wave of intense lust passing through his body. Odd, since the young man he'd spent two hours with on a blanket inside a clearing they'd driven to had been both passionate and solicitous of Ben's pleasure; Ben had felt both mollified and physically exhausted when they'd parted with a long, lingering kiss. Despite that, Ben now felt a biting, itching erection, a pressing need to masturbate as though he hadn't had sex in a month.

The fear returned. Ben almost shivered. He pretended to be disturbed in his sleep, mumbling loudly, rolling onto one side before waking up.

During his exertions, whoever had been at the foot of his bed left the room. Ben felt alone again. He listened for noises in the other rooms, waited a long time hearing nothing, then got out of bed and crept first into the corridor, then into the rest of the cottage. The doors were locked, the rooms empty. Puzzled, wondering if it were a dream, Ben went back to sleep.

§

Several nights later, he again awakened sensing someone at the foot of his bed. Once more he felt a scalding, sweeping lust over his lower limbs, the need to touch himself. Then fear reasserted itself, and he was cold again. While he was sleepily trying to get out of bed, whoever it was got away. He was certain it wasn't a dream this time.

Ben thought about the matter for the next two days and determined to ask Frances Ormond who else had a set of keys to the little cottage. Walking to the Ormonds' house, he came upon Victor Giove, surprisingly alone, sunning on a blanket spread over the grass behind his A-frame studio. Victor was clad only in a pair of red, worn swimtrunks and his gloriously tanned body.

Ben moved on with a wave, but Giove hailed him over so insistently that Ben reluctantly joined him, and even took off his shirt to get some sun.

He was "pale as February," Victor told him, and would burn unless he put on some suntan oil. When Ben began to splash it on, the older man said he was doing it all wrong: he would show him how. As Ben lay on his stomach, he expected to feel the large strong applicating hands transformed into messengers of caresses. They weren't. They were brisk, efficient. They spread the lotion evenly: nothing more.

Giove didn't seem to have noticed that Ben had been avoiding him. Their conversation was the usual: what Victor was writing, what Ben was doing, what was happening among the others at the colony.

Ben stayed for almost an hour—once his disturbance at their near-nude closeness had vanished. When he got up and put on his shirt Victor said:

"You ought to get more sun. And rest more. How are you sleeping? You look sort of done in to me."

Ben was so stunned he couldn't answer. Why would Victor say that to him—unless it was Victor himself who was visiting him every night?

When Ben finally did say he was sleeping well, Giove seemed skeptical, then added "Well, you know best." He rolled on his stomach, and his wide shoulders, his long, muscled back, two solid buttocks stretching the bright red nylon of his swimtrunks, his thighs and legs—honeybrown and flecked with sunbleached hairs—all jumped out at Ben. He wanted to fall down there and kiss and lick every inch of that body for hours on end. The black curly ringlets of Giove's hair shone like white gold in the sun. Shoving his itching hands into his trouser pockets, Ben managed to mumble a super-erogatory good-bye before tearing himself away from the spot.

He was imagining things, Ben told himself, walking away. Victor had only asked how Ben was sleeping because he'd probably heard Ben driving past his studio late every night for the past three weeks and was concerned.

Frances Ormond confirmed that she had heard Ben's Volvo at two and three in the morning at least a dozen times. She was far less subtle about it.

"That's the way Stephen Hunter began his terrible descent," she said, "staying out late, getting drunk in roadhouses, coming home late. Summer after summer. Night after night toward the end."

Ben thought it was none of her business, but defended himself by pointing out that he had written the two required stories and had already begun his novel. Late hours helped him work, he said.

She pursed her lips as though to counterattack, but changed the subject, feeding him coffee and freshly baked berry pie instead.

She told Ben no one else had keys to the little cottage. None were needed; the locks didn't work; anyone could get in if they wanted. Stephen Hunter had once told her he'd had enough of locks in the city. He wouldn't have functioning ones out here. It was his undoing, she added, because it enabled his murderer to get at him so easily.

Without much prodding, she narrated the grisly tale of three summer's past. The young vagabond had been captured in a saloon a few towns away. He'd confessed and was imprisoned. At first he made some foolish claim about Stephen owing him money and refusing to pay; about them being friends for years. Under pressure, his story changed into one of revenge. Stephen had molested him, he said. It wasn't convincing, even to the unsophisticated local sheriff.

Back at the little cottage, Ben discovered she was right—both doors could be opened, the locks just flapped on their hinges. Should he have them repaired? Yes. But whoever was visiting him at night did nothing but look at him. Was that reason enough to change something Stephen Hunter had done? Ben would never bring anyone back to the colony. He congratulated himself he never had. And he still couldn't get Victor Giove's words earlier that day out of his mind. He was almost certain it was Victor.

So he didn't repair the locks. And the next time he was awakened in the middle of the night and sensed a figure at the foot of the bed, Ben felt only a few seconds of the usual fear. The figure remained motionless. It seemed to be the right size for Giove. Then Ben began to feel the intense warm itch sweeping from the tips of his hair to the soles of his feet.

Slowly pushing down the light blanket, Ben let the dark figure warm him with its gaze, then began touching himself on his legs and groin. He thought he heard a sharpened intake of breath from his visitor, and Ben let go, slowly, luxuriously caressing and stroking himself, thinking of Victor at the foot of the bed watching him, wanting him, not daring to touch him. His climax that night was shared: he was certain of it.

When he opened his eyes, the room was empty.

§

He was visited every night for several weeks. Every night Ben awakened, sought out the outline of the figure against the lighter darkness of the room and succumbed to fantasies and sex.

During the day he often told himself he ought to be sure it *was* Victor and not someone else. But who else could it be? He searched the eyes of the other colony members he saw, looking for any signs of guilty secretive interest. He found none. Then he would come upon Victor—racing around the lawns with the big Irish Hound, or sitting reading in a hammock strung outside of Joan's studio—and, though they seldom exchanged more than a few words, every word, every phrase seemed so couched with meanings relevant to their shared nights, Ben was convinced it was Giove.

Didn't everything point to it? Victor's insistence Ben remain at the colony that first night? His friendliness? His increased reticence with Ben since the night visits had begun? He seldom spoke to Ben of Joan, or of their work—as though it had only been an excuse. Ben came to believe their new silence—when they met at the local grocery store, or out on walks—was more eloquent than words. It spelled content.

Ben would be a fool to spoil it. The impossible had become the possible. Not in the open way he'd first naively imagined, but tacit, secretive, and for that reason somehow more passionate than he'd ever fantasized. Victor must still have hurdles of attitudes, ingrained prejudices to jump before he could admit what he was wanting, feeling. Ben would give him time. Who knew what the next step would be in their growing closeness—so long as Ben didn't force it.

§

Ben had been visited that night as usual, all his lust and wakefulness drawn from him, as it always was, replaced by deep, calm, dreamy sleep.

People were marching down a small-town street. Batons twirled, trumpets blared, signs and crepe-covered floats sailed past. Children bounced eagerly behind. The drums passed by very close, going bam bam BAM! bam bam BAM! again and again, sounding lovely and rich and mellow at first, then ominous, then emergent.

Ben awakened to someone hammering on his front door. He thrust open the bedroom window to the cool mountain summer morning. It wasn't quite dawn.

"Ben! What do you know about drugs?" It was Eugene Ormond, evidently recently awakened. If he didn't look so panic-stricken, Ben would have laughed.

"Joan Sampson's taken a pile of them. We're sure they're some kind of sleeping pills."

"What did they look like?" Ben asked.

"We found one that feel on the floor," Dr. Ormond showed Ben the red and blue shiny capsule: Tuinals.

Ben dressed and ran out to Ormond's pickup idling in front of the cottage.

"She's got to vomit them up, I suppose," Ben said as they drove toward her studio. "Then black coffee, to keep her stimulated."

"Frances thought the same. I hope she's all right."

"Where's Victor?" Ben asked. "He would have known."

They pulled alongside the studio. Ormond looked at Ben oddly, then said:

"Didn't you know? He's back in New York. Has been for three days. That's what all this is about."

Before Ben could register the news, Dr. Ormond had stopped the truck and was urging him to come inside.

Joan was audibly vomiting. Frances, as audibly, cursing about the stupidity of trying to kill yourself over a man, for Chrissakes, even one like Victor. There was a final spasm of vomiting, quiet, then Frances Ormond half dragged the small woman out of the bathroom and spotting Ben, asked him to help her walk Miss Sampson around a bit while Eugene made coffee, doubly strong coffee.

Their charge was light, but weak; her arms were useless, her head kept lolling against Ben's shoulder; words and saliva dribbled out of her mouth.

They wheeled her around for another five minutes. Another fifteen minutes were spent feeding her the coffee and ensuring she didn't vomit that up too. Then more walking around.

Joan was visibly recovered by the time the phone rang. She still looked awful and had allowed Ben to bring her into the bedroom where she was noisily sobbing: but at least she was safe.

"Get that, will you Ben?" Mrs. Ormond asked, looking up from where she was cleaning the bathroom tile floor.

Ben lifted the receiver and said hello. There was a confused mumbling from the other side. Then:

"Joan. Is that you?"

Victor Giove: perplexed.

Ben looked away from the phone, unable to say anything for a minute. Holding his hand over the phone, he barely murmured, "It's Victor." Saying the name was more difficult than almost anything he could remember in his life.

"Of course it's Victor!" Frances Ormond said, and came to take the call.

"You see!" Joan sobbed, standing at the threshold of the room. "He's seeing her again. He was with her all last night. He couldn't stay away from her. That's why he went back."

Frances Ormond hushed her. Ben moved away from them, feeling as though he were on the set of a movie where everyone was playing a known role and only he didn't know the scenario. He couldn't believe that Victor was in New York; yet there he was, calling long distance in response to a call Mrs. Ormond had put through.

Ben walked slowly back to the little cottage. He felt dazed by the morning's events, but not so distracted he didn't notice it had rained the night before: the dirt around the cottage was still damp enough though drying fast. Two sets of footprints led to the tire tracks of the pickup. No other marks of someone walking around were visible.

That night he drank some brandy which kept him awake longer and made his sleep lighter than usual. When he was awakened during the night by the urgent panting breath at the foot of his bed, he immediately turned to the bed table and turned on the lamp.

The room was empty.

Energized by the need to know, Ben leapt out of bed and ran out into the other rooms. He even looked outside. When he returned to the bedroom a few minutes later, he thought he saw a wisp of smoke curling into the lower edges of the large storage closet. The closet was empty. But the morning chill caught up with him there, and he began to shiver so badly he had to get in bed and pull up the covers, waiting for sunlight.

§

"Stephen Hunter was homosexual, wasn't he?"

Frances Ormond looked across the distressed oak parquet of the old table at Ben.

"I guess they still don't talk much about those matters in college do they?" she asked, instead of answering him.

"The vagabond who murdered him was a hustler, wasn't he?"

"You seem to know all the answers. Why ask?"

"In the bedroom?"

"Stephen tried to get away," she said. "In the closet."

Ben wasn't surprised to hear it: only vaguely chilled to know his line of reasoning had been so on target.

"And Victor and Stephen were friends, weren't they?"

"Not by then, they weren't. They had been close friends. That summer they had a falling out."

"Because Victor wouldn't sleep with him?"

"You do have all the answers, don't you? Yes, Victor looked up to Stephen as though he were a god. But he couldn't bring himself to love him that way. Generous as Victor is with himself, I sometimes think he's too generous sometimes. People want more than he can give."

"And that's when Stephen began picking up hustlers?"

"No, he'd done that long before he met Victor. You've read the sequence called "Broken Bones," haven't you?"

"Years ago," Ben admitted. He'd never thought it was about hustlers.

Frances got up from the table and went to another room. She returned with a copy of Hunter's *Collected Poems*. Ben found the page and reread the first few poems in the sequence. He was shaken by the harsh, beautiful images of lust and fear.

"And this is why you said you thought I was heading in the same direction?" Ben asked her.

"I don't care what you do. Just be careful."

"I've never brought anyone back to the cottage."

"Borrow the book," she pleaded. "Read him again, Ben. He has a great deal to tell you. All great poets do. But I think he has a special message for you."

§

Like every literature student of his generation, Ben had read several of Stephen Hunter's poems in class, and had even memo-

rized one—a sonnet: "August, and the scent of tragic leafburn."
Aside from that one, however, Ben had always thought Hunter
overrated. He had preferred the more formal poets—Stevens and
Auden and Aiken—to what he termed the wild men: Dylan Thomas,
Lowell, and especially Stephen Hunter. Not that his opinion made
any difference. Hunter was in every anthology; his work was written
about, eulogized, discussed, reinterpreted.

Ben rediscovered him, reading through the poems in two days,
reading them again, then selecting out single poems and analyzing
them.

Hunter's famous *Odes to an Unruined Statue* were suddenly
opened to Ben as though they had been written in a language he
could never understand until now. Victor was the beautiful man/ob-
ject—the unattainable; Hunter, the critical observer and adoring
fantasist. The *Window Elegies,* those five intensely wrought poems of
dense metaphors and precise yet oddly angled images were illuminated as though a light had been switched on in a basement room.
Their visionary style and metaphysical message were all held
together by carefully delineated details of different windows through
which the poet had seen a loved one. The description in the second
elegy was clearly that of Victor's A-frame studio here at the colony;
the window Hunter had looked through night after night, spying on
Victor.

Ben didn't go near the large closet, which he never used anyway.
Nor did he sleep in the bedroom, anymore.

He felt safe on the living room sofa, even though it was cramped.
And, whether it was because of his intense new fear, or whether
there was a natural boundary to the presence, Ben was not
awakened once by his nocturnal visitor while he slept there.

The locks were repaired, of course, just as a precaution. And he
began to haunt his previous places of fast, usually anonymous sex,
returning home late at night and sleeping deeply. When he didn't go
out, he would stay awake at night, working, and sleep during the day.
Everything he did seemed tinged by an undercurrent of excitement,
as though anticipation were slowly building, but toward what end he
couldn't even begin to say.

Giove returned to the colony. Ben sometimes came upon him
swimming at the pond. Although Joan was no longer with him, and
the older man waved Ben over to join him, Ben would plead an
excuse and quickly leave. The one time Ben and he were thrown

together—for dinner at the Ormonds'—they found they had nothing to say to each other.

What Ben had thought to be a mutual secret content, he now saw otherwise: Victor was perceptive enough to understand what Ben wanted from him; he was trying to avoid having the same kind of problem he'd had with Stephen Hunter.

Ben knew that evening he'd fallen out of love with Victor. The golden aura that used to light the other man's steps through the tall grass, the sparkle that used to dapple his dark curls as he lay in the sun were gone. His eyes seemed tired, his face lined, his laughter constrained.

Ben knew why too. No man he could ever deem desirable would have been fool enough to not give so simple a matter as his body to a once in a lifetime met genius like Stephen Hunter.

§

It was August when Ben moved back into the bedroom. "August, and the scent of tragic leafburn," he reminded himself, when he awakened once more out of a deep sleep. He knew instantly that the presence at the foot of his bed was Stephen Hunter.

His body was beginning to tingle warm under the blanket cover he had protectively pulled up in that instant of realization. But Ben still shivered. The air about him stirred in cool eddies unlike any air he'd ever known. He heard what seemed to be fragments of whispered lines from poems, pleas, demands, obscenities. Stephen knew Ben: knew who he was, what he wanted, what he'd given up. Ben's teeth began to chatter. All he had to do was to reach over to the lamp table and put on the light, and he'd be alone, well, out of harm's reach. But if he did that Stephen might never come back to him. Ben wasn't sure he wanted that either.

He suddenly thought of Victor Giove. Large, muscled, beautiful generous Victor. He thought of Victor's smile, the bulge of his crotch in those tan worn cordorouys, the roundness of his buttocks in those scarlet swimtrunks, his rippling chest, his furrowed back, those ringlets of black curls, his Florentine profile.

The room became warm and still. So warm. Ben had to push the blanket away from him, letting the heat seethe around his body.

Keeping his eyes closed, Ben thought of Victor walking, running, swimming. Then someone else pushed Victor out of the picture and came into focus: a broad-shouldered, tall, thick-bodied man with intelligent deepset eyes of indeterminate color, a craggy face, long straight honeycolored hair, straggly moustache and beard: the face, the body, the very photograph from the frontispiece of the *Collected Poems.*

Stephen Hunter was a great poet. A genius. A man who'd felt as deeply as spontaneously as an oil geyser. He'd flown higher than a parachute jumper on mere thought. He'd filled himself with wisdom and suffering equal to any philosopher, any monarch. Compared to him, Victor was an oversized primate.

Ben relaxed, seeing without sight the figure moving in front of him, as though undressing, feeling the figure reach out and slowly caress Ben, the multicolored eyes gleaming softly, the mouth working to form wonderfully original words of manlove lewdnesses. The raking gaze swept over Ben's body like electric fire. Only such a genius could provoke, could produce such utter pleasure, Ben thought—as he gave in.

He was only slightly jolted when Stephen Hunter accepted. The sudden touch was of large warm hands pressing upon Ben's spread thighs, the brush of warm skin on either side of his loins, like a soft large cat. But the tongue that invisibly licked before engulfing him was that of a man, the long bony nose and unkempt facial hair, when Ben reached down to gingerly touch them, those of Hunter's photo-image; and Ben knew he had finally found what he'd come to Sagoponauk Rock Colony looking for, and why that first sunset had been filled with implications he could not at first decipher.

§

By the end of the summer Ben was a complete recluse. He had not been seen by anyone in the colony in weeks when most of the members went back to their teaching posts around the country. Joan Sampson and the Ormonds—the last to leave, in mid-September—tried to find him, but gave up after a series of attempts.

Both the Ormonds and Victor Giove used the house on a long late October weekend. The little cottage was empty, lived-in, although increasingly messy, dusty, ill-cared for. Victor felt guilty about the boy, and waited for Ben hours one afternoon, then he searched the area until sunset made it impossible. He left notes that were never answered and were never found on subsequent visits.

On his Thanksgiving break, Victor again drove up to the colony, this time to close-off the water pipes against the winter and to make certain all of the houses were locked. He once more drove to the little cottage, hoping to find Ben and to talk him out of his foolish decision to remain isolated. He didn't find the boy; but walking away from the little cottage, he gasped when he noticed the roof of Ben's Volvo sticking up out of one edge of the pond.

Although the pond was dragged by State and local police for two days, no body was ever found.

Victor relayed the sad, ambiguous news to Frances Ormond, who contacted Ben's family in Eastern Long Island. Neither of them heard from his relatives again.

The last two days of the Christmas holidays, Frances Ormond drove up to the colony by herself. She found several studios broken into: cans of tinned food opened, eaten, discarded. She cleaned up, repaired the windows and doors with local help, gathered all the remaining canned foods in the studios, bought more at the grocery store and dropped them off in a large cardboard box near the little cottage. She never told anyone she did this. Secretly, she was proud and envious that Ben had gone and done what she'd always wanted to do—to live here all year.

It turned out to be an extremely fierce New England winter. Storms raged weeks at a time. All but main highways were blocked by high snow drifts, and after, by ice layers most of which lasted until late March. Livestock froze in heated barns. Old people were stranded and died. Children and stragglers from stalled cars were lost in blizzards. Many local farmers closed up their houses and went south. Others remained indoors, barely surviving.

. Even though they managed to get into the colony by early March, the snow plows couldn't get anywhere near the little cottage.

Easter brought the first thaw. Victor drove up to the colony, bitterly hoping he would find the boy, and that Ben would finally listen to reason.

The door to the little cottage was still iced over and had to be kicked hard to open.

Inside, the main rooms were icily cold. Fires had been built, tin cans charred over the fire. Kerosene liters and sterno cans littered the living room floor. But Victor couldn't tell how long they'd lain there, a day or a month. It did seem as though the boy had gotten through the winter. That was a relief. He'd probably suffered so much he'd return with Victor to the city without much urging. Victor sat down to wait.

Although it was still cold, something else seemed to be missing from the cottage that Victor couldn't at first define: a disturbance he'd almost subconsciously felt every time he'd been here since they'd discovered Stephen Hunter's corpse in the storage closet.

When it finally was too cold to stay seated, Victor got up to leave the cottage. He wrote a note to Ben saying he would be at his studio; Ben could find him there. He was about to walk outside when he realized the bedroom door was closed.

Could the boy be hiding there?

Victor opened the bedroom door and remained still for a very long time.

The nude emaciated body of Ben Apres was stretched out on the bed as though in utter ecstasy. His skin was ashen, pale blue with frost, perfectly preserved down to the few frozen drops of semen that had splattered his gaunt abdomen and hung off the tip of his erection.

Victor understood why he no longer sensed the supercharged presence: the insatiable Stephen Hunter had finally found someone worthy of his love.

A Stroke

It happened on a Wednesday. On Thursday, Ron's sister in law, Annette, called him in the middle of a surprisingly pleasant April afternoon to tell him his father had a stroke and was hospitalized.

Ron's first thought was, why are you telling me this? His second was, what does this have to do with me and my life? I'm going to the periodontist's this afternoon for a checkup, then, because I'll be near Joan's office, I'll stop there, say hello, have a cup of coffee and commiserate with her over her new boss. After, I'll stop into that new bookstore for a while, long enough to miss the rush hour crowd on the bus. Then back home for a light supper, and the rest of that composing I should have done already. What does my father's stroke have to do with all this?

"How bad is it?" he asked.

"Pretty bad. He had the stroke getting out of the bathtub. Janice heard him fall. She said she had to put a bathrobe over him and call the ambulance."

That detail did it. Ron could picture the sprawled, overweight body on the bathroom tiles, twitching and convulsing. His own well ordered day suddenly burst like an overripe peach splitting its skin. Although he was sitting down with the phone, he felt weightless, floating. Things kept eluding him. His mug of cooled coffee was suddenly too far away to reach, his address book was on the other end of the big desk, out of reach. As though everything had been blasted away by the force of the news.

"We have to go see him, Ron. He's your father, you know."

"I know. When?"

Annette must not have heard him. She went on saying, "You only have one father, you know, Ron. My own father is dead, but ..."

"I said when?" He'd managed to reach over for his Day at a Glance planner, he held a pen poised above the next few days.

"I thought tomorrow afternoon," Annette said. She sounded disappointed, as though she planned a long list of reasons to counter him with, reasons carefully, eagerly prepared that she wouldn't be able to use now.

They agreed on a time. The hospital wasn't in Manhattan. His father lived in Queens. Still, Ron was surprised when she told him which hospital it was, one not three streets from where Ron had grown up. When he was young, he'd bicycled down the curving road past it a thousand times. Every time he'd remarked to himself how unlike a hospital it seemed with its Frank Lloyd Wright low slung lines, its wood and stone front, a discrete tinted glass foyer set deep off the road amidst heavy foliage. He'd always wondered who could see out of those high clerestory windows above the expanse of rough hewn brick, who sat looking up through the green glass solarium dome partly revealed between two parallel wings of the building. Ron had sped down the road, pedalling like mad, then coasting, wondering what kind of people were in such a place. It was difficult thinking of his father there.

"What does Dave think?" Ron asked. Dave was his brother.

"He'll go," she said so succinctly that Ron immediately understood Annette's careful arming to persuade him. Those same arguments must have been used on Dave already—successfully.

"It wasn't hard," she admitted. "Janice called last night. It was Dave who picked up the phone."

Janice was the woman their father lived with. A young woman, younger than both he and Dave. Dave had never talked about her to Ron; he hadn't even mentioned her name in the last four years.

"We'll come pick you up," Annette said. "Dave took off from work tomorrow. We'll have the car."

Ron wondered if Dave were sitting next to his wife, overhearing her end of the conversation. Or would he be at work at this hour? Ron realized he didn't even know his brother's work hours. So, he pictured Dave at home, in the room they insisted on calling the den, in the reclining chair, his feet up, their dog nearby, a newspaper opened in Dave's lap, the radio station tuned to his favorite easy listening station, "the dentists station" Ron always called it, music to have root canal done to. Dave wasn't even forty, and he'd already embraced the conventions of middle age.

"What about Larry? Does he know?" Ron asked. Larry was their youngest brother.

"I wanted to call him. Dave said not to bother."

"He should know, shouldn't he?"

"*I* think so," Annette said, sounding martyred. Evidently this was one front of the battle she'd already lost on.

"Do you want me to call him?"

"Do whatever you think is best."

The invisible shockwaves that had exploded around Ron's desk the minute his sister in law began talking, had spiralled out as far as they were going—and were now beginning to spiral back. It seemed as though every object on the desk was now in his hands or lap.

"How bad is he really?"

"You never know," she said.

Never know, she implied with her tone of voice, this might be the last time you ever see him.

When they hung up, the shock waves had all sprung back.

What would it be like to go to his own father's funeral? People did it all the time. Marty had just a few months ago, gone back to Columbus, Ohio. To be without him, though, that was the real question. What would that be like? Ron tried to picture his father. He hadn't seen him in five years, not since his parents had divorced, and it was difficult for him to get a solid image. The divorce had been rough on everyone in the family. But this, this would be a real change, final, irrevocable.

The phone was ringing again. Ron hesitated, then picked up the receiver. It was business.

§

He was ready too early the next day. He'd re-arranged his entire weeks' plan for this, spoken to various friends, especially Marty last night, explored his feelings, and come up with a series of tentative but more or less real emotions. This morning he felt vaguely annoyed that it wasn't over yet. He felt washed out. He waited, coffee mug in hand, a Bach cantata on the cassette player as the only suitable background music.

He'd also been on the telephone, trying to reach Larry where he worked. He tried once again.

Someone Ron didn't know answered, and after asking him to wait, found his brother.

"Hi!"

How young Larry's voice seemed, surprised and pleased by the call. They didn't talk much on the phone, although far more often than the twice a year either of them called Dave and Annette. They saw each other more often. They'd always been friendlier, Dave always set apart—first by being older, then away at school, then in the Paratroopers, later on married. Unlike Dave and Annette, Larry came downtown. He and Tina spent evenings in a cabaret on University Place. Sometimes they'd stop at Ron's first, invite him to join them. He'd gone once, but hadn't cared for the music, which was country, and had found the patrons too young. Ron and Larry didn't really share interests—Larry was into photography—but they did have the same values, formed at the same time by Lennon and McCartney, Robert Heinlein, The East Village Other and The Students for a Democratic Society. Ron couldn't see Larry at thirty nine—or even at seventy five—in a recliner with a pipe in his mouth, pooch at his feet.

"Bad news," Ron announced. "Dad's had a stroke. He's half paralyzed. He might have another. If he does, it will probably kill him."

He'd begun boldly, to shock Larry into the seriousness of the situation. Now he knew how Annette had felt calling him—like a hit and run driver.

"Yeah?" Larry said. He seemed thrilled, excited, and a little frightened too. It was the same tone of voice he'd used seven years before when Ron had pulled out two tiny tabs of blotter L.S.D. and had said, "You're going to try it anyway, so you might as well take it first with someone you trust."

"He's really bad," Ron said now.

Silence for a few seconds. Then an affronted "So?"

"So, we're going to see him. Dave and Annette and I."

"Does Mom know?" Larry asked, less hostile.

Ron hadn't thought of her at all. The divorce had been such a mess. His father had felt betrayed, had been negligent about payments during the separation. He'd finally realized she wasn't teasing and hadn't contested the action. But for years before, he'd put everything he owned in her name too, for tax purposes, and they were still in and out of court, lawyers haggling over property settlements.

"She'll hear soon enough," Ron said. "But she won't come to see him. So, there's no sense in telling her. The hospital isn't too far from where you work. We're going there now. You could take a few hours off and come meet us."

"No way."

Ron expected that answer. "Why not?"

"I hate him. He hates me too. You know that."

Like all their conversations together, it was at least honest.

"If I showed up he'd probably croak on the spot."

"That isn't funny, Larry."

"I'm not going."

"He's an old man," Ron began, then stopped. He wanted to say something decisive, something that would explain what he had felt yesterday when Annette called him: something that would hit Larry with the full weight of the possibility of having your life completely changed without your doing anything. As though you'd stepped out five minutes for a newspaper, and come back to find your apartment gutted by a flash fire. Larry had to understand the finality of it.

"Listen, Larry..."

"I don't want to see him again."

"Just like that?"

"You don't know the trips he put me through. You weren't at home then. You were in Amsterdam or England or someplace. And I don't want to remember. Which I will if I go. I don't want to see him again," Larry repeated with such sombre bitterness in his young voice that Ron understood that for his brother their father would never be dead, would always be alive, a knife turning in a wound.

"And Ron. Don't bother calling me tomorrow to tell me how spastic he is. Okay?"

§

Ron sat in the backseat. The mongrel had her own frayed pillow and only nuzzled him a little before going to it and sitting quietly. The car had the air of being much used. There was a styrofoam hamper behind the backseat, probably holding an empty thermos. A package of facial tissues bounced along with an old pair of galoshes and an implement for scraping ice off windows.

They'd reached the Grand Central Parkway before anything was said. Dave looked outside and Ron couldn't be sure whether he was admiring the warm clear day or the newly cleaned side windows. Annette, in the front seat, added touches to her make-up, a dangerous chore, Ron thought, with all the stopping and starting, but one she was evidently used to. Occasionally she would say something to Dave, to which he grunted a response that seemed to satisfy her. An odd match, Ron thought, although Annette's general affability made it easier to understand. Dave had always been so quiet, so private, it was hard to think of him sharing anything with anyone. At home, growing up, he would stay in his room for hours, sometimes doing nothing at all; daydreaming Ron always thought. Of course, Dave had also led a wilder life: parties, girls, motorcycles, dubious friends. Now he drove along with the pipe in his mouth, his large, dark eyes gleaming as he half turned to say something comforting to the dog, his long hair frizzed with gray all over. (Of all the things from the Sixties, he hadn't given up his long hair!) Dave appeared pleased his day off from work was such a sunny one. He seemed almost smug about the immediate rewards of following his duty.

It was difficult for Ron to reconcile this placid graying Dave with the moody, impulsive, sometimes violent brother he'd been. Difficult to see in this driver the teenager who'd one day flung a hammer at Ron to end an argument. Flung it so hard, straight at Ron's head, that it had whizzed by his ear, missing him by an inch, and had stuck by its claw in the plasterboard wall. Even more astonishing than the homicide atttempt had been Dave's attitude: he hadn't stayed to see it hit or miss. He'd thrown it, and left the garage with the hammer in mid air.

Ron wondered if Dave remembered that incident. Or, if he remembered another, on another afternoon. It was early winter and the pond across the street from their high-set house had frozen during the night. How hard was it, Dave wondered aloud when they'd arrived home from high school. They'd gotten out of Dave's car and raced through the bare little woods. When they reached the edge of the pond, Ron stopped, but Dave kept on going, shouting, clambering over the thickened white edge of the ice, sliding, jumping— Ron watching. And then the inevitable happened. There was a series of pistol shot reports as the ice cracked around Dave. He fell through to his chest. A great thump resounded out of him. Ron stood on the bank breathless at his brother's antics, then began laughing. He kept on laughing, through his surprise, through his fear the pond was deep where Dave had gone through, through his relief that it wasn't, through his shouting to Dave that he was coming as he edged carefully out to him and finally pulled the shocked, frost rimed scowling Dave out of the water and onto his hands and knees. He'd been unable to stop laughing as he got Dave onto earth again, and pulled him, threading through the bare trees, and finally into their basement. Dave stood shuddering, shaking, unable to speak although he tried to, with stunned outrage in his eyes, and Ron had still laughed. Laughed while he ran upstairs for towels and warm clothing, stopping in the kitchen to heat up water for tea. Later on, when Dave had been stripped and dried, brought upstairs and warmed with tea and Brandy, Ron had gone back down to close up the house, and had let out an unearthly howl of laughter. Ron hadn't been able to look at his brother for two days without at least a giggle. Thinking about it, he laughed again.

Smiling, Dave half turned, his lips parted to say something to Ron. He must have changed his mind. He turned back to the road.

"Did you talk to Larry?" Annette asked, offering Ron a cigarette over the carseat.

"Forget him."

"What did I tell you," Dave said.

"Dave's got as much to resent as Larry," Annette said. "We're still getting bills from their bankrupt business. Your father! He made Dave a partner just in time to go out of business. Just so there would be another address for the bills to go to."

"He tried to screw me good," Dave said without any rancor.

"He gambled," Annette said. "He lost thousands of dollars. He went on trips to Mexico, to Rio. He paid for Janice's abortion. That's why he went bankrupt."

"I got out of it," Dave said. "I went to a lawyer and showed him I was on the payroll until the day we closed. I never received a share of the profits."

"Can you imagine a father doing that to his own son?" Annette asked.

Dave suddenly laughed. "What a nut he is, you know, Ron. To think he could get away with it." He laughed again. "What a nut, to go on making babies at his age. He's sixty-three!"

"He's still your father," Annette said, recalling the seriousness of their visit. "The only one you'll ever have."

"That crazy Roumanian doctor friend of his shoots him up with something," Dave said. "B-Twelve and Monkey enzymes."

"Even so," Annette intoned, "Dave is responsible, mature. Much as he didn't want to come, here he is." She turned front again and patted his shoulder, murmuring some endearment Ron didn't catch.

"And what about Mom!" Dave continued loudly to Ron. "Who ever thought she'd get married again? She was seeing this guy before the divorce was final. That was fast, wasn't it?"

"They knew each other for years," Annette said. "They were kids together, she told me."

"Living in a little mansion upstate," Dave went on. "Buying cars, furs, furniture, trips to Hawaii and Tokyo. Boy, I'll bet she's laughing up her sleeve."

"She's got a bad heart, Dave," Annette admonished. "She didn't feel at all well last week."

"Who ever thought they'd become such screwballs," Dave said. "Did you, Ron?"

"Well, I'm sort of a screwball too," Ron said. He didn't know what Dave and Annette really thought of him, of his life and friends. Whenever he was with them, he always found himself going out of his way to make it seem more free and irresponsible and glamorous than it really was; as though to counter their own staid boredom. Though lately, with the revue he'd written a hit Off-Off Broadway and even a few album cuts of his songs, they must have started to believe all his glosses.

"What screwballs!" Dave concluded, ignoring Ron, but in such a loud, gleeful, all encompassing voice, he seemed to mean not only his parents and Ron, but the dog and his wife, and the occupants of all the cars around them on the cloverleaf, as they pulled off the highway.

§

From the clear glare of the day they entered a shadowy garden-world. The back entrance of the hospital, like the front, was deepset, surrounded with rosebushes in bud. Directly inside, the walls and floors were painted a cool blue ornamented with taupe. The sofas in the central lobby were cinnamon colored leather. It looked more like a Palm Springs hotel than a place where people had to have bedpans emptied and stitches taken. The woman at the information desk gave them a visitor's pass and directed them up a wide stairway. She also wore street clothes. Ron hadn't seen one medical uniform so far.

On the long, bright, skylighted second floor, he did see uniforms, those of nurses and orderlies, but they looked as though they had designer labels: soft pastel colors, cut like clothing he'd glanced at in the color fashion spread of last week's *Times* magazine.

"Here we are. Room two fifteen," Dave announced. He didn't seem as awed—or bothered—by the luxurious civilian look of the place as Ron. He did, however, seem excited for the first time today.

Ron's first impression as they entered, was that the room was the wrong one. It was filled with slightly greying ladies. He almost pulled back out, before one of them recognized Dave.

All three women—mother and daughters—turned away from someone they were looking at. They were his father's sister—Aunt Lisa and her daughters Jean and Dolores: all of Ron's relatives, his favorites. Their soft, smiling, similarly pretty faces suddenly relaxed.

"Look, the children!" Aunt Lisa said. "The children," she repeated turning to the others. "The boys. Ronnie and Dave and his wife."

There was a general rise and flurry of greetings.

"I told you they would come," Lisa softly admonished the person in the wheelchair. "They're good children."

It was then Ron realized who the person she talked to was: his father, but so suddenly old, as to be unrecognizable. Ron wanted to leave the room. Instead, foolishly, he smiled.

Dave too seemed at a loss.

Not Annette. Well schooled in such encounters through her own father's long illness (or was it from watching daytime TV serials, Ron wondered), she knew precisely what to do. She flung herself at the wheelchair. "Papa!"

Dave was brought forward to his stricken father. Ron saw his brother's eyes darting about the figure in the wheelchair, looking for some clue to begin the encounter. Dave's ears were burning red.

His aunt had Ron by the hand, suddenly, thankfully. He no longer had to worry about not being able to look at his own father. She led him a few paces away, telling him that she'd spoken to his mother that morning.

"I told her about Mark," she said, and glanced back at his father with such a look that Ron could tell that she was indeed glad he and Dave had come. They'd no doubt been sitting there patiently, consolingly, three mater dolorosa. But they were good people—

quiet, polite, charming. So unlike his own immediate family. His cousins were high-school teachers with teenaged children. Their older brother Dean, who'd been on the first nuclear submarine when Ron was only a ten year old, was now a Commander in the Navy, teaching at Annapolis. So unlike Ron's own rowdy, demanding generation, he didn't wonder why he'd seen so little of Aunt Lisa and her children when he was growing up. "He didn't think you were coming," Aunt Lisa whispered to him, as though she hadn't already loudly announced it.

Too soon it was his turn to confront the unavoidable. Dave had moved off the armchair placed next to his father. Annette had taken up a nearby position, close enough to converse with the other women, yet easily overhear whatever was said to her father in law.

His father's hair was white, thin. Had he been dyeing it all these years? He was settled in the wheelchair as though dropped into it. His skin looked like onion-paper, especially one side of his face. He was wearing hospital pajamas—a sort of cantaloupe color, wrapped in a brown bathrobe. Was that the same one Janice had wrapped around him when he'd fallen? One of his legs hung off the chair's front edge. His father's eyes—once as dark and glittering as Dave's—were now washed out, the corneas tearing, the irises bruised looking. He appeared pleased to see Ron. But there was another look on his face too, one Ron had never seen there before, and he couldn't be certain what to call it.

"How are you doing?" Ron asked.

His father kept looking at him, but said nothing. The watery eyes took him in greedily.

Ron tried to recall if Annette said he was temporarily aphasic.

"Can you talk?" Ron asked.

His father took his hand and held it. Some strong emotion filled him. He clearly just wanted to sit like this. His leg off the lip of the wheelchair bothered Ron; as did the bathrobe twisted around his back which couldn't be very comfortable. The leg had an ace bandage around the shin. If it were injured, why wasn't it in a cast or splint?

Ron looked down at the mottled hand loosely holding his. It's grip was weak, but that made it easy for Ron to hold it. When was the last time he'd held his father's hand?

He remembered. Remembered that same hand held up to strike him at the conclusion of an acrimonious argument. It had been a strong hand then, unmottled, decorated with expensive rings. But Ron's own hand had been strong too. It had shot up and stopped his father's in mid air. Mark had been so outraged then, he'd pulled his hand away, let it fall to his side, and had shouted "Get out of my house!" Suddenly frightened, the eighteen year old Ron had. And never lived at home again.

He remembered that hand another way too, holding the steering wheel of their Oldsmobile, loosely, confidently, in the style of a racing driver, fooling around, the white plastic hub slipping easily through the curved palm. Ron was a teenager then, his father, too busy to read, used to keep the car radio tuned to talk shows while driving. He always had some scientific fact or anecdote to tell whenever they drove together. "You know Ron," he would begin, "this guy was on the radio yesterday. A biologist. And he said..." Because of all three brothers, Ron was considered the smart one, he was certain neither Larry nor Dave ever heard these impromptu lectures about the Wasps' methods of queen selection or how sea birds had internal radar pointed to the magnetic north pole.

He remembered that same hand larger. His own two small ones holding tightly to it, as his father ducked him in and out of a swimming pool at a summer place they'd taken for years at Locust Manor. He remembered that same hand huge, lightly holding the top of Ron's head, as he stood shivering on the bathroom tiles of their first home his father urinating, legs like tree trunks, then lifting Ron to do it, then carrying him back to the crib.

"Why is your leg like that?" Ron had to ask.

His father gurgled. Spit came out of one side of his mouth: the paralyzed side, Ron decided. Then his father looked down and leaning over with effort, tugged at the knee of the dangling leg, lifting it to sit firmly on the wheelchair's edge.

This mechanical, impersonal treatment of his own body was more than Ron could stand. He wanted to run from the room.

"I hurt it a little," his father managed to say, the words slurred, "when I fell."

When he fell. That was the euphemism he and Janice had chosen. It infuriated Ron.

"Look, Dad. You didn't fall. You had a stroke. A cerebral hemorrhage. It's very severe. Half your body is paralyzed, I can hardly make out what you're saying. You're going to have to take it easy for a while. Have physical therapy and all."

"Ron!" Annette interrupted. "What are you saying to your father?"

Ron ignored her. Looking at his father's watery eyes, it was now clear to him what that unfamiliar look was, it was fear. He'd never seen his father frightened before. Never thought to see him terrified like this. It made Ron afraid too, as though he were suddenly cut loose from his moorings.

"I don't mean to be cruel," he said. "I just want to make sure you know where you really are."

The old man murmured something, and Ron had to lean forward to hear. The hand in Ron's trembled.

"I know," his father said.

But he continued to stare stupidly, desperately, a crooked smile on his half frozen face. Ron could now make out healing bruises on his father's temple and cheek. He could see his father standing up in the bathtup and clutching at his head, then dropping like a dead carcass to the tiles.

"Is this place all right?" he asked. He couldn't believe it wasn't, but felt he had to say something. "Is there anything you need? Does Janice come to see you? Are you getting compensation insurance or what? Who's paying for this room?" And how, he wanted to ask, but couldn't bring himself to do it, are you in here, if you're bankrupt, as Dave and Annette said.

They passed another long, halting, difficult five minutes more of such conversation. It was some relief for Ron to find so obvious a way to help—since it was the only way he could now.

He soon ceded his seat to Dave, and went out into the lobby for a drink of water and a cigarette. He toyed with the idea of finding the doctor in charge to get more information.

"You must be one of Mark's boys," a well-dressed elderly man said, coming up to him. "I'm Doctor Ballin, your father's physician. An old friend from when you lived here. I remember seeing a lot of you. The way you used to fly down this road with that bike, I swore we'd get you in here one of these days."

§

Ron followed the doctor back into the room. Later, Dave took Dr. Ballin aside to ask the same questions Ron had. He could make out Dave's earnest face saying the words "how long, how much, how often, when, where, what."

"We saw your show," Ron's cousin Dolores suddenly said. Ron was surrounded by his relatives. "We liked it very much."

He was more than surprised. "You did?"

"Gary was told that it was a little racy," she admitted. "But we both thought it was cute. Your mother said they were planning to make a movie of it."

"Not quite. We've gotten some nibbles for a Broadway production. It's only a little revue."

"And my Jill—she's fourteen," his other cousin said, "showed me a record album with two of your songs on it. You're famous."

"We're all very proud of you," Aunt Lisa put in. "We've never had an artist in the family before. Not a musician."

"Didn't Uncle Ted play piano?" Ron asked."

"That was just fooling around," she said.

"I was thrilled," Dolores said, "to see your name in lights on the theater marquee. My students ask if we're related all the time."

Ron doubted that, but liked to hear it. He happened to glance past her. His brother was still at the door, talking to the doctor. Annette was at his father's side, patting his leg, rearranging the bathrobe. His father paid no attention to her. He stared at Ron, surrounded by his female relations. Ron was sure his father had heard their conversation, they were only a few feet away. He searched the half paralyzed face for a sign of what he thought. The half crooked smile was still there: the watery, weak eyes.

Then, out of the left eye—the unparalyzed side Ron thought—he noticed a flicker, a glimmer of the old, hard, appraising brightness. Yes, and there it was again.

Ron continued talking to Jean and Dolores and Aunt Lisa, saying yes, it had been difficult for him getting his songs recorded and published, getting the show staged. He'd fought a great many obstacles, he'd been patient, unwavering, perservering. He felt half performer, half charlatan saying it: it seemed so trite. But he said it loudly, clearly, so his father had to hear it too. And a curious feeling swept over Ron then. He was filled with a power he'd never possessed before. He was aware of himself standing straight, healthy, a fine, grown man, an individual, achieved, even respected. And it was as though he was viewing himself not from the familiarity of his own mind, but from another's. He instantly knew who's—from behind that half-paralyzed face, from behind those watery eyes, from within that figure half collapsed in a wheelchair. It was less than an

instant, *ein Augenblick* Heine would have called it, the blinking of an
eyelash. But intense for all its brevity, filled with grim pride, and
resentment that he, Ron, had accomplished what he'd set out to do,
in defiance of the odds, despite his lack of contacts, in opposition to
Mark's own wishes, fighting Ron every inch of the way, mocking him
on one occasion, even bribing him to give up his dream and return to
the supposed security of the family business. And with that double
perspective, Ron realized that he now understood something about
his father—that he too had wanted something—not in music,
perhaps—but something he'd failed to accomplish in the world.

Then it was gone, and Ron was back with his aunt and cousins.

But it wasn't over completely yet. Ron disregarded the others,
looking hard at his father, feeling all of his strength gathered, and said
to himself, as though both of them could hear it, yes, neither you
nor anyone else could stop me.

The old face flinched and looked away from Ron.

With that, Ron felt triumphant. He'd accepted his new power, and
flashed it in his father's face, as though to say, your life is over; but
mine has just begun. The room seemed too small, far too crowded
and dim. Ron needed air, light, space.

Visiting hours were over, a young woman's voice announced over
the P.A. system.

Annette and Dave rose, saying they would come visit often.

Ron waited until they were out of earshot, then said, patting his
father's one good hand, "I'll see you as soon as I can."

§

Although it was only three p.m. when Dave dropped Ron off in front
of his apartment, the afternoon seemed shot.

Ron wanted to sort out his thoughts. In the car, riding back to
Manhattan, he'd put aside the strange experience he'd shared with
his father, to daydream, every once in a while joining in the other's
conversation. Now he was torn between staying out and going for a
walk or going back in. He bought a newspaper and that partly
decided him. Sunlight streamed into his living room. The classical
music station was playing Mozart's Clarinet Concerto. He reheated
the morning's coffee, and sat sipping, reading the paper slowly,
deliberately, fully, stopping at tiny filler items, even completing the
crossword puzzle.

When the Mozart was over, he felt empty. He dialed Marty at the studio.

"Was it awful?" Marty asked.

"He's a mess," Ron said, then went on to describe his father's appearance, the prognosis (chancy this early, but quite good), his visitors, and the hospital's decor. As Ron talked, he could visualize Marty leaning over the slanted table, sketching or filling in one of those ornamental designs with colored pencil. The deco-style lamp's light would cast a half shadow on the upper portion of Marty's face, so his honey hair seemed darker, his eyes more serious.

"Well," Marty finally said. "You sound pretty chipper. Are you glad you went?"

"I sound chipper?"

"Not at all depressed. Chipper. That's the word."

"Well it's over. The visit I mean." Then, because that sounded lame, "Marty, something happened in that hospital room between us. I don't know exactly how to describe it. It was so fast and complicated."

He tried to tell Marty, but after a little bit, he could see it wasn't coming across. Marty sounded perplexed, a little bored.

After they made plans to go to a movie and rang off, Ron looked at himself in the bathroom mirror. Nothing was changed. Yet....

"And what kind of a day have you had?" he asked his reflection.

"A good day," he easily answered. "A good day for killing old demons."

Both faces smiled; then conspiratorily winked. *Ein Augenblick*.

An Asian Minor
The True Story of Ganymede

Prologue

Although it's been a very long time since anyone has heard from me or even about me, I understand that my name and story are currently a hot topic, due to a certain group of overconcerned busybodies intent on making me a symbolic victim of an old pervert's lust; and contrarily, by others saying the perversion is fine, and neither I nor my human rights have been violated.

So, to clear up the conflicting charges, I've decided to spend some time during my break here up on Olympus to tell you what *really* happened some 4,000 years ago—and not so incidentally, to give the current crop of good-looking young guys what I hope are a few hints as to how to get themselves a sugar daddy who really counts, rather than settling for whomever comes along.

My own main man, Zeus, or Jupiter, or whatever you want to call him, is sleeping, as he and most of the other folks up here have been doing since you people stopped offering sacrifices and asking for our intercession in various affairs. A sort of extended hibernation, you might call it, with restless me awakening every few centuries to make sure no one needs a drink—that, after all, being my main job as an immortal, in case you forgot.

This time, when I woke up, a few other minor deities—Rumor and Discord—were jawing on about world events, and with those two going at it it didn't take long for me to catch up on recent developments and to decide to spill the beans.

So listen carefully, and even if you aren't knockdown beautiful, you might learn a thing or two.

I am born and made the subject of prognostications

Now in my time, folks usually began stories, and especially stories about themselves, by giving extended family trees, with capsule histories of everyone on the branches, relevant to the story or not, including people they'd never met and relatives they mostly hated. Not me.

I'll just tell you that I was one of about two dozen children born to King Troas, third of a line of kings who founded and ruled the city of Troy, on the northern coast of what you would call Turkey. Troas had six wives, one of whom was my mother, and a pile of daughters. Of three sons, the others were Ilos and Assandros, but as they were much older, I never saw much of them.

Nothing else about my family is terribly interesting, except that somehow or other my granddad, Ericthonios, in his senility had come to believe that his father was sired by Zeus himself. So Zeus was the god my father paid especial attention to, which seemed pretty good politics and religion, if you ask me, since he was the strongest and the leader of the rest.

Whatever the reason, we had a really rich city and province. Great agriculture, some light industry, and trade that extended as far as Egypt and Spain. In short, everything was pretty hunky-dory in Troy when I was born.

And went on that way, until I was ten years old. No one paid any attention to me. The palace was filled with children—sisters of all ages, nephews, nieces, servants' kids, courtiers' scions—all kinds of brats running around. Why should anyone notice me? I got all the usual childhood diseases, got over them without too much trouble, proved to be healthy, agile, out of the way when not absolutely needed, and not too much of a smart aleck.

A few of the others did bring attention to themselves—Ibycus, one of my nephews, for example, who got so fat he had to be rolled around in a wheelbarrow. But at least he got to dress up as Bacchus during that god's festival every year and was allowed to clown around and get shit-faced drunk on wine for days at a time.

There were, however, a few disquieting omens forecast when I was born. At least that's what some of the nursemaids and tutors told me, although I always suspected that was to scare me into behaving myself.

According to them, when the horoscope of my birth was cast, it showed portents that I would become so outstanding that I would draw the attention of everyone, even the immortals. It didn't explain how I would do this, but it was not considered too great a thing to have happen. Look at Marsyas, the singer, who thought he was as good as Apollo—he had the hide taken off him for that. And Arachne, who boasted that she wove better than Athena— turned into a spider. And Midas. And Niobe. I could go on. All I want to make clear is that for months after I was born, everyone looked me over for signs of something extraordinary—an extra finger, two different-colored eyes, special athletic or intellectual abilities. They found nothing. I was just another kid.

When I was about ten, however, an inkling of what it would be showed itself unexpectedly.

We had visitors at our court from a neighboring kingdom called Phrygia. And while I was standing around in the palace reception room, along with all the other royal wives and kids, the Phrygian king, Sarpedon, happened to glance in my direction.

His minister had been going on and on in flowery diplomatic language about how terrific the alliance of the two countries would be, and turned to Sarpedon for confirmation of what he'd just said. The king didn't hear him. The minister then tried to get his attention by coughing and going "ahem." No luck. Finally someone in his entourage got up the nerve to touch him. Sarpedon looked around as though coming out of a dream. Ignoring the minister, he pointed me out and asked King Troas who I was.

Surprised as much by his strange manner as by his question, my dad said I was one of his children: number 19 or so, he couldn't remember exactly which.

"What a marvel!" Sarpedon said. "Bring him out. So all might see him."

So I was brought out from all the others and surrounded by these Phrygians, all decked out in their ceremonial black armor, who looked me over from head to foot.

Naturally Troas was a little put off by this, as he was just dying to show them some really important treasures he had—a hundred golden oxen; 12 snow-white horses (the result of the North Wind falling in love with a flock of our wild Trojan ponies); the triple walls of the city, with 24 gilded gates; two huge vats of yellow sweet wine from a place called Gaul; all kinds of jewels and handiwork of our world-renowned gold- and silversmiths. So, puzzled by the Phrygians' making such a fuss about me, he was polite too.

The inspection finally over, Sarpedon agreed to see the other treasures, and to my dad's satisfaction, he was properly impressed. He did, however, tell Troas that I was the rarest and best of all the city's wonders. Since Sarpedon traveled around a great deal, conquering and invading and trading and visiting, this meant something. In addition, this old guy traveling with his entourage, named Tiresias, who looked about a thousand years old and smelled like old goat's milk, told my dad—and this I quote out of modesty—that I was "the loveliest born of the race of mortals." Which was a mouthful, since he'd seen plenty.

Since Troas was trying to make a military pact with the Phrygians, he made me hang around while they feasted and talked business, all of which I found pretty much of a bore. I should tell you here that this Sarpedon was a grown man with several wives and kids of his own, but he couldn't take his eyes off me. During dinner he made me sit next to him, and later on when gifts were exchanged, he gave me all sorts of presents. The only one I really liked was an ivory-handled dagger he said had come from the dark continent called Libya.

After the treaty was signed and the feasting and athletic games concluded, Sarpedon and his gang went back to Phrygia, and everything in Troy went back to normal.

Almost.

For something had happened, I could tell. Sometimes, out of the blue, Troas would call for me and have me stand in front of him for the longest time, looking me over from head to foot, making me turn around, then back again. He never said anything, just sent me away.

After the Phrygians' visit, whenever any strangers of note were in Troy, Troas would invite them to the court, show them the city walls, the hundred golden oxen, the 12 snow-white horses sired by the North Wind, then call for me, which was pretty much a nuisance. Without a single exception, these kings and princes and merchants and other travelers would take one look at me and go gaga, saying how I was the most beautiful thing they'd ever laid eyes on, etcetera.

When they'd gone, Dad would make me come to him again, and look me over again. He couldn't make sense of it. My mom was no great beauty. No one had ever accused *him* of being terrific-looking. Where had I come from? Why hadn't anyone noticed me before?

He even had me measured by the court mathematician and philosopher, one Polycleites, a Chian. Every angle and relationship of limb to limb was ticked off—the distance between my eyes, say, or how widely my lips parted, the size of my ears to my head, of my index finger to my forearm, of my big toes to my feet.

Polycleites then devised a life-sized chart of me including all these relationships. Then my sibs and nieces and nephews and a whole lot of other kids from the city were called in, stood against it, and measured too. None of them had my exact ratios, although some had a few, and some had several.

This, the mathematician-philosopher said, was because my proportions were perfect, according to some formulas he made up of three to four to five to nine, which he said made me equal any geometry that existed.

After a few months of this, dad got involved in a small war and no longer bothered to show me off to visitors, or to call me to be looked over and remeasured. So I was, happily, pretty much forgotten.

For a while.

I am initiated and really found out

Two years later, when I was ready to be initiated into the Temple of Zeus, which would make me a bona fide and responsible citizen of Troy, Troas remembered me. This time he wasn't able to forget me so easily.

Part of the initiation was that you went downstairs in the temple to where a deaf old lady (who sat around a fire chewing on special leaves that kept her wrecked pretty much of the time) told your future. You would approach her, have your sponsor say some prayers, offer a decapitated chicken or some such petty sacrifice, and she would say what your vocation in life would be, when and whom you'd probably marry, how many kids you'd have, whether you'd be rich or poor, healthy or ill, powerful or disgraced, and any other tidbits she could figure out from the chicken-blood patterns splattered in front of her.

Well, the minute I walked up to her and dropped the chicken at her feet, this old Delphic jumped off the seat where she'd sat so long everyone thought she was glued to it, threw up her arms, let out a wrangled shriek, and bowed down really low in front of me. She placed her ratty old face on my bare feet, muttering under her breath. This went on quite a while, to everyone's consternation. Then she looked up at me with a toothless smile on her withered old face and said,

"Destined is he to never not be.
Serve the highest as equal.
Be revered by those higher.
Given. He will be taken.
Taken. He will give always."

...or some such gobbledygook no one understood, although like all forecasts it was duly written down by the temple scribe so anyone could read it.

Of course, now it makes complete sense to me. At the time, however, it threw all of the ceremonials into a tizzy that the old mess would bother to bow down to me, she who had never been known to get off her rear for priests or kings or anyone before.

Well, you can suppose that the minute we got back to the palace, King Troas called Polycleites and had me measured all over again. I was bigger, naturally, but my previous ratios still held good: three to four to five to nine: perfect as geometry.

All this razzmatazz annoyed me. I wanted the old bag to tell me I would be a soldier like my brothers, or a sailor exploring distant lands like my cousin Iolas, or *something* interesting. Instead, I'd gotten my feet kissed and a garbled oracle. Worse, not only my dad but everyone I came across in the palace looked at me a little funny for weeks after that. It was weird.

Meanwhile, Sarpedon and those other visitors had talked about me when they got home. People began coming to Troy for the special purpose of taking a look at me and wouldn't be put off by the triple walls or the 24 gates or the hundred golden oxen or even the 12 snow-white horses old Boreas had gotten on some unsuspecting mares. I'd be hunted out from wherever I was, made to take a bath, get dressed, and be paraded out to be gawked and leered at.

King Troas once asked an Egyptian prince—he was neat, with red skin and clothing so sheer you could see everything!—how he'd heard about me.

"All over the civilized world, the name Ganymede is known," the Prince said. "Known as the loveliest of all mortals."

"Do you think so?"

"He is equal in beauty to the gods," was the answer.

Knowing as I do now how Egyptian gods have jackal heads and dog faces and stuff like that, it wasn't much of a compliment. Still...as far as my dad was concerned, that was the limit to his patience.

The court astrologer was brought out and my horoscope reread. Hearing that I would be so special as to attract the attention of the gods, Troas got really worked up. He was sure they would get wind of how terrific-looking I was, become jealous, and then no end of mischief would occur to him, the city, the whole country.

I think he planned on having me smothered in my sleep or something equally treacherous and efficient. But he must have been talked out of it by the priests of the Temple of Zeus, who reminded him of the old bag's prophecy. If a mortal, even a king, destroyed what might after all turn out to be a gift from one of the gods (me!)—well, who knew what havoc that might cause?

The next morning, with no warning at all, I was awakened hours before I usually got up, dressed in commoners' clothing (which I preferred anyhow), and told I was going on a journey with Polycleites.

An hour out of the city, Polycleites let on that I was to stay with him in an isolated house another hour's ride away. King Troas had given him the house, some land, and a pension. In return, the scholar was to keep me out of Troy, away from the people, and also to try to teach me some mathematics and philosophy. Although he didn't say it outright, I got the impression that my dad figured that by hard study I would turn out as lacking in charm, grace, and looks as Polycleites.

Only 12 years old, and I was already an exile.

I match wits with a stranger

Under different circumstances, life with Polycleites might have been a real drag. But it wasn't bad. We had an old, mute house-keeper, and although she was a bit simple, she was kind to me and a good cook. Polycleites had just been waiting for a chance to devote himself to his mathematics. He was completely content.

We got along surprisingly well. As a rule, Polycleites found people both repulsive and unnecessary, but his attitude toward me was different—and not only because I was, so to speak, the goose that was laying his golden eggs. He had persuaded himself that I was physically perfect, and so he could look at me not as a 12-year-old boy who ate and pissed and occasionally got moody or bored, but as though I were a living, breathing, walking, talking justification of the rules of mathematics by which he had lived so long.

Sometimes he would stare at me as I lay out on the grass. It was never with lustful intentions or even vague aesthetic pleasure, like most men. All he saw were exact planes and volumes set against each other in absolutely perfect ratios.

So, aside from learning a little bit of mathematics and the merest smidgen of philosophy, I was pretty much on my own. I went into the fields and woods, hiked up into the hills that surrounded us, observed birds and animals, sometimes played with a herd of wild ponies (no relation to the North Wind's babies). Sometimes I stayed away from the house a week at a time. Polycleites didn't mind. And whenever I'd return he would greet me as though I were an old theorem he'd forgotten and was happy to be reminded of.

Occasionally we received news from passing visitors. Everything in Troy was fine. The small war had been won with no trouble. New trade routes had been opened. Everyone was getting richer. A few more nieces and nephews had been born in the palace, and a few more golden oxen to show off to visitors. I never knew how I was explained away. Perhaps Troas told everyone I'd gone off to school.

We'd been there a few months when I returned from one of my four-day solo camping trips and found a guest of Polycleites' house.

This was unheard-of: We were not allowed visitors. But the minute I walked in, the old mathematician took me aside to explain how this was a special case. The stranger was *also* a mathematician, one known by name all over the Aegean, and the most brilliant mathematician Polycleites had ever encountered. They'd already passed two days together, during which the visitor had presented startling new theorems and proofs and had demolished, or otherwise shown outmoded and fallacious in seconds, other theorems and proofs that my mathematician had been using for decades. There was no doubt that the old scholar was immensely proud to have been sought out in this backwater by so eminent a colleague. It would take years, possibly decades, Polycleites intimated, before he could sort out all the new information.

What he didn't say about our new guest was that he was just a shade odd. Picture a man of about 21 or 22, tall, slender, well-knit: a runner's body, with long, well-muscled legs, strong ankles, and large feet. He had a small but extremely handsome face, dominated by flashing brown eyes that seemed to be able to perceive absolutely everything around him. All of his gestures and movements were fast and precise. The minute I laid eyes on him, I suspected he wasn't your ordinary garden-variety itinerant mathematician, no matter how renowned.

He was certainly a fast talker. Polycleites had never been a terrific fan of mine—except abstractly, of course—but before this, he'd always been a dogged protector, as though if he didn't watch me every moment, I'd express symptoms of being sullied by contact with others—my proportions would get out of line or my ratios would slip. This day, with his head filled up with new axioms and his attention glued to the long sheets of proofs in front of him, I guessed that I was more or less on my own.

I ought to admit right away that while all those other folks were saying how scrumptious I looked, I always thought they were missing the point: If I had any real strength, it was my cunning. For the past four years I'd achieved the near impossible—living as freely as any child from any family of any class in the city of Troy. I'd sneaked away from the palace every chance I got, made friends with scavenger boys at the city gates, spent hours with petty-criminal urchins in the warehouse district, lived wild, made mischief, always just escaping capture and punishment. I may not have been what you would call hard-boiled, but I was nobody's fool. And I wasn't about to be talked into anything.

This was to be of some help to me, because soon enough I felt the traveling mathematician's charm and cultivation strike eerily sympathetic chords in my young nature. If he'd said that I had gorgeous proportions, eyes like glistening lakes, limbs of Parian marble, I would have been forewarned. Instead, he talked about subjects that had long piqued my curiosity—the flight techniques of predator birds, the evidences of earth history as displayed in the structure of rocks, the myths of creation and the probable realities behind such myths.

Right after dinner, the distracted Polycleites retired to his room to pore over his proofs. I realized his disappearance and my inebriation at the same moment—and, I might add, at the same time I felt the young mathematician's warm, rapid hands undoing my clothing.

My exertions to prevent this brought me to a few of my senses, but not enough. He was quick to explain the physical properties of wine, how rest and languor were needed to counteract its strongest effects, how loosening clothing allowed blood to course through the body more freely and thus dissipate the wine, how—why, look! Another of its effects was apparent: I was already tumescent.

So he talked on, and somehow or other we arrived at my little bed. In no time at all, he had me completely undressed and was fondling me, kissing me, caressing and servicing me—all with an exquisite little rapidity excelling anything my little waterfront buddy Autocylus (whom I'd sex-played with for years) had been able to accomplish, expert as he had been.

There I was, prone, overstimulated, panting, awaiting his long, firm body, poised above me now, to drop down and execute the coup de grâce—when I happened to feel, along the back of each of his shoulder blades, what seemed to be small folded wings.

I sobered up fast, recalling the Delphic's words about "serving one higher." Could this have been what she meant? Could this be…an immortal?

I pulled back from him so fast that he thrust deep into the bed-clothes and looked at me with an expression of great frustration and annoyance. I pulled away and huddled at the end of the bed, pretending to be more panic-stricken than I was.

"You aren't a mathematician at all! You're some sort of leg-endary beast!"

He tried to hush me, lest I draw the scholar into the room with my cries. I whimpered in mock terror.

"You aren't a man! You're some kind of bird! I felt your wings!"

I could already see his long, perfectly shaped member begin to shrivel up. He quieted me. He wheedled. He cajoled. He talked biology, ornithology, physics for 15 minutes, inching closer and closer. I moved farther and farther away, until I was off the bed. I wouldn't let him touch me.

Finally he had to tell me the truth. He was Hermes—the Messenger, the Thinker, the Scribe of the Gods. He'd heard of me in his many travels upon the earth, he said, and had determined to find out if I lived up to my reputation. To his surprise, he confessed, I far surpassed it. And he wanted me. If I became his boyfriend, he would provide me with a life unlike that of any other boy. He'd give me knowledge of all tongues of all nations, even of wild animals, birds, and lizards. He'd give me speed close to flight and the ability to come and go so rapidly as to appear invisible. He'd give me knowledge of mathematics, philosophy, the natural sciences. He'd ensure a life of renown in letters and the capability to persuade all men and beasts to believe and do what I wished. If I became his boyfriend.

I have to admit it sounded good. So good, I began to ask for more details. So good, after he gave me details, that I asked to have a contract drawn up, with all of his promises put down in writing. For if he *was* Hermes, then he was not only the messenger and thinker of the gods, he was the liar and trickster of the gods too.

Drawing up the contract took quite a while. We bickered over terms, negotiated fine points of his promises—such as whether the renown I was to have in letters was to be local or international, fleeting and widely popular or limited but ever-enduring.

Hermes got defensive and began requiring yet more specific duties from me as a lover. Hearing that, I got even more demanding, and so we had to negotiate our terms all over again.

Several hours later, we had a good half-dozen scrolls of a contract agreed upon and about to be signed, when I had one more idea.

"Of course, all of this is binding upon the mutual pleasure of both parties in the act," I said. "Since the act you wish to perform upon me is not known to me, I will have to insist that be in the contract."

"I can guarantee your pleasure," he said, but his bright eyes darkened the way a forest does just before a rainfall. "If indeed you have never performed this act."

I staunchly declared I hadn't. After all, I pointed out, I was only 12 years old.

"Perhaps," he said, unconvinced. But he did agree to my stipulation.

He was a wiser, gloomier, but no less lusty immortal when he finally did bed me. It was almost dawn by then, and I was so exhausted—what with the hour, our wrangling over the contract, and the excitement of meeting an immortal with wings—that, I have to admit, I fell asleep right in the middle of it.

The following day Polycleites awakened me, bursting into my chamber with an armful of papers in his hands, looking about wild-eyed and muttering where in Hades was that damned scalawag of a mathematician who'd tricked him with solecisms and solipsisms so cunningly devised that it had taken all night to figure out how they worked.

Hermes had fled, although whether from embarrassment or

boredom and disgust with me I couldn't say. The contracts were under my pillow, along with one tiny feather I'd plucked from the heel of his right foot. I still have it.

I become a soldier's boy and meet a hero

It wasn't long before word of how poorly I'd been protected by Polycleites got back to Troy. We never did discover who was the talebearer, although all evidence pointed to that sower of dissension and mischief, Hermes himself, a sore loser if I ever met one.

My dad promptly rescinded the exile, the retirement, the pension, and both of us were ordered back to the court. Not that he cared a whit about my virginity. If he ever did think about it, he must have realized that like most boys my age I'd lost it carelessly in the indiscretions of adolescence. What seemed to bother Troas was how fast the gossip traveled and how, even holed away in the hills, I just couldn't stay out of the news. The typical story: The young heiress skinny-dips in the Trevi Fountain and Daddy reads about it in the *Times*.

To end all of this "beautiful boy" reputation I had, Troas decided to make a man out of me as soon as possible. Thus I was forced to join the army at the age of 12½.

Not as a soldier. Not even a lowly foot soldier. First I was made a junior adjutant—a glorified water boy—to one of the most important generals, so my father could keep me closely monitored. This was Melampus, a battle-scarred, rough old codger, who, however, melted so under the force of my mere presence in his tent in such a short time that he could no longer carry on a sane conversation, let alone plan out battles and strategies while I was around.

So I was shunted off to a lesser man, a corporal named Leonides. But even though he had a reputation for being the cruelest of taskmasters in the great allied army of Trojans, Phrygians, and Sardinians getting ready to invade the northern states on the Pontus Sea, Leonides became a babbling pussycat whenever I stepped into his tent. He wouldn't even let me help scrub him in his great tub, as the lower adjutants were supposed to do, lest he lose the final little bit of control he still retained over his lust.

In the space of a few weeks, I was ordered to an even lower rank: apprentice to the blacksmith. It was evidently thought that I would get so sooty, burned, scarred, that it would destroy my fairness, and so I could no longer cause any trouble.

I wasn't very happy about this post, not because it would mess

up my looks, but because it seemed to me too far away from the
real army life and any potential action. But both Melampus and
Leonides, having seen the fatal peril of my beauty firsthand, insisted on this course to my father, who, once hearing their arguments,
agreed readily enough.

It turned out to be a far more interesting spot than I had first
supposed. The forge was always filled with soldiers, coming to
have a hilt rewelded or a sword sharpened, or occasionally a cloak
clasp or belt buckle repaired. The blacksmith was a small, dwarfish
fellow from Smyrna, with weeping eyes and timid disposition away
from the fire, who nevertheless became a veritable fire-breathing
Titan when facing the glowing coals. He was a kind man and treated me gently, feeding me well, never mistreating me, teaching me
a few of the more basic skills of his craft. He even allowed me to
tinker with odd pieces of metal I found lying about the forge. I
would form these into trinkets, and eventually brooches and rings
for the soldiers to give to their lovers in the ranks and their mis-
tresses in the city. Like all blacksmiths, mine was nicknamed
Hephaistos, after the deity ruling the forge.

The soldiers' company was constant and relaxed. I saw more of
them and heard more of their stories at the blacksmith's than I ever
had before. Their talk was all of battles, near escapes, batallions
mowed down to a man in cunningly laid traps, wild skirmishes with
barbarians. They talked of the Celts, who painted themselves
before fighting; of the Gauls, who were gigantic and wore the skins
of wild animals; of the Scythians, who after eating cleaned their
teeth with the rib bones of infants they had slain for sport. I could
listen to them talk for hours.

Months passed. I got sooted over as planned by the general and
my father. I got tiny nicks and scratches from flying chips of metal,
but they healed without leaving scars, due to Hephaistos' atten-
tions and balms but also because they were already cauterized from
the intense heat. I became an ardent soldier worshiper and a tolerable jeweler. I also developed a wonderful tan.

Among the lower ensigns and the most experienced soldiers, no
name was spoken more often for glory of arms and intensity in
passion than that of Hyllos the Thracian, who had recently joined
the allied armies. Some of the younger soldiers claimed that he was
the son of Ares, the God of War himself, who had spent himself
out of pure lust into the air, impregnating a bathing maiden half a
league away.

I had often devised trinkets that other soldiers, enamored of Hyllos, had given to him. But one day the Thracian himself finally appeared at our forge. He stood out among his companions like a hero out of legend. Handing Hephaistos his famous sword, Hyllos complained that its edges had grown dull in recent weeks from lack of killing.

Hyllos was the reddest man I've ever seen. His skin was so ruddy that if he were to blush, one would have to search to find it. By contrast, his hair was the blackest I've ever seen, blacker than soot. His eyes were pale blue, the cool shade of newfounded iron. His arms and legs were heavily muscled; his straight stout torso was like the trunk of a great tree. As a boy my age, he had wrestled and taken the palm at the Olympics, and it was rumored that he would throw down any pretty boy he wished, wrestle him into an unbreakable hold, and possess the lad—all in the time it takes for a kettle to boil over. Nor were grown men safe from him. We gauged his age at about 25. None of us had ever laid eyes on a more handsome man.

Hephaistos exercised his usual skill with the sword. Satisfied with the new edge, Hyllos called to me.

"They say you are a trinket mender. Mend this brooch if you can."

I caught the piece and inspected it. It bore his seal—a rampant, sexually aroused bull in onyx on a brass ground—all of it battered, as though worn much in battle.

I told him the underplate had to be replaced. I would hammer out a new one for the onyx.

"Hurry up, then," he said. "I must have it for a gift."

This caused a commotion among the other soldiers at the forge. However, one glance of Hyllos' anger silenced them, and they cleared out quickly. I prepared a new brass piece, working steadily at the now cooling forge. Hephaistos left to take dinner.

"You work slowly for a slave," Hyllos said. "If I were your master, I'd beat you into a craftsman. But I forget, it's rumored that you were once highborn. Well, you're nothing special now, are you?"

This was said so candidly and so arrogantly that I felt free to speak likewise to him.

"If it is my destiny, great Hyllos, to be made a lowly forgesmith's boy, at least it has been brought upon me by others. Unlike you, who are walking into certain humiliation by the giving of a trinket. You were born only to receive gifts."

For a second I was sure he would cuff me, but he laughed

instead and inspected the brooch. Seeing good work and no flaws, he pocketed it, threw a copper at my feet, and said,

"So do we hear truth from the mouths of babes. I thought to give this brooch to a friend. But you are right. When I next give away anything, it will be to whomever plunders my corpse."

So saying, he walked out. Although I could not hear what he said outside, the other soldiers laughed and whistled. A few even came in to peek at the impudent forge boy who'd had cheek enough to talk back to the Thracian.

If I had any doubts then that I was being courted by yet another immortal in disguise, they were quickly overcome.

Hyllos seemed to hold the power of command over everyone in the army but me. Even the oldest and most experienced generals bent to his wishes. Not me. For one thing, I was out of his reach.

So *he* came to *me*. Not openly, of course. Hyllos would appear at the forge at odd hours, when no other soldiers were there, wanting this, then that, then something else to be repaired, rewelded, sharpened, or created for him. As most of this work was for Hephaistos, I could ignore him—which I did, quite pointedly. And even when the work to be done was for me, I remained silent, out of the way. In turn, Hyllos never looked directly at me, never said more words than were necessary, and then stalked glowering away.

He began inviting Hephaistos to his table, where the old smith's work was praised and displayed. I too was invited and placed at the lowest part of the servants' table, yet always in Hyllos' full view. My master was then asked to late-night orgies in the Thracian's tent. Whenever he arrived, Hyllos would drunkenly greet him and ask him where his boy was—the dirty flower of the forge. In short, the Thracian contrived every manner of having me near him, without ever seeming to wish it.

This went on for some weeks, with no change, before soldiers began speaking of Hyllos' oddly transformed behavior. Always rowdy, he now was quiet, meditative. He no longer joined his companions on the hunt. He was given to making instant unreasonable demands of his servants, and striking them when his wishes were not met. He would sulk for hours. Already feared, he was now dreaded, even by his countrymen, due to the increase of his ungovernable rages.

One evening I was ordered to his tent with my small tools and told to fix a clasp on his ceremonial armor. From his bath he greeted me gruffly, then dismissed his adjutant. When we were alone, he began to berate me for earlier work, saying it had broken or bent under pressure. I didn't say a word. He then began recounting rumors of my being a child prostitute for my old mathematician and his friends. Yet still I held my tongue. He began to accuse me of all sorts of lewdness. Not a word out of me.

Finally, unable to contain himself, he jumped out of his bath, grabbed me to throw me onto the floor. But my foot was so positioned that I fell into the bath instead. This was an unexpected treat. I thrashed around in the luxury of a hot scented bath until I felt cleaner than I'd been in months.

When I emerged from the tub, he was sitting down, barely covered in a small cloth, staring at his feet in gloom. I removed my wet clothes, dried myself off slowly, even massaged myself with his body oil.

By the time I was ready to dry the wringing-wet ringlets of my abundant curly hair, he was transfixed watching me. His eyes were open so wide, each seemed like another sky. His mouth was agape in wonder. His face was immobile and stupid with lust as an idiot boy's.

"Listen to me, Hyllos," I said. "Great as you are, you will never win possession of me by harsh words. Woo me with kinder words, words that you feel in truth, and I will give you what you want."

Disbelief passed over his face. Then his arms reached out for me.

"Do you love me, all-conquering in battle?"

He mumbled, stuttered that he did.

"Am I not the most beautiful human you have ever seen?"

He admitted that even the gods could not compare; that cinched it as far as his being an immortal, for no human could dare make such a statement.

I let him touch me—at first only with his fingertips, then his hands—then I allowed him to draw me to him.

"Once, only once will you possess me, great one," I said. "Promise that you agree."

"Once, yet once. I must have you," he panted, his words almost lost in his kisses all over my body.

"Only once, because of who you are," I said.

"Once. Once will be enough," he said, his lips hidden now in the small of my back."

"Promise!"

"I promise."

I'm sure he would have agreed to anything at that moment.

Luckily he did promise, because his now-naked beauty—unsur-
passed by any in manliness I'd ever seen—and the heat of his passion in those few seconds of touching and kissing were so intense
that I would have had to give in to him even if he hadn't promised.

Hyllos bedded me with a passion that sent exploding volcanoes
through my flesh. His desires were so manifold, his lust so
extreme, that long before he was able to take his fullest possession
of me I had passed into a state in which all my senses were so over-
taxed, I could no longer tell what was occurring; I suppose I
blacked out then. What I do remember of the first part of his catalogue of acts and positions still causes me hot flashes. Not for nothing had he been married to the Goddess of Love.

The following morning I was sore all over.

Hyllos was already awake and beginning to repeat his passions
on my battered young body. Gently but firmly I pushed him away
and got up, reminding him of our deal the night before.

He begged me to reconsider. He promised he would deliver me
from the depredations of the forge. He would make me his ensign,
his favorite, his declared friend and lover. He would grant me glory
in battle, eternal military fame, the generalship of an invading
army when I came of age. We would fight together, side by side,
until we were old and honored and faithful and yet still horny as
this very day. Our deaths would be the most revered, he said, we
would fall in battle before enemies who outnumbered us a hundred
to one, but only after we had slain a legion of them. In death, our
souls would not descend into Hades but would be plucked up by
the gods and cast into the heavens to form a new constellation,
larger than Orion, greater than the Twins.

All in all it was tempting…if he could only cool down long
enough in bed so I could get a little fun out of it. But thinking about
it, I wondered if a long life of marching and fighting and passion
was completely inviting. Of course, military fame was more suitable
to a prince of Troy than Hermes' offer of literary renown and the
knowledge of all languages. But with it I foresaw complications,
endless scenes of jealous rages, even deeper immersion into some
of the more kinky sex games he'd indulged in the night before.
Handsome as he was, passionately in love with me as he was, surely there were alternatives—surely something better awaited me.

So I held him to his promise and quickly escaped his tent. Back
at the forge, I got myself sooted up again and went to work.

Thereupon Hyllos went into a towering fury. He set fire to a

dozen tents and beat the fleeing soldiers senseless with his bare
hands. Soon after that, he sunk into a melancholy so utter that all
shunned his company. He hadn't touched food for a week and was
reported to be drinking heavily and using Egyptian potions for for-
getfulness.

Despite all this, he looked no less divinely handsome when I next
encountered him.

It was in the afternoon of a blazing hot day, and no one was
about. Hephaistos had gone to sleep, giving me the afternoon to
myself. I was wondering whether to go take a dip in the river
Scamander to cool off and was leaning against a stone wall eating
a plum when Hyllos approached.

He stopped short when he saw me. I first pretended not to
notice him. But he came closer. I deliberately continued to suck on
the juicy fruit. This excited his memory so intensely that, as I
watched, his entire body became rigid. Then his tunic stood out
from his loins and he had a spontaneous emission. Days later,
where his semen had struck the ground and hissed into the earth,
several bright flowers herbalists call Marswort and value for their
antiseptic value sprang up, almost fully grown.

His immediate lust quenched for the minute, Hyllos handed me
an object wrapped in a small leather packet and looked at me
gloomily, as though waiting for me to change my decision. When
I merely put the packet in my belt, he turned away and stalked off.

When he was gone, I opened the leather. Inside was the very
brooch I had repaired for him. Scratched into the underside of the
brass in a rough hand were the words

"Ganymedos—
Inflamer of loins,
destroyer of souls."

That night I heard that Hyllos had taken ship with his 4,000
Thracians, back to his homeland.

I am hidden among women and meet a blind musician

Hyllos' defection from the allied armies of Asia Minor on what
was more or less the eve of a major expedition against the Pontian

states was seen by King Troas as a major disaster. The troops—or at least those who were not aware of his real reason for leaving—quickly lost morale. Some said that Hyllos had sent scouts, who had discovered the enemy's superior strength; others said he had secretly consulted an oracle and had been warned of a great defeat.

Those and other rumors were repeated many times over, naturally, with the result that loose talk circulated throughout both the army—camped out on the Trojan plain—and the city itself. Confusion ensued. The invasion was delayed. Treaties among our neighbors were broken. The Temple of Zeus was quickly and expensively refurbished in order to allay that obviously angered deity.

When the truth was finally brought to General Melampus and then relayed to King Troas, I was thrown out of the army PDQ and dragged back to the palace. I was bathed and oiled and rubbed for two days to get the army life out of me. Then my dad called for me.

I had been away long enough for him to gloomily ask if my measurements were the same as before.

"I've grown a little," I admitted. "But I think all the ratios are holding up pretty well."

"So it appears."

After much rumination and consultation with his by now over-worked and bewildered ministers, it was decided that, lest more of my mischief making bring a real catastrophe down on the city, I should be exiled again, this time where I could be watched more closely. I was to be hidden in the women's apartments of the palace, where the chance of a straying male was minimal.

This same ploy would be utilized a few centuries later by an enemy of our royal family, when the famed Achilles, in order to avoid getting involved in the mess of the Greco-Trojan War, hid out among his palace women. Achilles was also a good-looking guy, with a real doll for a lover, Patroclus, whose death in that war sent the Greek hero on a bloodletting spree that lasted for months and decimated Troy's citizenry. Still, he ought to have known better than to try an old trick like hiding among women again, especially since he was a grown man when he did it, not a kid like me.

I protested the decision of Troas and his counselors. I whined and carried on about the gross indignity of a former soldier being thrown among old nurses and chambermaids. But I calmed down fast when Troas said I should consider myself lucky that nothing worse was happening to me, and I'd better get moving because he was going to prepare a sacrifice to Zeus.

To tell the truth, the women's apartments weren't so bad after all. I was imprisoned, but quite luxuriously. There were four or five girls my age—cousins and other relations—and we began hanging around together. After a while, we even began playing together. I became intimate with all of them, but the notion of being utterly unmarriageable unless their virginity was intact had been knocked into their heads so often that we had to content ourselves with kissing and touching games.

The older women—my aunts, older sisters, and my mother (who was delighted to have her boy around again)—went out of their way to spoil me. The choicest cut came to my plate, the fanciest tidbits too. Special hors d'oeuvres and sweets were devised to tickle my palate.

Most of the early days there I lolled around on pillows for hours, daydreaming, wondering how I would next be approached and by which immortal. For while Troas really believed hiding me was a brilliant solution, I knew immortals a lot better than he did, having had truck with two already.

I thought perhaps this time Aphrodite, the Goddess of Beauty and Love, might come take a peek at me. But I remembered she already had a boy—Eros—not to mention scores of guys, mortal and immortal, of all ages. So that eliminated her. Athena? She was too honest to cheat or lie her way into what, after all, was a private dwelling. Hera? Possibly. But I eliminated the males. These women's apartments were guarded outside by men and inside by older women.

When I grew bored lazing around and felt I needed a little action, I began setting up athletics among the girls my age. We'd play ball games out on the women's lawns. I would persuade them to go swimming or running with me. I taught them how to use a bow and arrow, how to wield a dagger, how to wrestle off a grown man. Among them, only my cousin Althaea ever proved any real competition.

So, restless again, I began to teach those of my new companions who couldn't how to read and write, and those who did have some smattering of these arts how to do it better. Those who were proficient readers I taught mathematics and philosophy. By unanimous consent, they appointed me critic over all their efforts, not only over what I taught them but also over their drawing, needlepoint, and song making.

Should any man come near while we were outdoors, I had to put up veils and remain absolutely silent, not because of my voice—which was still unbroken—but because my talk itself—that of a boy who'd lived among soldiers and other grown men—would give me away. None of the women wanted that. Because within a short time I was utterly adored by all of them—not only, and not specifically, for my physical charms (which they all agreed outshone even those of my cousin Canothe), but because, knowing no better, I had treated them as equals, as individuals, and had artlessly taught them what had been hidden from them for years: men's knowledge: arms, athletics, science, reading. They gobbled it up as though it were the best Miletian honey.

Toward the end of the third week of the festivities for the newly decorated Temple of Zeus, I decided to make a temple visit of my own. Disguised, accompanied by Althaea and old Kantarene, our chaperone—a sweet thing, but a veritable monster to any man who came near us—we left the women's apartments one night and went to the small, elegant temple of Hermes, near the gymnasia dormitories, where by all rights I ought to have been staying. I bade the women wait in an antechamber, then I revealed myself to the priest of Hermes and sent him outside too. Alone with the idol, I threw off my cloak.

A single dish of fine oil was burning at the altar. I dipped in one edge of the contract the god and I had made and made a brief invocation. The statue came to life.

"Hermes, it's me, Ganymede."

"Ganymede! I knew you'd reconsider and come back to me."

"I haven't reconsidered, and I'm not coming back to you. I'm taking you to court. You reneged on your contract."

"Court?" he said. "What court?"

"The court of the gods. You reneged on your contract. There were supposed to be no recriminations if we didn't agree."

This was so; as to the court of immortals, that was pretty much a wild guess. Yet one like it must have existed, because he was suddenly defending himself.

"How have I reneged? What recriminations?"

"The rumors, lies, ambiguities, confusion, communication foul-ups, loss of important papers, nondelivery of crucial messages..." I began.

He denied it all. But when I began to describe some of the more bizarre mix-ups and their results, he couldn't hide his pride in his own ingenuity; so he was caught out. But still unrepentant.

"Who do you think will listen to your word against mine at a trial?" he said.

"I'll get the God of War after you," I retaliated. "He'll do anything for a single night with me. Anything."

That seemed to work.

"It's unsuitable to threaten a god," he said a bit huffily, but added, "I'll clear everything up. I wouldn't admit it to anyone but you, but some of the snafus I set into motion have become so complicated I'm losing track of what belongs where. By the way, you're looking tastier than ever. Sure you won't reconsider on that agreement?"

As an answer, I tucked it away in my clothing and gave him one light, brotherly kiss on the cheek, which he received with a resigned sigh. But I could tell he was pleased. If I'd denied him, at least I'd not given in to Ares (disguised as Hyllos) either. And after all, Hermes was a rather happy-go-lucky, forgive-and-forget immortal.

Communications did settle down after that encounter. Of course, Troas attributed that to his repairing Zeus' temple. I knew better, but figured why disabuse him of his notions and put myself further in Dutch by having to explain how I knew.

So a few months passed by. I got lazier and more and more inured to being waited on hand and foot, having the lute played to me when I wanted, having my toes rubbed, taking long, luxurious scented baths.

One day a few of us were outside, tossing around an early version of a Frisbee—made out of inflated oxen bladder—when a stranger approached. The girls shrieked and warned him away. But he continued coming toward us. Finally they ran to hide me from his sight.

They needn't have bothered—he was blind. He walked with a long, thin staff, which he used to test the ground in front of him as he advanced.

Across one shoulder was slung a bag of the most supple leather we had ever seen, which he told us came from the underbelly of unborn deer. Within the bag were marvels—pieces of folded paper which, when he opened them and sent them into the air, formed remarkable sculptures of horses, birds in flight, men's heads.

Even more wonderful was his lyre, made of wood so light a baby could lift it, yet strung with threads so fine as to be almost invisible which, when we tried to make music on them, would not be plucked, they were so taut. More astonishing than the lyre, however, was the blind man's voice. We'd never heard a more mellifluous voice from man, woman, or child before. Every word seemed music, every phrase a song, every sentence a lyric poem.

He called himself Philanthropos, lover of humanity, and like many blind wanderers he was a minstrel and epic poet. But he also claimed to be a healer of ills, a calmer of tensions, a destroyer of conflicts. Indeed, he himself seemed perfectly serene. Not a line furrowed his large shoulders; not a scar, blemish, or spot marred his perfect tanned skin. Softness, gentleness, and grace characterized his every gesture.

Rumored of for years, Philanthropos was brought before the king and welcomed with great show, hailed by Troas as a guest of the highest importance, to which he responded with great modesty.

His presence at the court made quite a difference. Calm descended instantly. Peace was quickly concluded with the enemy state to the north. New trade agreements, including cultural exchanges, were effected. The allied armies, who'd been causing trouble since they'd arrived a year before, were sent back home following a week of feasting and celebration.

Soon men of learning from other parts of Asia Minor began arriving daily at Troas' court to meet Philanthropos—some to sit at his knee and hear him sing, others to listen to the old myths and legends dramatically retold, still others to have bothersome wounds healed. A few wished to learn the healing arts of which he was a master. Several merely wanted to bask in his presence and find peace of mind.

Naturally my dad believed that Philanthropos' presence was Zeus's gift in response to the city propitiations. He did all he could to satisfy his guest so that he would remain in Troy as long as he lived. Since Philanthropos seemed no older than 30, that would have been a good many decades.

Like everyone else, I too fell under his spell. Because of his blindness and his absolute purity of morals, of all men only Philanthropos was allowed into the women's apartments, so we too could enjoy his manifold talents and benefits.

I might have become jealous, since all the attention I formerly received from the women and girls was now given to him. But he was known to be chaste, so I was still sought after by my younger friends for kissing and play. And to tell the truth, I'd never met a more spiritual man before. I bore him no grudge.

When he sang the story of Orpheus in the underworld, I was so moved I wept along with the women. When he recited tales of the battle of the gods and the Titans, of the Pygmies and Centaurs, I was stirred to go out and fight myself. When he told of the mysteries of the olden times before the great flood, of the sinking of that center of the world, Atlantis, I was fearfully awed.

He spoke of the origins of human beings. How all people were divided from a single dual being. Men who loved other men and women who loved other women derived from a primal being of a single gender. Men and women who loved each other came from a being of mixed gender. This explanation satisfied me on this question, which I had sometimes pondered. For while I enjoyed my luxurious imprisonment and the company of women and girls, I still longed for the company of my own sex and often wondered what had become of the little friends with whom I had wandered the city streets and alleys, having fun and making trouble.

Of course Troas was a dolt for thinking that anyone as wise as Philanthropos, even though blind, wouldn't soon enough guess that I was a boy. He did guess quite early on, but weeks passed before he said anything—and, as was his great diplomacy, that only when he and I were alone for the first time.

He had just completed reciting a lovely poem, for which I thanked him, and we were refreshing ourselves with iced water, brought daily from the slopes of Mount Ida, when he said,

"Do not thank me, Prince Ganymede. For if I come to these apartments more often than is seemly, it is to bring you the pleasure and knowledge denied you by your sad destiny."

Discovered, I admitted who I was. Philanthropos was so sympathetic to my plight that he soon gained my confidence. I complained of my wasted youth; he counseled patience and offered comfort. I worried about my growing restlessness; he proposed to soothe me with massages he had learned from ancient men in the Far East. I exposed my deep conflicts about the reason for life itself, especially a life as filled with reversals as mine had been; he presented many cogent and well-reasoned arguments of the meaning of life, and how to accept both happiness and misfortune.

During the first private massage, the idea crept into my mind that perhaps this was no ordinary minstrel, poet, healer, and saint, but another immortal—a fleeting thought soon banished.

After that day, Philanthropos and I spent more and more time together, sometimes with the women, but more often in private. I soon confided my complete past to him—short but eventful, and strange of late. Thus he learned of the Delphic oracle I'd received upon my initiation into the Temple of Zeus and the promise that I was to serve and be served, that I was "never to not be."

He began to explicate these ambiguities in various manners, which somehow or other always led back to our meeting, our being together, our remaining together. I began looking forward to his daily massages. They had become experiences wherein I would approach what I could only describe as a totally sensual-spiritual trance state, yet which I could never construe as being in the least bit lascivious.

Philanthropos had been at our court almost two months, and our meetings in private had been going on half that time when, in the course of one of his massages, he once more went into an interpretation of the oracle I had received.

"It is clear to me, dear Prince. What higher cause could you possibly serve than to become my apprentice? You will serve others by poetry and music and healing and pacification—the highest of human arts. And you will serve yourself too—by meriting the love and honor of all people.

"All you need to do is express your wish to join me in my work, and I will teach you all. I assure you, I have your father the King's heartstrings. He will readily assent if I ask for you.

"We will remain here in Troy, bringing the city and its culture to a height never before ascended—no, not even in antediluvian Atlantis. At the same time, and by methods only I hold the secret to, we shall travel to neighboring kingdoms, and then all over the world.

"We shall teach and learn everywhere we go. See the painted barbarians in the frozen north who speak in the tongues of animals. Go to Cathay, where the mountains themselves have been turned into terraced gardens."

I knew then that he was an immortal. No one but a god would ever dare to make a promise like that.

"If that is so, dear Philanthropos," I replied, "then I will serve you and thus be served. But one matter still is not clear—the Sibyl's words about my never not being."

"That is fame and glory never-ending."

"Surely. But doesn't 'being' mean actually being alive?Many men, and women too, have been famous and honored, although long dead."

"Am I not the sun itself?" he asked rhetorically, for by now I realized that he was indeed. All I had to do was look at him. He seemed utterly life-giving, like the sun. And more than that: the absolute fulfillment of every even half-formulated idea or desire I'd ever entertained of an ideal lover.

"Apollo!"

"Lighted by the sun's beneficent proximity, Ganymede, every day of your life will seem a decade. You will go everywhere in the sun's dominion, experience all there is to experience, know all there is to know, feel, see, hear, smell, touch, taste, intuit all. Living a life fuller than any mortal before or after, you will leave this veil of flesh utterly fulfilled in extreme old age, your hand firmly clasped in mine. Then I will burn your flesh to a single ash, so that no earthly material shall ever touch you again."

I swooned.

"Each time we touch, Ganymede, each time we make love, you will be transported to another existence. You will become youths transformed into flowers, maidens metamorphosed into trees, you will be a child driving the chariot of the sun across the heavens, a woman seduced by a shaft of pure sunlight through the angle of a shutter slat."

With that we began to make love. The solar system tumbled past. Comets whizzed by.

I'll skip the historical and terrestrial parts and get to where I really wigged out. Picture the planet Earth as seen from beyond the crescent moon. The huge planet Jupiter, with its dozen satellites, shot past. Then Saturn, with its silver score of rings. Then out, out past them to uncharted worlds. Novas exploded. Huge gaseous clouds folded and expanded. Galaxies fell into dancing patterns. I lost my sense of self, my sense of individuality, altogether. I was but a tiny mote of pure diamond in the midst of billions of other tiny diamond motes. All was seen, felt, known to me in that moment.

Amidst all this knowledge, something tugged at what remained of my consciousness—irritating me, pleasantly but insistently. I realized that I'd been whirled far past the sun's influence, way past his control and scope by a force—dared I think it?—a force larger than *him*. This lasted only an infinitesimal fraction of an instant, yet it gave me pause, like a tap you think you've heard on a door. I suddenly knew there was someone greater than Apollo, the sun— grand as he admittedly was. In this portion of an instant, I resolved to set my cap for this greater being. For spectacular as Apollo's promises were, he still hadn't adequately explained the oracle's first point to me.

So I relaxed into the trip, finally settling back into the solar system again, stopping near the asteroid belt—and there I took my mental-spiritual-physical enjoyment of it very well, thank you.

Wise as *he* was, there was no possibility of hiding my odd little realization and my decision from Philanthropos the following day when he came to the women's apartments. True to his word, I'd gone places with him I scarcely knew existed; and, completely the opposite of my experience with Hyllos, instead of being exhausted by the experience, I was revivified.

He asked whether I'd made my decision to join him.

I began to explain what had happened to me during our many hours of lovemaking. It wasn't too difficult for him to understand.

"It was thrilling," I admitted, trying to somewhat soften my refusal. "But after what I've seen, I simply can't settle for the ideal."

Without another word, and with absolute tolerant sadness, he withdrew.

I am exiled again and meet an old shepherd

He also withdrew from the palace, and though King Troas begged him to stay, making outlandish offers (including several of his wives, daughters, nieces, half of the more than hundred golden oxen, and even a few of the snow-white steeds sired by Boreas himself), Philanthropos would have none of it.

Only after he was gone from Troy a week and it was gloomy and overcast for the eighth day in a row did anyone realize that we'd had nothing but sunshine the two months of his visit.

One of the minor chambermaids had been spying on me and blabbed. So I was torn from the warm nest of the women's apartments, dressed as a boy once more, and dragged before my father, who was sullenly contemplating yet another rainy day.

"Don't lie to me, Ganymede. I want to know exactly what happened."

Indifferent at this point, I told him the truth: that Philanthropos was the god Apollo in disguise, that he had had his way with me but could not win my devotion. I mentioned his promises for our life together and his explications of the early prophecies of my own life. I also tried to explain the spaced-out condition I'd been in when I made my decision. But Troas couldn't grasp any of this, as he was scarcely able to believe those tiny lights in the sky were entire worlds, never mind accepting the other wonders I'd glimpsed beyond them.

"How could you refuse Apollo?"

Once more I tried explaining the greater destiny I'd sensed for myself. Completely exasperated, he hushed me.

"I said you'd bring trouble, and you have. I ought to have exposed you on a mountaintop at birth, as my counselors suggested.

"Look at all the harm you've done. We'll probably never see the sun again. Our crops won't grow. Our trees will die. Our livestock will shrivel. We'll have to become a fishing town again. Or glib-tongued merchants like those smarmy Greeks with no goods of their own to market. Who would believe it! When they predicted you'd be outstanding at the time of your birth, they must have meant outstanding in madness and folly. No sun! Think of it. No, don't. I can't bear the thought. No one will sing or recite poetry any more. Doctors will go berserk, or worse, sink back into their usual incompetence. The peace and happiness that settled on us is fled. Already our decline is being bruited about in the marketplaces of second-rate villages."

I tried to tell Troas that this return to normalcy wouldn't be too bad. Unlike Hermes, who was tricky, or Ares, who was tempestu-ous—both of whom I'd turned down as well—Apollo was at least honorable. He was moping at the moment. But he'd get over it. All would return to as it was before his visit: sunny and rainy days intermixed, scandal and glory, ability and incompetence, loss and gain. He'd see.

Troas went pale, stared at me agape.

"Hermes? Ares? A son of mine refused three immortals! Barely 13 and a whore already to three immortals! I can't stand it!"

So I was disowned and banished from Troy, never to return. The decree of my disfavor was hung on every public wall in town. One notice was even offered up in a solemn rite at the Temple of Zeus, in further propitiation. Naturally, a new round of refurbishings and sacrifices to that all-potent god were set off.

One afternoon, following an incredibly rowdy send-off by those acquaintances of my earlier warehouse and back-alley days—now accomplished young thieves, con men, and murderers—I left the city. They were supposed to stone me out of the gates as I went, but they did this halfheartedly, only tossing a handful of pebbles at me. Most of them were too exhausted from their revels the night before and too hungover to do much else. All of them were secretly proud of my success: I'd made a worse name for myself than any of them had managed to do.

Despite that, I journeyed joylessly for three days on foot before reaching the midslopes of Mount Ida.

There, on a beautiful fresh morning, I found a shepherd's hut perched high upon a crag of rock; the man's flock scattered in a meadow in front of him.

He hailed me and called me over.

This shepherd was an aged but amazingly healthy old pastoral, fully white-bearded and shaggy-haired, dressed in the roughest of cloaks and chiton, but withal quite clean, vigorous, and even muscular from all his outdoor work and simple living. He had no name but that of his occupation, he said, and invited me to share some bread, cheese, and water with him. Hungry, I thanked him and joined his repast.

Sitting on a rock ledge that formed a little terrace, we could see miles across the hills and valleys, clear across the plain of Troy to where the city's 24 golden gates and triple walls shone in distant miniature. The broad river Scamander threaded the plain like a flat, shiny snake. Even farther away we could see the Hellespont, glittering on the horizon.

I couldn't restrain a sigh. Who would have thought eternal banishment would become my lot, I who was born a royal prince of the great city of Troy, I who had been promised so much?

This was a theme I'd mentally embroidered a great deal since leaving my old mischief-making companions. Perhaps I'd been a fool to expect so much. I'd had three chances to fulfill my promised destiny of serving one higher—and each time I'd turned it down out of pride in myself and in my predicted fate. That pride was the real cause of my father's insistence that I get out of Troy.

I wondered what imp of the perverse had gotten into me during that supererotic trip Apollo sent me on. What self-destructive impulse had made me throw away a life no human before me had even been offered? I must be as crazed as Troas thought.

Naturally, I said nothing of this to the old shepherd. He asked only a few questions of me, and I told him little, not even my name. He offered to let me remain in his hut for the night rather than wandering the great distance to the next poor habitation. I declined, explaining that I was a curse: Wherever I remained I brought trouble and woe.

This didn't seem to bother him a bit: Although I repeated it, he still didn't seem at all upset, which I attributed to his ignorance of such matters.

When I thought I had lingered long enough, I stood up to leave. But he pointed west, where a huge storm—not visible moments before—had suddenly gathered over half the sky. Would I help him round up his sheep and get them safely penned?

To pay him for the meal, I said I would, and did, executing this task so deftly that although the storm came on with astounding alacrity we were ready for its onslaught.

At the first immense thunderclap, it was evident to us both that I could no longer refuse his offer of lodging. Every inch of the nearly black sky seemed ready to hurl itself down upon us, and the nearest shelter was a small wood a mile off.

"There," I said. "I told you. It's the curse again."

He pulled me into the little hut just as the squall slammed into the mountainside.

It was a frightful storm, the worst I'd ever experienced. The rain beat down in twisting sheets that seemed deliberately to strike the flimsy walls of the hut. Leaks sprung all over the place. The wind howled and shook the hut, threatening to topple it. Thunder surrounded us, right at the door. The very land beneath our feet trembled and shook, as though we were in the midst of an earthquake.

The sheep out in their pens began to bleat in such terror-stricken tones that the old man finally wrapped himself in a blanket and went out to soothe them, although I tried to dissuade him this perilous course.

I finally fell asleep from fright and exhaustion, huddled in a corner. When I awoke, the shepherd was back inside, attempting to dry his old bones by a pitifully small fire. That too flickered out before long. He continued to shiver and chatter his teeth. Certain I had caused this old innocent's death by my very presence in the hut, I began to bemoan my fate.

"Forget about yourself and your fate," he said, not at all harshly. "Come help me."

"How?"

"You are young, and the heat from your blood flows easily through your veins. Come warm and dry me with your body's heat."

I found this idea vaguely repellent. (After three gods, culminating in the perfect Apollo, who wouldn't?) I suspected he wanted more than mere heat from me too. But I felt guilty and so went to where he lay shivering.

Outside, the thunder settled into low cannonades. I first covered the old man's back and legs, then one side, then the other, and finally lay up against his chilled chest. He was a very healthy old man, it seemed to me—firm of flesh and remarkably smooth of skin, I supposed from a simple diet and much exercise in the out-doors. He was soon warmed, then heated up, then...

He began to cuddle me. He confided that he had never encoun-tered a youth so pleasing to him as I was. He made many jokes and pleasantries, told me stories about his life on Mount Ida, how he had seen nymphs and satyrs, how he had even once seen hoof-prints that must have belonged to the oldest of earthly gods, Pan, conservator of nature. He caressed me gently, warming me, and in short, was so unusually modest and considerate and delightful that I thought perhaps the Sibyl had gotten her oracle mixed up. Perhaps I was destined to serve the lowest, not the highest. My greatest pleasures before this had not been with immortals—even in disguise—but with knavish pickpockets and street brawlers. Who could be lower in rank than this old shepherd?

This reversal cheered me up so well that I was soon laughing and kissing him back. I told him he might do with me what he wished, for I was his for the night (and—who knew?—for as long as he might want me, since no one else did).

Whereupon he took me like a man half his age—and was so moderate and humanly passionate, compared to those superse-ductions of my recent history, that I responded alike, clasping my arms and legs about him and gazing fondly into his eyes.

Many folk aver that men become pure dolts, mere animals, dur-ing this act—their faces expressionless, their eyes like unreflecting mirrors. But I had seen lights of laughter and affection in boys' eyes at those moments, and when I looked into the old shepherd's eyes I noticed those same lights, which gave me such comfort that I hugged him even closer.

Strange to tell, as I continued to stare, those little lights seemed to grow, to become rainbow-hued, to brighten and expand as though they were stars, to spread out into galaxies, nebulae, novae.

But I blinked, and they were resolved into mere lights of pleas-ure in loving human eyes. All so fast, I was certain my eyes had deceived me.

Afterward the old shepherd hugged and kissed me a great deal, telling me that I was born for love and had given him the greatest pleasure he had known from another. I slept within the curve of his body as though inside a large warm cloud and awakened in that position to a morning of more pleasure—and a bright, shining sunny day.

I became his apprentice after that, and we spent many weeks together. He talked seldom at first, often sat perfectly still for hours, alone on the ledge outside the hut with a full view of the valley and plains. Yet he would awake and be aware of all that happened around him, his sight so sharp he could spot a sheep about to wander too close to a ravine or point out a peacock on a distant lawn.

When he did begin to speak, he was extraordinarily wise for such an unlettered recluse. He admitted his learning came from observation, investigation, and contemplation of the world, and suggested that was the best way to know anything for certain. He began to teach me what he had absorbed of the history and geography of the countryside around us, of the world as he had heard it described by travelers, of the heavens as he had deciphered them from watching the starred skies at night. He would draw diagrams on the dirt with a little stick, which were so concise and clear that I sometimes felt I was witnessing the primeval chaos being divided into space and matter, time and nature, land and sea, air and fire, darkness and light.

I related all I had been taught already by Polycleites, Hermes, and Apollo as Philanthropos. The old shepherd amended those teachings, correcting some, expanding others, eliminating the more fanciful and elaborate features. He insisted on showing me that I existed only in terms of the construction and interacting relationships of tiny, invisible particles he called atoms, generated during the spontaneous burst of the creation of the universe untold eons before, which had been set into a motion that would continue indefinitely.

Other times he told me how all living creatures were composed of the same materials, also invisible, which were merely arranged differently, so that some creatures were plants, some birds, some insects. He spoke of what lies within the earth, too, how the explosions of volcanoes show that our mantle of rock—apparently so hard and enduring—was merely molten liquid cooled by the air. The air itself, he said, was composed of numerous materials which could not be seen by the eyes or touched, but could be known by other means.

He instilled in me the principles by which men had lived and ought to live, how the fates shaped all human lives, but some lives with more interest and imagination than others. He thought my own life was one of the special ones.

The old shepherd was the best-tempered man I'd ever met, and if he had a fault, I was not able to find it during our time together. I came to love him even more easily than my little alley-friend Autocylus, more naturally than my mother.

So I was astonished one day when, after our morning lovemaking and simple breakfast, he announced with no alteration of expression or voice that he had to leave Mount Ida. He would not say why, nor for how long—only that he would return for me. I was to watch over his flock until then.

I knew better than to complain or argue with him. And it was only when I could no longer make out his retreating figure in the distance—a gnarled stick, his old cloak, a rough hemp bag slung over his shoulder, hat pulled down over his face—that I was saddened by his departure.

As the days passed, I saw evidence of him and his teachings, memories of his affections, everywhere I cast my eyes. I trusted he would return to me. Still, I passed that week missing his presence more and more.

I might have remained that way—a solitary, love-stricken shepherd on Mount Ida—the rest of my days. But one night, long after I had fallen asleep, my hut door was broken down and a squadron of Trojan soldiers awakened me, bound my hands, and dragged me away.

I become a human sacrifice

Before I even had the chance to get washed up and dressed, I was brought up in front of King Troas, who looked me over, muttered that I was looking gangly, and immediately sent for Polycleites. (He was now returned to favor as court mathematician and philosopher, his previous failure to keep me out of trouble overlooked because a more-than-human force had been involved in the business.)

My old tutor arrived and began to measure me head to foot, finger to forearm; writing down and computing all the ratios on a

counting board. As Polycleites worked on his calculations, I breakfasted under the curious gaze of my father, who seemed to have
some new scheme in mind for me.

While I'd been away Polycleites had much improved his theory
of the necessary perfect proportions, supplementing his old ratios
with new ones of one to two, two to five, and two to eight. He told
me these reflected his newest studies in music and astronomy. For
proportions to be be perfect, they must now not only conform to
geometric equivalents but also fulfill certain musical progressions
and even be relevant to the dynamics of Celestial Harmonics in a
grand mathematical-musical-astronomical schema he'd devised.

This interested me, and I attempted to explain to him how he
might have to revise his theories to include the three planets I'd
noticed—complete with satellites and even rings—whirling about
beyond the orbit of Saturn, outermost of the worlds in his plan. He
never once looked up from his scrolls; when I pressed him on the
point he dismissed my comments, saying I was an ignorant sheep boy
and knew no more of planets than I knew how to keep continence.

I proved, however, to be as physically nonpareil in his new system of ratios as I had in the older one.

"Then he is perfect?"King Troas asked.

"As perfect a 14-year-old boy as ever trod this earth," the mathematician reported. "Physically, mathematically, musically, and
celestially perfect!"

My father seemed pleased upon hearing this, which caused me
no little concern. Now, however, he rubbed his hands together in
glee, ordered more juice and honey for me, bade me eat my fill of
breakfast; then amended that so that I would eat enough but not too
much, lest I alter by a jot my perfection. After all, he said, tomorrow was the morning of the rededication of the Temple of Zeus, and
I must look my best. I was to have a key role in that occasion.

"But I thought I was banished and proscribed."

"Were. But on my orders you are now exonerated. And tomorrow you will be the first citizen in the city of Troy."

This was such a dizzying turnabout that I asked for details.

With much hesitancy at first, then with gusto, my father
explained how this had come about.

After my banishment following the Philanthropos episode, when
the rains finally let up and the sun began to shine, everyone was
startled to see a new crop began to sprout—the second that year—
stronger, healthier, and tastier than the one before. Fruit trees that

had already dropped one full load were now in flower again. Wheat fields were abundant with young kernels. Flowers, ferns, even weeds grew with incredible speed and fullness. As the people harvested these new crops they wondered how it had come about, and concluded that the Sun God's visit—brief as it was—had completely revitalized our land. Even areas that hadn't been sown in years spontaneously brought forth plants. Only one person could be responsible for this sudden bounty—the cause of Apollo's visit to Troy in the first place: me.

The people then recalled how both of my earlier contacts with immortals—disruptive enough when they first occurred—had also ended up in enduring good. Communications and learning had never been so fast, clear, and esteemed since the recent great confusion in these areas due to Hermes' vexation. The bravery, strength, and repute of our army, although untested by a war with the Pontian states, remained high. But we were now known not as a warring nation but as an imperial peacemaking people—which brought even greater repute among faraway civilizations. The musical, poetic, and healing arts had never flourished so well as they had since Apollo's visit and his instigation of many new practices in these arts.

My name was no longer gadded about in the lower quarters of the city as a swearword or euphemism for a boy prostitute. I was no longer held up as a warning example to errant youth. Among the noblest born (including, naturally, many relatives), my best qualities were recalled with increasing frequency. Women meeting together in secret hailed me as their only friend among the opposite sex. Someone had even written an ode praising me higher than the original founder of Troy—anonymously, of course, as the proscription against me was still legally in effect. All over Troy and the surrounding countryside pregnant women had begun placing offerings upon secret altars dedicated to me, hoping for sons as beautiful, wise, and fortunate as I.

Word of all this didn't take long to reach my perplexed father. He went back to the Sibyl who had given my oracle and had her predictions rechecked against my natal horoscope. These he and his counselors discussed at great length and with the seriousness usually reserved for state affairs of the gravest sort.

They arrived at the following conclusions:

(1) I was the most beautiful boy—most beautiful human—on earth; by all evidence the most beautiful that had ever lived, proved

mathematically as well as by much observation.

(2) My horoscope predicted that I would have qualities so out-standing as to make me famous from my tenth year on, attracting even the attention of the immortals. This had happened.

(3) My initiation oracle said that I was to serve the highest and in so doing be served by the highest. This could only refer to the highest of the immortals, Zeus himself.

From all these axioms they concluded that I could best fulfill all the prophecies—and my personal potential too—by becoming a sacrifice to Zeus the following day in the rededication ceremony. Not only would this ensure the city's good fortune to come, it would get me out of the way, eliminating further—possibly less for-tunate—contacts with other immortals.

Without waiting for my reaction, Troas had me sent to a guard-ed chamber, where he hoped I would meditate and otherwise pre-pare myself for my special fate.

I don't think I was terribly upset by the news. It was evident that I had driven my father, his counselors and priests, and probably most of the city quite insane (those poor pregnant women with their secret altars!). For this alone I deserved extraordinary punish-ment. I also rethought the Sibyl's oracle. I suspected Troas and his friends had hit on as correct a solution as any other.

Killing me, they would ennoble both me and themselves. Politically and religiously (which amounted to the same thing), it was an inspired idea. By destroying the most perfect human on earth they would affirm their own fear of perfection, their willing-ness to be imperfect, their voluntary submission to a higher force. With all these implications, how could any immortal refuse such a gift? And so Troy would be blessed forever.

Amen.

I did have one compunction: that my old shepherd would return to the hut and find me gone, the sheep all dispersed, and think I'd been irresponsible and unfaithful to him. As I'd never met a better-natured, more intelligent, more truly affectionate man, this natu-rally saddened me greatly. I wondered how our lives would have been different if he hadn't gone away; whether he would have fought the king's soldiers for me, or somehow intuited their com-ing in advance so we could escape.

A temporary reprieve seemed in sight the next morning. It was a gray, blustery, stormy-looking day, and I was certain the rededi-cation would be called off.

I couldn't have been more wrong. In fact, the priests of the Temple had been hoping for just such a day, Polycleites told me as he urged my attendants to hurry and prepare me for the ceremony. Only in such weather, he explained, could there be any true proximity to Zeus. The inclemency showed that the immortal was already approaching, looking forward to his gift from the people of Troy.

The storm was more than fortuitous. It was also necessary. It was to be the method of my death. While other immortals accepted the freshly dead, and some minor ones even settled for a bowl of blood, Zeus only took the living. Those dedicated to him were wrapped in metal bands attached to lightning conductors on the roof of the Temple. When the lightning—Zeus's power—took the offering, the priests would know they had won his favor. I was assured my death would be instant and painless. You might say I was getting a primitive forerunner of the electric chair.

I won't go into the elaborate details of the rites—the chanting and marching and incense burning, the swaying and dancing. I will, however, note that it was an eerie scene. The huge, freshly cleaned, newly repainted Temple chamber and restored altars were lighted only by a few torches. But every once in a while there would be a great flash of light from a thunderbolt that shot down the attracting rods from the central open roof. Those gadgets, of which there were several, went into operation early on in the ceremony. Not wanting to take any chances that Zeus would not be satisfied with me, Troas had arranged for 24 of the more than hundred golden oxen to be sacrificed first. As each of these big oxen were struck by lightning, they shuddered, stiffened, and fell down on their sides— to the great jubilation of the throng inside the vast hall.

When all the oxen were done, it was my time.

I was placed inside one of the contraptions (modified to fit my arms, legs, and head). Several speeches and prayers were quickly made; then all was ready and the mumbling crowd drew back, all eyes turned heavenward, awaiting the approach of the death-dealing thunderbolt.

At that moment, someone dashed out of the mob and pulled me free of the metal bonds—my old shepherd!

Before I could hug him, before the crowd could surge forward to seize the blasphemer, an enormous thunderbolt boomed directly above the Temple, and lightning shot down the rod, brightening up the darkened cavernous space so every detail could be seen.

My shepherd grabbed onto the headpiece of the metal and the billion-watt wrath of Zeus raced down the rod into him.

Instead of shuddering, getting stiff, and falling down with a thud as the oxen had—and I most assuredly would have—he became a human torch. The lightning raced around and through him and out again. He seemed to glow from within.

A great murmur went up as all cowered back against the walls. All but me. I thought fast. What could this sudden rescue with fireworks signify? There was only one answer. My old shepherd was an immortal. Not just any immortal, for only one god could play with lightning and enjoy it—Zeus himself.

Sure enough, he turned to me, smiling, and held out his hand.

"Come, Ganymede," he said. His voice rumbled like earthquake tremors about six points on the Richter scale. The people behind me, still awed, were delighted that Zeus had seen fit to come in human form to accept his gift.

I wasn't so pleased. In fact, I was downright suspicious.

"What happens when I come to you?" I asked, and answered myself. "I become barbecued boy, right? Well, forget it!"

His glow dimmed slightly. "You won't join me?" His voice thundered throughout the Temple.

"If you're Zeus..." I began.

"How can you deny it?"

"Don't interrupt. If you're Zeus, then who was my old shepherd?"

"I am he. I am all people, everyone in the world—yourself included. But I am especially your old shepherd. That was the human form I chose to take. Come now, Ganymede."

"If that's true, what am I promised?"

Behind me I could hear my father saying that I must be truly insane to be dickering with the king of the immortals. I would ruin them for generations to come. I ignored him.

"The other immortals promised me all sorts of terrific things. If you want me, you're going to have to do a lot better than they did. I'm not going to be known as the idiot who threw over Apollo and Hermes and Ares for an instant baking."

He flared up with impatience.

"I'll be your old shepherd,"he said. "Your true love. Always."

That sounded like it had possibilities. "But you're already married," I pointed out.

"That was for convenience's sake. I couldn't create *everything* for myself. I needed a woman for some things. Besides, Hera and

I haven't slept together in eons."

"What about all those others? Leda, Danae, Europa, Io, Callisto? Don't think I haven't heard about them."

"Look," he said, and his incandescence immediately split into two glowing old shepherds as bright as the original and as identical. "Wherever I am, you'll always have one of me at your side. You'll have an honored place at the table of the gods. You'll be my favorite. My cupbearer."

Still not bad, but here I felt we were approaching the key point in our negotiations—the whole curious "never not to be" business the Sibyl had forecast. None of the other immortals had ever given me a straight answer on this promise.

"I'll look pretty silly as your cupbearer at 88, won't I? Bent, arthritic, toothless."

Behind me I heard a commotion. I turned to see that my dad had collapsed and was gibbering mindlessly on the floor.

Zeus became one again and smiled. "I grant you eternal youth, then. Satisfied?"

"Not quite. Fulfill the oracle. It was yours, you know, made right here in your own Temple."

"Well, what is it?"

"I want what no other human has ever had: immortality."

Well, you can imagine how the Trojan people liked that. Not only was I arrogant and filled with hubris such as they'd never heard before, but I was downright cheeky too. I could imagine them all hoping he'd strike me dead for being so pushy. But I didn't give a hoot about them. This was between Zeus and me, and frankly, it really was the only way I could see things working out, mutually loving though we might be.

He suddenly brightened up so much everyone had to turn their eyes away so as not to be blinded. Even I was blinking. He extended his hands to me. From each finger a needle-thin beam of white fire shot out at me. I was engulfed in white fire. My clothing was burnt off in a second; I expected to see my skin blacken and peel off too. Instead, I began to glow. Then there was a great thunderclap.

"Ganymede," he said, with what I can only describe as infinite love, "be immortal."

Well, I'm really glad he only pulled that act once. It was a staggering experience. His fire burned into my skin, setting off a thousand million orgasms. I had believed him when, as the old shepherd, he had told me I was composed of all these tiny molecules.

Now I felt each one of them going off inside me. Each one becoming immortal.

When I came to my senses, my old shepherd was holding me around the waist. The lightning was gone; we were both glowing. I can't begin to describe how I felt, but it wasn't human.

"King Troas," Zeus thundered.

My dad stumbled forward.

"Zeus accepts your gift of golden oxen and a new Temple and grants your family and city ten generations of the greatest good fortune."

There was much cheering and applause at this.

"But Troas, because you offered Zeus a gift you were not free to give—one he very much wanted, but had to win himself from the will of Ganymede—your city's fortunes will last *only* ten generations, then end in a terrible catastrophe."

There was much moaning and weeping at this.

"But Troas, because your seed has provided the rarest gift Zeus has ever been offered—that same Ganymede—even after your people are gone and your city demolished, you will live on in glory, as long as there are generations of men capable of hearing and understanding your nation's story."

With this speech national pride was restored, and there was great jubilation, music, dancing, singing, and swaying.

In the midst of all this, my old shepherd bade me grasp the attracting rods. As I looked up through the roof of the Temple, a huge bolt of lightning shot down toward us. Wrapped in his arms, I shot up the rod—out of the Temple and to Olympus—in a flash.

Epilogue

How my story got changed to Zeus taking the shape of an eagle and flying off with me I can't say for sure. There was a large statue of a golden eagle in the Temple, and I suspect that as the legend was repeated over the centuries the lightning rods were forgotten and this impressive but accessory statue was mentioned more often, until, through further embroiderings of the tale, it became the only logical method by which he could have gotten me off the ground and to Olympus.

I have just one final word of advice for you younger folks. Take my word, it really does help to know beforehand the kind of person you're going to spend eternity with.

What's life with Zeus been like since then? Well, like all couples we've had our ups and downs, our squabbles and reconciliations. But in general I'd say it's been...heaven!

alyson
books

ARE YOU READY? *by Rik Isensee.* Many gay men enter midlife unprepared to face the challenges of living in a youth-oriented culture. Isensee, a nationally renowned clinical psychologist and the author of the best-selling *Love Between Men* and *Reclaiming Your Life,* brings years of practical experience and research to this vital guide for gay men on celebrating this new period of their lives.

B-BOY BLUES, *by James Earl Hardy.* A seriously sexy, fiercely funny black-on-black love story. A walk on the wild side turns into more than Mitchell Crawford ever expected. An Alyson best-seller you shouldn't miss.

CALIFORNIA SCREAMING, *by Doug Guinan.* Kevin is a fashion photographer with a stalled career, perfect looks, a chiseled body, and no future. Brad Sherwood, a multimedia mogul, rich beyond belief and the world's most eligible gay bachelor, has everything except what he needs most: someone to adore him. When the two men meet, it looks as though happily ever after has finally reached the Hollywood Hills. Until Kevin breaks the rules—and falls in love.

DESMOND, *by Ulysses G. Dietz.* When gay vampire Desmond falls in love with a human man, his dark world will be forever changed.

JOCKS, *by Dan Woog.* An intriguing look at America's gay male jocks as the locker-room closet opens up. Is there life after coming out to your teammates? Is there life before coming out? This collection of more than 25 inspiring real-life stories digs deeply into two of America's twin obsessions: sports and sex.

LIVING WELL, *by Peter Shalit, MD.* This handy guide provides simple, practical advice on looking and feeling your best. Shalit brings his experience as a physician and as a gay man to play as he addresses issues of concern to gay patients. In an often humorous and always approachable style, he covers issues from the typical (finding a doctor, dieting, and exercising) to the more sensitive (body modification, substance abuse).

MY FIRST TIME, *edited by Jack Hart.* Hart has compiled a fascinating collection of true stories by men across the country, describing their first same-sex encounters. *My First Time* is an intriguing look at just how gay men begin the process of exploring their sexuality.

2ND TIME AROUND, *by James Earl Hardy.* The seriously sexy, fiercely funny sequel to the best-selling *B-Boy Blues.* Raheim Rivers (a.k.a. "Pooquie") and Mitchell Crawford (a.k.a. "Little Bit") are back—back in love, back together, and back to stirring up the hip-hop community and the rest of New York.

These books and other Alyson titles are available at your local bookstore.
If you can't find a book listed above or would like more information,
please visit our home page on the World Wide Web at **www.alyson.com**.